Carl Melcher Goes to Vietnam

Carl Melcher Goes to Vietnam

Paul Clayton

Thomas Dunne Books
St. Martin's Press ⚏ New York

THOMAS DUNNE BOOKS.
An imprint of St. Martin's Press.

CARL MELCHER GOES TO VIETNAM. Copyright © 2002 by Paul Clayton. All rights reserved. Printed in the United States of America. No part of this book may be used or reproduced in any manner whatsoever without written permission except in the case of brief quotations embodied in critical articles or reviews. For information, address St. Martin's Press, 175 Fifth Avenue, New York, N.Y. 10010.

www.stmartins.com

Library of Congress Cataloging-in-Publication Data

Clayton, Paul, 1948–
    Carl Melcher goes to Vietnam / Paul Clayton.—1st ed.
        p. cm.
    ISBN 0-312-32903-2
    EAN 978-0312-32903-7
    1. Vietnamese Conflict, 1961–1975—Fiction.   2. African American soldiers—Fiction.   3. Americans—Vietnam—Fiction.   4. Race relations—Fiction.   5. Soldiers—Fiction.   I. Title.

PS3603.L455C37 2004
813'.6—dc22

                                                                    2004041300

First published in the United States by Booklocker.com, Inc.

First Edition: July 2004

St. Martin's Press

10 9 8 7 6 5 4 3 2 1

To Willie Morris and his friend
James Jones, both gone now. . .

There is no better man, no braver heart,
Than he who shares good Fortune's grace,
For love of muse, for sake of art,
With those inclined to join the race.

AUTHOR'S NOTE

I would like to thank Colonel David Hackworth and Jay Acton for finally making the publication of this book possible. I would also like to thank my mother for instilling in me a love of story, and my father, for his wonderful example of hard work and stoic determination.

CHAPTER 1

I looked out my window. We were cruising above a plateau of shaving cream clouds. That bothered me; I didn't like not being able to see the ground. A missile could be racing up at us right now. I looked over at my two friends. They were talking excitedly about something, and that made me feel better. Friends are the key, I think. If you have good friends, you can get through anything, even Vietnam.

Two seats over sat my Reb friend from Georgia, B-O-B. B-O-B had once told me the meaning of his name, Brook something-or-other, the third, or esquire. Like everyone else, I just called him Beobee which is how the letters B-O-B sounded when you said them quickly. Beobee was about five-foot-eight, one hundred and seventy pounds, with a receding hairline and a permanent, reddish flush to his cheeks. The guy sitting between us, my other friend, McLoughlin, got up to go to the bathroom.

"They don't have any missiles down there, do they?" I asked Beobee.

Beobee's ruddy face brightened with interest. A bit of a windbag, he liked to be asked questions. "You mean the enemy?"

I nodded.

"Of course they do."

I suddenly wished I hadn't asked. I liked Beobee, but his monologues wore you out. I'd gotten to know him at Fort Lewis, Washington, where we had waited to ship out to Vietnam.

"They're the ground-to-ground kind," he said, warming to the subject, "122's mostly. They might have some ground-to-airs now, but I believe the Navy and Air Force keep the approaches to Cam Ranh pretty well patrolled."

"Good," I said, hoping he'd leave it at that.

"If they did have them though," Beobee went on, "and they managed to launch one at us, I don't rightly know if it could climb this high."

1

"Oh." I looked out the window. We were still well above the clouds. I felt a little safer.

"Of course we've been descending for the past ten minutes," Beobee said, "that would make a difference . . ."

He went on and on and finally someone on the other side of the aisle asked him a question. Beobee had already served a tour of duty in Vietnam as a machine gunner with the Air Cavalry, and he fancied himself an expert on just about anything that had to do with modern warfare. Because of his age (he was about twenty-five) and his campaign ribbons, I knew that most of the stories he told were true; there were just too many of them, that's all. I really did respect the guy.

Jack McLoughlin, or Glock as he had been known in Infantry training, took his seat between Beobee and me. Glock and I were very different, but had become good friends anyway. Glock was six feet tall, with broad shoulders, one-hundred-eighty pounds. He had a bright intelligent face, blue eyes, and was outgoing and friendly. He was married but they had drafted him anyway. He was the kind of guy you'd expect to have been the star quarterback on the hometown high school team, and indeed, he had been. Everybody liked him. I could see him as President someday, like John F. Kennedy.

I'm different from that. My name is Carl Melcher and I'm five-five, weighing a hundred and twenty. I was never good at sports. I'm more interested in books and music. I wasn't married when I got drafted and I had broken up with my girl. The only reason Glock and I got to be friends during basic and infantry training was our proximity to one another. The army did everything alphabetically, and I'm an "ME" and he's an "MC," so we'd usually end up bunking nearby, or I'd be one or two behind him in all the lines you had to wait in. I'm really glad I got to know him. He was a really solid guy.

I turned and looked at the rear of the plane. It was a regular commercial jetliner. Back in the States before they drafted me, I never would've imagined they'd send guys to war in a jetliner, but here we were, a bunch of Army, Navy, Air Force, and Marines, all jammed into a DC-8 with pretty, young stewardesses moving through the aisles, collecting the empty trays and pillows.

I turned to Glock. "There must be a hundred and fifty guys on this plane."

Some Air Force guy behind us leaned over the seat. "They say that ten percent don't go home."

Glock got in his face and laughed, "hah, hah, hah," really slow. Then he turned away. I think it was the whiskey he'd had; the blonde stewardess liked him and had slipped him some.

The Air Force guy blinked a couple of times and watched us, waiting for somebody to say something. I didn't know what to say.

Beobee turned to the guy. "You mean, don't go home alive."

I thought, here we go again.

The jet engines wound down in pitch and volume. I felt us losing altitude and held tightly to my seat. "Everybody goes home," continued Beobee. "It's not like the old days in Europe. We got thousands of men buried over there. But this here is different. Conditions have changed. We got us a whole new ball game here. Everybody goes home."

"Cool it, Beobee," I said. Glock and I exchanged looks as Beobee rambled on in his southern drawl about helicopter medevacs and the modern, military morticians' techniques. He was on a roll. The Air Force guy made his escape by claiming he had to go to the bathroom before they put on the FASTEN SEAT BELTS sign. Glock and Beobee argued about the number of guys that were killed in an average week here. I'd read it was a hundred and twenty.

The plane banked dizzyingly and the coast came into view. White waves rushed onto a tan beach. I saw a fishing village with palm frond-thatched huts. It looked peaceful. I wondered what it would be like in whatever part of Vietnam I'd be assigned to. I still didn't know where that was. Hopefully it would be the same place as Glock and Beobee. When I had first realized I might have to go to Vietnam, the idea had seemed dangerous, but exciting. I would go because my country ordered me to. But the more I thought about it, and about the possibility of getting killed, the more frightened I became. So I thought about other things, and I read a lot too, mostly science fiction, to keep my mind off it.

"El is probably asleep by now," Glock said.

"Huh?" I said.

"You know, Eleanor, my wife. It's eleven o'clock at night back there." He took her picture out of his wallet and looked at it.

"Oh," I said. It's funny. I didn't think about the States much. I didn't have anybody back there to think of, to wonder what they were doing right now, except my parents. My girlfriend at State University, Linda, had broken up with me. It was my first semester and it'd put me in a deep depression. My brain turned to oatmeal and the only things I passed were Literature and Basic Piano Techniques One. All I remember from my four months at State was reading about Ulysses sailing across the wine-dark sea, and sitting in the music room at a piano playing scales or "Fifteen Miles on the Erie Canal." I flunked out and got drafted.

Glock looked at me sadly. "You know, we were going to buy a house. I was making big bucks, but when they drafted me. . . ." He looked sadly at her picture.

Glock rarely got like that. It was the whiskey. I felt sorry for him. In a way, maybe I was lucky that it was all over between Linda and me. At least I didn't have to worry like Glock. Once, back in basic training, Glock had snuck a bottle into the barracks. He'd gotten drunk and we stayed up half the night talking on the front stoop. The conversation got around to home and he started crying. It really surprised me, a guy like him crying. Another thing that amazed me about him was that after four weeks of basic training he started to like the army. He would never admit it, but I could tell. He'd really excelled in the training and I knew they wanted to send him to Officer's Candidate School, but his wife had put her foot down. In order to qualify he would've had to reenlist for another year. That's probably why she said no.

The jet's flaps lowered with a whine and a groan. I looked out the window and saw we were coming in for a landing. The others craned their heads to look out the windows, their faces twisted with awe or fear, like we were landing on the moon. That's the way I felt too, like we were about to land on an angry, red planet full of dangerous aliens.

We glided over some warehouses and the runway came into view. Off to the right about a dozen fighter aircraft sat in sandbagged enclosures. Technicians moved about the sharp edges of the planes with carts and tools. As our wheels hit the runway with a loud bang, I had a thought. I had a year to do in Vietnam, three hundred and sixty-five days, and the clock had just started ticking. I didn't go to church much, but I said a prayer anyway that Glock, Beobee and I would all come home, and that whatever happened, I wouldn't turn out to be a coward, or let my friends down.

They opened the door and the air hit us like a blast from an oven. I followed Beobee and Glock out the door. Cam Ranh was big and modern, with lots of planes and hangars. But the sky was a shade of blue I've never seen before, and the air smelled different too, as if some long-familiar ingredient was missing.

Four Military Policemen, or MPs, carrying M-14 rifles ushered us to a waiting bus. We drove a short distance to where another plane, a smaller, camouflage-painted C-130, with its props turning, was waiting. As the hot exhausts of the turboprops blasted us, I shouted at one of the MPs, asking him where they were taking us. He shouted back that we were going to a big 4th Infantry Division camp in Pleiku Province, in the Central Highlands. It was named Camp McGernity after a Sergeant Mack McGernity, the Division's first casualty.

The flight was hot and noisy. The C-130 was a stripped-down version, used primarily to haul cargo. There were a few porthole-like windows, but they were up high up. I stood on the seat rack and looked at the flat, green-and-tan plains, the snaking rivers. I felt like talking but Glock, Beobee and the others lay sleeping on the racks, mouths open, like a bunch of desiccated corpses. I tried reading but I couldn't concentrate. For some reason that song, "Come Sit On My Cloud," by Steem Masheen kept popping into my head. During my last two years at East Catholic High I was in a Rock and Roll band and we used to do that number. I played rhythm guitar and sang harmony on the backups. Everybody said we were pretty good. We were called "Terry and the Tense Moments." Terry sang lead; he'd coined the name. He and I arranged all the material. We never had to buy sheet music because I could listen to a song once and figure out all the chords, while Terry worked out the bass for Wayne, and the leads for himself.

I've always had a way with music. I can remember every note in a song after I've heard it a couple of times, the rhythm, the bass, the lead riffs—all of it. Back in basic training, when they had me guarding the Motor Pool in the dead of night, I'd remember songs in my head. I'd hear them perfectly, as if the records were playing somewhere between my ears.

Man, my high school days were something, but they didn't last. The band broke up after graduation. Herb, our drummer, got drafted. Terry married his girl, Mary, and moved away. And I went to State College, flunked out and got drafted.

We arrived at Camp McGernity about an hour before sundown. I liked the primitive, Wild-West quality of the place. We rode in a bus along dusty dirt streets, past wooden barracks encircled by wooden sidewalks. There were sandbags all over the place; low walls of them surrounded the buildings, and they were stacked in orderly layers over the mounds of underground bunkers. A pretty Vietnamese woman in a conical hat swept off the stoop of one of the barracks. She smiled as we drove past.

We entered our barracks, our boots clomping on the wooden floor. The place was full of cots, but no people. The emptiness of the place bothered me.

"It's a sad place, isn't it?" I said.

"When you find yourself out in the boondocks," said Beobee, "you'll wish you had such a sad place to sleep in, believe me."

"All right," I said and laughed as I looked at Glock. "You're right. It's a great place. It's quaint and, you know, rustic."

Beobee shook his head as if realizing for the first time that I'd never be the soldier he was. I was bone-tired and I didn't care. From the moment the army had sworn me in, I never thought of myself as a soldier. I felt more like a prisoner. Getting drafted had been like getting shanghaied.

"I'm going over to the Air Force base to see if I can find a friend of mine," Beobee said. "You guys want to come?"

Glock shook his head.

"Thanks," I said, "but I'm gonna read and then take a nap. You never know, they might want us to pull KP or guard tonight."

"All right," Beobee said. He walked out the door.

Glock poured some water from a canteen over his head and rubbed it into his face. He turned to me. "Whew," he said, "my ears were getting numb. I'm taking a walk. Be back in an hour."

"All right," I said, wishing he'd asked me to come with him. I didn't really want to sleep; I wanted to look around, but Beobee's constant talk had worn on me.

I must've napped for three hours, because when I woke, the sun had set. The barracks was dark and quiet and a heavy homesickness came over me. I wished I had someone to talk to, even Beobee.

There was no moon and the night air was hot and dry. Wearing flip-flops and a towel around my waist, with only the faint light of the stars to see by, I walked along the wooden sidewalk toward the showers. Every now and then I'd wander off into the sand and have to prod with my toes to find the wooden walkway and get back on. I continued on in this way for about fifty meters when I heard someone coming. I stopped and listened as booted footsteps approached and stopped right in front of me. Whoever it was, was no more than a foot or two away, but I couldn't see them. They'd obviously been aware of me, as they'd stopped, yet they said nothing.

"Who's there?" I said. No answer. I waited another few seconds, the hair on my neck standing straight out.

"Who is it?" I said. Still nothing. Then I heard him, or her, start to cry. It was strange; I couldn't tell if it was a man or a woman, but it was the most pitiful crying I'd ever heard. A shiver ran through me. The crying stopped and I waited a few more seconds and then moved forward again, this time with my hand thrust out before me, the way you'd wave cobwebs away from your face. I didn't feel anything and continued on my way. There was no one in the showers, and only a single, dim light bulb to see by. I showered quickly, looking over my shoulder every so often.

Back at the barracks, I thought about the incident for a long time. I'd read about things like that happening to other people, but I'd never experienced it myself. I think it was some kind of spirit, a lost soul, maybe somebody that'd died in the war. I don't think I'd been in any danger or anything. It was more like the thing, whatever it was, had come to warn me, to tell me something. Finally I fell asleep.

Someone bumped into my cot, almost knocking it over. It was dark. I recognized Beobee's voice.

"We got incoming, boy. 122s. Get in the bunker."

I followed him out of the barracks and down the earthen steps while the sirens wailed sorrowfully in the distance. Inside the bunker, it was so dark it didn't make any difference if my eyes were open or closed. An enemy rocket slammed to earth with a thunderous boom and I jumped. Fortunately nobody saw me.

"Yeah, they're 122s all right," Beobee said.

I heard Glock agree with him, as if he knew a 122-millimeter rocket from a Roman candle. In the rear of the bunker some guy started sobbing hysterically. Nobody laughed at him.

"You know," said a faceless voice behind me, "the psychic Jeanne Dixon predicted that Camp McGernity would be attacked and overrun by the communists on Christmas."

"Yeah, I heard that too," said a solemn voice to my left.

Another rocket crashed closer. The bunker shook, timbers creaked. A couple other guys speculated on Dixon's predictions. The idiots, I thought, why didn't they just shut up? They were only making things worse.

Everyone fell silent as we waited for the next rocket. I heard Beobee patiently explaining to someone that, "Yes, indeed, a direct hit from a 122 could easily pierce the roof of our bunker. But," said Beobee with assurance, "that would never happen because the base is large and our barracks, along with the hospital buildings, is positioned in the center, well out of range."

"Aw, shut up, will you," someone yelled from the darkness.

"Yeah, you're only making things worse!" said somebody else.

"That's right, keep your big mouth shut," yelled a chorus of voices.

In the rear of the bunker, the one guy continued to sob. Rockets fell in quick succession, shaking the bunker as if a giant were striding our

8

way, ready to slam a huge foot down and squash us like bugs. People screamed and I was scared, expecting the ceiling to come crashing down at any moment. The rockets stopped suddenly and a hundred sirens wailed in the night. I thought of that science fiction movie, *The Time Machine*. After a nuclear war, the Morloks—radiation-deformed humanoids—used sirens to lure the normal humans into huge underground air-raid shelters. Instead of finding safety there, the humans were slaughtered by the Morloks and eaten.

These sirens sounded the same—long, drawn-out sorrowful wails— and I thought that if the enemy caught us in here, all without weapons, we'd be slaughtered, too. Finally the sirens wound down and stopped. For a few minutes nobody moved, and then Beobee said, "It's over now."

We started up the earthen steps, our arms on one another's shoulders like blind men, when suddenly there was a flash of light and a series of booms shook the earth. People shouted and somebody's head butted me in the gut, taking the wind out of me and knocking me down. Something knifed into my leg. Others fell and people stepped on us as they ran back down the stairs.

"Outgoing! They're our guns!" someone yelled.

"That's right," Beobee said. "Our artillery's trying to catch them before they crawl back into their rat holes."

Nobody moved for a moment and then lights came on. Beobee helped me to my feet. "You okay?"

I looked up at the light and nodded.

"Wait a minute. You're bleeding."

I looked. My pants were torn and bloody at the knee.

"C'mon," Beobee said, "you're going to the aid station."

The aid station was bustling with activity. Medics moved between the rows of several dozen cots. Beobee and I sat down on an empty cot. After a few moments a woman wearing fatigues came over to us. She was pretty and wore her hair in a little pony tail. She looked at my leg and then asked me who I was and what happened. She wrote it all down on a clipboard. Then she took out a needle.

"I'm going to have to anesthetize your leg and give you a few stitches. I'll give you a shot for tetanus."

I stretched out while Beobee went to talk to some guy outside the tent. I looked around at some grungy-looking men laying on the cots. "Were they hurt in the shelling?" I asked the doctor.

"No," she said as she worked. "They're infantry. They got it in a firefight. They're the lucky ones. Six men were killed."

In the morning we were issued our bedding and fatigues. After that we went to the armory and got our M-16s, a magazine of rounds, web gear and two grenades. Initially I felt uncomfortable with the rifle, afraid I'd trip and shoot somebody. After I'd zeroed it though, I felt more comfortable with it. With our rifles slung over our shoulders, our gear on our backs, and our new Combat Infantryman's Badges, CIBs, pinned proudly to our chests, we clomped noisily along the wooden sidewalks back to the transient barracks. After we'd put everything away, I told the guys I had to go back to the aid station. They said they would go with me.

It was a hot, cloudless day, the temperature in the nineties. Glock wore a black beret he'd picked up somewhere. For infantry like us, berets were not considered uniform wear. Military people were touchy about their hats, scarves and things.

We stepped into the dusty street. Glock stopped. "You guys want to see where the rockets landed?"

"Will it take long?" I said. I was curious, but I didn't want to keep the doctor waiting.

Beobee checked his watch. "It'll only take ten minutes."

We came to the six-foot-high chain-link fence separating the runway from the rest of the base. On the other side, a hundred feet away, a mob of guys in tee shirts, armed with sledge hammers and crow bars, were removing some twisted steel plates from the runway where one of the rockets had landed. I spotted a jagged, sharp-looking piece of metal as big as a pen knife about ten feet away on the other side of the fence.

I pointed. "Look, a present from the enemy."

Glock looked around quickly, then hoisted himself up on the fence.

Beobee grabbed his shirt. "You can't go over. Why you think they got it fenced off?"

"Oh no? Watch me."

The metal fence jangled as Glock climbed over, jumping down with a thud. He walked toward the shrapnel and an Air Force lieutenant turned and saw him.

"Hey you! Where you think you're going?" The Lieutenant's fists balled at his sides.

Glock picked up the shrapnel. Standing, he was a head taller than the Lieutenant. "This is for my little brother back home."

The Lieutenant frowned as he looked up at Glock. "Don't they teach you army boys how to address an officer?"

Glock smiled down at him. "Yes, Sir. Sorry, Sir."

The Lieutenant's eyes flitted from Glock's face to his beret. He was on the verge of saying something, but couldn't quite get it out. He suddenly smiled a little, as if he'd just realized it was all a joke or something. "Okay, soldier, you have your souvenir. Now get back on your own side of the fence."

"Yes, Sir!" said Glock, with a little bit too much emphasis on the "Sir."

The Lieutenant hesitated and my heart sank. I thought Glock had gone too far, but then the lieutenant shook his head in disbelief. "Army draftees! Kee-riest!" He went back to the others.

Glock climbed back over the fence. I couldn't believe it. Glock had met the lieutenant's eye and won him over.

We continued to the aid station. A tank and a deuce-and-half truck rumbled by, raising clouds of dust. We turned a corner, coming upon some guys yelling and jumping as they played volleyball.

Beobee scowled. "Damned Base Camp Commandos."

Glock looked like he wanted to join them.

I was never really fond of sports, but the life of a Base Camp Commando looked pretty good. One of the guys in the transient barracks had said that last night's rocket attack was the first one in two months. He said that there was a constant stream of infantry guys coming in here on litters, all of them shot or blown up. No doubt about it, the life of a Base Camp Commando was a lot safer than life in the boondocks. I put it out of my head though. I was infantry. Period. And soon they'd be sending me to the field and there wasn't a thing I could do about it.

We walked on. An electrical generator droned behind some big tents. A dozen or so Vietnamese soldiers, ARVNs they called them, and a couple of new recruits like us passed, talking loudly and laughing, probably on their way to the chow hall. We slowed and I heard that song, "Fire In My Soul," by Steem Masheen blaring through the wooden walls of one of the barracks. It made me think of Terry and the band. We loved Steem Masheen; they were our heroes.

Inside the barracks a drunken voice tried to match the pitch and passion of Masheen's lead singer, Turk and, failing miserably, ended in a croak. Glock and Beobee and I cracked up. We stopped and listened to the organ solo and the hairs on the back of my neck stood straight out. It was a wild and happy moment.

When we got back to the barracks, Beobee got a metal canteen out from under his cot. He shook it, rattling the ice inside it, and said, "Kool-Aid . . . lime. Very hard to come by." He gave us a conspiratorial look. "I have a friend in the chow hall."

"Beobee has a friend everywhere," Glock said.

Beobee produced three paper cups and filled them with the cold, green liquid. He passed the drinks to us. "And now we have to toast our friendship. To us."

CHAPTER 2

There were about eighteen guys at the chopper pad when we arrived. A young lieutenant with a clipboard came and stood before us. He told us about the chopper blades, how they've been known to droop on occasion, and how, if we didn't want to lose our heads we would have to bend from the waist as we approached the aircraft. We were assigned six to a chopper.

We'd spent three weeks at McGernity. There were no more nightime rocket-attacks, but a couple of times we saw battles raging out in the distance. You couldn't hear the firing, but you could see machine-gun tracers like red stitching across the black night sky. Sometimes a round ricocheted off the ground and went bouncing off wildly. Now we were going to the boondocks, closer to the enemy.

I heard the first of the choppers approaching, its blades going, "thock-eh-ta-thock-eh-ta." A few moments later the first helicopter settled down like a duck on a pond, raising a storm of dust. One of the door gunners waved us forward and we ran, hunched over, and scrambled quickly inside. We all crowded in the center, our knees pulled up under our chins, as far away from the open doors as possible. Then I noticed Beobee and Glock sitting calmly with their feet hanging out the door. I followed suit.

The pilot wore a helmet with a mike. After looking around to make sure we were all in, he eased back on the stick. The chopper shuddered like a washing machine on spin with an unbalanced load as we lifted a foot or so off the ground. We started moving forward and Glock and I broke out in ear-to-ear grins.

It was magic. With our feet dangling earthward and the wind whipping through the cabin, we climbed quickly to four or five thousand feet. Soon we were over the jungle, and from this height it looked like a green sea with mountainous swells. The pilots seemed like young gods with fantastic powers as they worked the various controls that kept us shuddering and swaying through the sky like a great metal bird. I would have given anything for the guys in the neighborhood to have seen this.

As I looked down, I was reminded of riding the Chesapeake Ferry as a boy with my father. I would hold tightly to his hand as we stared down at our shadows on the foaming bow wave. I was afraid of that cold, green abyss under the boat, sure there was something horrible down there. I guess I'd already seen too many horror movies because I was sure some huge monster would surface at any moment, turn its angry eyes on us and pull us down into the water, leaving not a trace behind. The jungle below us seemed like that too, full of hidden horrors. What was below its surface? Was the enemy watching us right now? Maybe they were shooting at us, or getting ready to launch a rocket at us. I wondered if we would be able to see the bullets? And if the chopper took a direct hit, could the pilot land it?

This wild, shaky ride, our introduction to the war, reminded me of another movie I'd seen as a boy about a lost world. It too had started with a helicopter ride. Then something went wrong and it crash-landed inside the cone of an extinct volcano. The passengers discovered a hidden world there, complete with dinosaurs and natives. A few natives were eaten; one was squashed by a dinosaur; half a dozen fell to their deaths from a jagged cliff, and some guy, the villain, got a spear in the back. Finally the hero and a very cute blonde, the old professor's daughter, managed to escape. I must've seen a thousand Saturday matinees like that when I was a kid. They were great because no matter how bad things got there were always survivors. Survivors! I suddenly realized why I'd loved those movies so much. After all the death and destruction, when you walked out of the movie house into the bright sunlight, you were a survivor. That's what I wanted to be. That's what everybody wanted to be.

Beobee tapped me on the shoulder and pointed to a brown smudge in the distance. "There it is," he yelled over the noise of the engine, "Firebase 29."

The Firebase was slightly higher than the surrounding peaks. Its trees and foliage had been scraped off, giving it the appearance of a reddish brown island in a sea of green. About twenty-five 105 howitzer artillery pieces were arranged around the perimeter, and I saw men carrying boxes full of rounds from a big pile over to one of them. Then the ground was rushing up at us as we came down, and the people down there turned away and covered their eyes as our chopper's blades whipped up a storm of dust. I hopped off with the others and ran behind a sandbag wall. The next bird landed before the wind from ours had died down and then they were both gone, the "thock-eh-ta" sound echoing off the hills as the dust cloud slowly drifted away.

A sandy-haired guy with a clipboard took us to the Command Post bunker, or CP as they called it. The light was dim inside and it took my eyes a moment to adjust. The Captain and his First Sergeant sat at a makeshift table of ammo crates. They were both about fifty or so. The Captain was thin, with a kind face and a bald spot on the top of his head like a yarmulke. The First Sergeant had the face and barrel chest of a bulldog and wore his brown hair straight up at attention like a scrub brush. A younger Sergeant sat in front of a big, green radio reading a comic book. A large map with ridge lines like fingerprints, and white and red flags stuck in it, hung on the wall behind them. Web-gear, rucksacks, canteens and M-16's hung from wooden pegs hammered into the other dirt walls.

The guy that brought us in addressed the Captain. "Sir, these are the new replacements in from Pleiku."

The guy next to me saluted nervously and the Captain waved it away. "We don't salute officers out here in the field, son." Getting to his feet, the Captain looked us over silently. He seemed to be a pretty decent guy for an officer.

He started pacing. "Okay men, relax. Welcome to Company B. My name's Captain Harris. There's not much I can say that'll make your stay out here any easier. A lot of what you need to know you'll pick up from your buddies, so pay close attention to how they handle themselves out here."

We really were "out here." From the chopper, the base had appeared as a mere speck of brown on a green planet.

15

The Captain pointed to the map behind him. "We're situated near the tri-border area of Vietnam, Cambodia and Laos." He ran his finger along a line on the map. "We patrol this entire area, from this grid on down." He pointed to a ridge of mountains. "From here to McGernity. The enemy operates a system of trails that'd make the New Jersey Turnpike look like a country road. We're also in what we call a free-fire zone. That means if you see somebody, you better shoot first and ask questions later."

"What about civilians, Sir?" I said. I didn't want to shoot anybody by mistake. The Captain looked at me sternly. "In this area there are no civilians, son. If you want to go home you better remember that." He turned to the young Sergeant. "Do you have that list I marked up showing who goes in what squad?"

The Sergeant shook his head.

The Captain smiled kindly. "Hang loose for a moment, men, while I find out where we're going to put you all."

He went into the next room of the bunker. Nobody said anything and it suddenly hit me. I was finally in Vietnam, in an infantry company. All during training I'd avoided thinking about it, hoping that I'd be one of the lucky ones the army sent to Germany or Korea, or Iceland, places where there was no war. That accounted for only about a half-dozen guys. The rest of us, about a hundred and fifty, got our orders for infantry training which meant, "you're going to Vietnam."

I remembered a conversation I'd had with a friend of mine back home, Tom Hearst. He'd asked me why I was going. Tom's parents had managed to get him in the Coast Guard Reserve. All the reserves—Army, Navy, Air Force—were packed with guys who didn't want to go to Vietnam. And there were long waiting lists to get in, so you had to know somebody. My parents didn't. So, Tom didn't have to sweat anything, yet he had the nerve to ask me why I was going? Like I really had a lot of options! Civilians who evaded the draft were getting five to ten years in federal prison. Soldiers who refused to go to Vietnam ended up busting rocks in the stockades. Some guys ran away to Canada. The way I looked at it, Vietnam was my best option . . . as long as I didn't get killed.

The Captain came back in with a clipboard. He cleared his throat. "Our job is to keep the enemy from running supplies through this valley and so far as we know they've been confining their activities to the other side of the border." He stopped pacing and tucked his hands behind his belt. "We run a lot of reconnaissance patrols and if we spot anybody out there, we simply move back and call artillery in on them. We have enough firepower here to level one of those mountains across the way, so if you keep track of where you are, and you know how to use your radio, you'll be all right. In a few minutes you'll meet your squad and they'll answer a lot of your questions. Battalion flies a hot meal out to us just about every other day now, so relax and try and get used to the hill."

He made it sound a little too easy.

The Captain turned to the young guy who had met us at the chopper pad. "Ted, are we getting hots this afternoon?"

"Yes, Sir. Meatballs with mashed potatoes and string beans."

We followed Ted through a shoulder-high trench which snaked from bunker to bunker. Twenty-three line-bunkers encircled the hill. Ted dropped Beobee at the machine gun squad. I was glad to find out that Glock and I would be in the same squad, the third squad. As I looked out over the jungle, I hoped my luck would hold out when I went down there on a patrol.

I've always been an especially lucky person. In fact, I've cheated death twice: once when I almost drowned in the surf at Atlantic City, and another time when I was a kid and got hit by a car while riding my bike. In my senior year of high school I had read a little about Buddhism. The theory of karma held the key to my luck, I think. It explained that what happens to us now is the result of everything we've already done, even in past lives. Christians have a similar belief, you know, where the bible says, "What you sow, so shall you reap." I figured my karma was probably okay because, while I'm not a saint or anything, I'm not a bad person either.

Third squad's bunker was on the steepest side of the mountain. Here the hill fell away sharply into a fifty-foot drop full of concertina wire rolls and tautly stretched barbed wire. Beyond the wire the foliage began and the angle of the slope decreased slightly. From the trench I could

17

see all of the valley and the mountains rising on the other side. A brown gash of earth, running for maybe a thousand yards, was visible in the middle of the valley. Glock pointed at it, wondering what it was. Ted said it was a bombed-out part of the Ho Chi Minh trail complex. As far as the eye could see, that scratch of brown was the only evidence of man's presence.

Inside the bunker, a man sat at a crude table, smoking a pipe and writing a letter. A picture of a woman and two children was propped up in front of him.

"Fellas," Ted said to us, "this is Papa, your squad leader."

Papa took the pipe from his mouth and rose to greet us. We shook hands. He looked to be over thirty, with a Mediterranean tan and big, brown eyes that had a fatherly warmth to them. I liked him right off. The only other person in the bunker was asleep in the top bunk, curled up like a cat, with his back to us.

"Well," said Ted, "I have to get back." He shook hands with Glock and me. "I'll see you guys around the hill." He walked out.

Papa smiled warmly. "So, how was your trip out?"

"Great," I said, "I really liked the chopper ride."

Papa laughed. "Yeah, they're a lot of fun." He pointed to some boxes. "Sit down, guys."

I sat and enjoyed the coolness of the bunker. After being outside it was like air conditioning.

"What's going on back there with all those demonstrations?" Papa asked. "Have you seen any?"

Glock laughed. "Not in my hometown."

"I saw some National Guardsman in the Washington, D.C. train station when they took us down to Fort Bragg," I said. "He had twigs and leaves all over him like he was on some kind of bush patrol."

Papa laughed and shook his head. I was glad I ended up in his squad. He seemed like a nice guy. He showed us where we'd be bunking and we started putting our things away. He tapped the sleeping guy on the butt. There was a grunt of complaint.

The guy spoke without turning around. "Okay, Jackson, you'd better have a good reason for waking me or we're gonna fight!"

He had a funny accent I couldn't place.

Papa and Glock laughed.

The guy sat up, looked down at us angrily, rubbed his eyes, and said, "Oh!" His angry look faded to a shy smile. He was tall, maybe five-eleven, but skinny. His face was very pale, almost sickly, and he had black, olive eyes.

"Lee, these are the new men," said Papa in his mellow voice.

We all shook hands. Lee seemed friendly, although intense. He was from some small town in Ohio and my age, eighteen. We talked about home. Then Papa showed us some more pictures of his family. He was from St. Paul.

"How many guys are in the squad?" Glock asked.

Papa smiled. "Well, now that you guys have finally arrived, seven. There are three more guys out on patrol."

I started putting my things in one of the empty top bunks. Even though I had finally ended up in the boondocks where who-knows-what could happen, it felt good to have a home of sorts. This seemed like a really close squad.

I stared out the little firing port built into the side of the bunker at the dirty green surface of the jungle below. Back in Basic Training when we had bayonet practice, the Drill Instructor made us scream at the top of our lungs, "Kill! Kill!" while we thrust and parried with our rifles. I had always cracked up. I didn't hate anybody and I wasn't a killer.

Lee climbed down from his bunk. "So, you say you're from Philadelphia, Carl?"

"Yeah."

He laughed, his face tense. "When I heard we were getting replacements, I thought for sure we'd get more New Yorkers."

Papa looked at us and winked. "Lee doesn't like New Yorkers very much."

"Really? Why?"

Lee's face was pinched. "I just don't like them."

Papa smiled. "Aren't they supposed to be rude?"

"I heard they were always in a hurry," Glock volunteered.

"I remember a waiter in a deli like that," I said. My friends and I went up to New York once in a while after we graduated. "The waiter walked away when we didn't make up our minds right away."

Papa interrupted. "Speaking of delis, fellas, it's almost chow time. We should get in line."

We filed out the aperture, but Lee stayed behind.

"Aren't you coming?" Papa asked.

Lee shook his head. "Nah. Not hungry."

The line at the mess tent was short when we got there. Papa turned to Glock and me. "Lee was on Firebase 99 over at Ben Me Gon. They had incoming mortar fire day after day for over a month. He never got over it. That's why he's so angry. I'm trying to arrange a job at the Base Camp for him."

Glock and I nodded. I guess that would make a guy irritable. The line moved up and I slopped a mound of mashed potatoes and meatballs onto my paper plate. There was a tub full of purple Kool-Aid, and I ladled my cup full.

I followed Papa and Glock back through the trenches to the bunker. We sat on the bunker roof under the bright sunlight. Below, the vast expanse of jungle shimmered in the growing heat. We ate quietly.

Ted, the guy that met us earlier at the chopper pad, came over carrying a green patrol radio. A loud, staticky voice issued from it, saying something I couldn't make out.

Ted decreased the volume. He called over to the guys at the next bunker, "Friendlies on the way in." Then he yelled to Papa, "I've got Ron on the horn right now. They'll be coming up through the wire any minute, okay?"

"Okay," said Papa. He put down his plate and stood. We moved to the edge of the bunker and looked down to where the maze of barbed wire, mines and trip flares met the tangled green of the jungle. I could barely make out something moving through the greenery. Then bamboo crackled loudly and they emerged, hunched over, the green rucksacks high up on their backs like humps, weapons cradled in their arms. They plodded slowly up the winding path like a team of mules tethered together, three black guys, soul brothers they liked to be called, and a white guy bringing up the rear. One of the soul brothers carried an M-79 grenade launcher and another an M-16 rifle and the radio. The point man was very dark, and carried a sawed-off, automatic shotgun. The white guy carried the M-60 machine gun. All four of them had belted machine gun ammo X-ed across their chests like Mexican banditos.

Papa yelled down to them. They looked up and waved feebly. I think they were too winded to yell or say anything. The dusty-colored guy lost his helmet as he leaned back to see us. He quickly grabbed it and laughed. The darker point man's eyes were hidden behind a pair of wrap-around sunglasses.

Once inside the wire, they dumped their rucksacks and sat. They were all sweating pretty bad; it must've been a rough climb up from the valley. The white machine gunner collected the extra belts of ammo and left.

The three soul brothers regarded us casually as Papa introduced us. The older, darker guy, Ron, made me a little uncomfortable. It was the wrap-around sunglasses, and not being able to see his eyes. He bent to his rucksack and took a map from it, never offering to shake our hands or anything. The tall, light-brown, thin guy suddenly reached out to shake my hand and introduced himself as Mike. He seemed friendly and outgoing. The tan-colored guy was Puerto Rican. I could tell by his accent. He smiled and said his name was Chico. They were all from New York City. I suddenly remembered Lee's comment about New Yorkers and understood what he'd really been saying. He didn't like black people.

Normally, Glock was really outgoing, but he seemed shy and unsure of himself. "I never heard of the army issuing shotguns?" he said to Ron.

I had never heard of it either.

Ron sort of smiled. "What shotgun?" he said, as if he didn't have one lying at his feet. He laughed and turned to Papa. "I'm going to the CP for my debriefing." Then he picked up his weapon and walked off.

Glock watched him go, shaking his head. There seemed to be bad chemistry between them already. Maybe Ron didn't like Glock's beret. After all, Glock was a new recruit like me, yet here he was sporting a black beret like he was part of some elite commando unit or something.

Papa turned to Glock, saying "according to the rules of the Geneva Convention, we're not supposed to have shotguns here."

"Is that right?" said Glock.

"Why?" I said.

Papa shrugged. "I guess they're supposed to be inhumane or something."

"That's right," said Chico. He wiped his face with the green towel draped around his neck and threw me a wink. "Inhumane."

"Dig it," said Mike, the tall, skinny guy.

Glock still had a strained look on his face. I guess he wasn't used to people like Ron.

Mike looked up at Papa. "Hey, Papa, any hots today?"

"Yeah, but you better hurry. They'll be closing the chow line down any minute."

Chico pointed at Papa. "We call him Papa cause he's an old, old man." He laughed.

I turned to Papa. "They didn't draft you, did they? How'd you end up in the Infantry?"

Papa smiled. "No, I was too old for the draft and I had a little baby, too."

"So, how'd they get you?" Glock asked.

Papa gestured at the black square of the bunker opening. "Let's go inside, guys. It's too hot to talk out here."

It seemed odd, someone as old as Papa, being a Specialist Fourth Class in the Infantry. If you enlisted in the Army, you usually got to go to a school and learn a trade. The Army filled out the ranks of the Infantry with draftees like me. Nobody enlisted for the Infantry, at least nobody in his right mind.

When we were seated inside, Papa continued. "It's true. I did join the army. But not the Infantry."

"So what happened?" Glock asked.

Papa sighed heavily. "There were extenuating circumstances." He leaned back against the sandbag wall and crossed his legs. "I was married, with one little kid, and between jobs. The recruiter told me that if I signed up I could go to Electronics School. Well, about halfway through school the second baby came along." Papa pointed to the picture on his writing table. "The baby was colicky and cried all the time. I couldn't sleep. I couldn't concentrate on my studies. Many's the night I spent in the car with a flashlight and my books, cramming for a test."

Lee came running into the bunker. "Air strike," he yelled.

We followed him up onto the roof of the bunker. The jets looked gnat-sized, they were so far away. I watched one rush down at a steep angle, release its bombs and pull up sharply for a getaway. Seconds later a bright orange napalm flower blossomed, quickly turning into a puff of jet-black smoke. Then the sound of the explosion reached us. As the two jets made repeated runs, Mike and Chico returned and watched from the trench.

"They're puttin' down some heavy stuff on them," Chico said.

"Dig it," Mike said.

The jets were so tiny the whole thing seemed unreal. It looked more like a movie. When it was over, Mike and Chico wandered off again and Glock, Papa and I went back inside the bunker. Lee stayed on the roof with his radio.

Back inside, Papa seated himself comfortably and leaned back against the wall. "So, where was I," he said.

"You were in your car studying with a flashlight," said Glock, throwing me a look as if Papa was goofy or something.

I didn't smile back.

"Well," Papa said, "to make a long story short, I flunked out and they put me in the Infantry."

Ron's voice came from out in the trench. He and Lee were arguing about something.

"That's a shame. Couldn't you take the course again?" I said.

Papa laughed. "No. They said they'd send me to school and they did. I was the one who flunked out."

"Well, they need more bodies in the Infantry than they do in electronic school," Glock said.

Outside, the others were still arguing.

Papa threw up his hands. "Eh! That's life. I'll be going home soon anyway. I came in with the monsoons and when they return I'll be climbing into a chopper, heading out." Papa smiled.

"When's that?" Glock asked.

Before Papa could answer Ron, Mike and Chico entered. Ron was carrying a clear plastic sack full of cigarettes, soap and candy, everything you couldn't buy out in the boondocks. "I got the CPs," he said as he sat the bag down in front of his bunk.

"What's 'CP' mean?" Glock asked.

"Care Package, maybe," said Ron. He started going through the bag as Lee came in. Ron took out a pack of Blasto Mints.

Lee's eyes went wide. "I get the Blastos this time. You had them last!"

"No, I didn't," said Ron, "there weren't any last time."

Lee advanced. "Yes, you did!" He tried to grab them out of Ron's hand and they were pushing each other, about to fight.

"That's enough, Lee," Papa said, rushing to put himself between them.

I looked at Glock and the others. Nobody moved. Maybe this wasn't such a great squad after all. I'd been looking forward to some quiet so I could write a letter to my folks. And now this.

Papa separated them. Lee jerked his arm out of Papa's grasp and moved toward the aperture. "I'm going to see the Captain. I'm not staying in this squad anymore!"

"Lee! Wait a minute." Papa moved to catch up with him.

In a slight depression, away from all the noise and activity, a huge, wooden potty, built on a platform of rough-hewn timbers, squatted in the center of a circle of seven-foot-high sandbag pillars. Seven steps led up to a white enamel seat, the only thing made to human scale. It looked like some kind of ancient astral observatory, or altar, that had been left behind by a race of giants. There was a rack built into the side of the structure full of magazines and newspapers. Underneath was a big, black 55-gallon oil drum with its top cut off to collect the droppings. A camouflaged awning crowned the entire affair.

I climbed the steps and sat down. All my life I'd never had much exposure to black people. When I was a child, there were none in our neighborhood. I'd heard about them, but I had never seen one until I went to the first grade at Saint Michael's. There was only one there, a tall, skinny girl named Beth Blakey. All the black people lived across the fields in the government housing, "the projects" we called them. They never came into our neighborhood and we never went into theirs.

The only time we ever saw them was when we, I must've been eight or nine years old then, when we ventured out into those fields to play war. We'd take our plastic carbines and our sixguns in holsters, our toy bazookas and maybe a neighborhood dog or two, and we'd skulk through the tall grass. If we saw any black people, it was usually from a distance and we'd all stop and hide ourselves and watch them until they went away.

One time we didn't see them right away and about a dozen black kids came around a corner about twenty feet away, almost bumping into us. This one guy's eyes locked onto mine. I can still see him. His face was very dark and he was wearing a pair of red shorts and a torn undershirt with a couple of dime-sized holes around the neck. His arms and legs were long and skinny. I knew his eyes wanted to slide off mine, as much as mine did off his, but we didn't dare. We just stood staring at each other and then our gangs started backing off and we searched for rocks to throw. In another second the barrage began.

I heaved a rock and ducked into a clump of bushes. Inside it was cool and fragrant with wild honeysuckle, and I felt as though I were magically insulated from the battle. I ran out and heaved another rock and ducked back into my green sanctuary. Straining to hear the muted sounds of the battle outside, I looked over into the eyes of my friend Jimmy Gallagher who had also discovered the safety of the grove. We burst out laughing, not having had this much fun in a long time. Then, just as I was getting ready to go out again, the relative quiet of our hideout was pierced by a tiny sound overhead. Both Jimmy and I heard it and looked at each other and then up. It became a quick clipping noise and then something cracked into my head with such force it knocked me down. I felt dizzy as thick, salty-tasting, sticky stuff poured down my face, blurring my vision. I saw the rock at my feet, the size of an egg. Bright, red blood stained my clothes and hands. I had never seen that much blood in my life. I ran back to my house. When my mother saw me, she screamed and cried, confirming my worst fears.

25

I vaguely remember a trip to the hospital, lying on an X-ray table, then someone sewing up the side of my head. It was as if they were sewing up a hat I had on and not me. That was the first and last exchange I had with black people until I was drafted. There were a couple dozen of them in high school, but they kept to themselves and so did we. In basic training about thirty percent of the guys were black, but it was the same thing. Then I came to Vietnam.

It was a messed-up situation. We were supposed to live and work together, but racial tensions were evidently as high here as they were back in the States. Back home you couldn't pick up the paper without reading about some race riot somewhere.

Two days later Papa had to take out a patrol. Glock and Lee would be going. That morning I watched them get ready. Glock had evidently managed to talk Papa into letting him carry the shotgun. He looked pretty thrilled about it, sitting there wearing that black beret of his while he oiled the wooden stock of the shotgun, a wad of gum working in his jaw. Lee seemed glad to be getting away from Ron. It bothered me that now, after all this racial trouble had been stirred up, I'd be the only white guy left to spend the next four or five days with the black guys. I wished I was going with them.

CHAPTER 3

I sat up in my bunk and tried to read. Below, Chico was trimming his nails and across from him, Ron and Mike were playing poker. Someone approached out in the trench. Ted, the company clerk, called in. Ron went out to see what he wanted.

"Hey, Melcher," Ron said when he came back in, "go see Gene-the-medic up at the giant potty. He needs some help."

"Okay, what is it?" I said.

Ron wiped his face with a towel. "You'll find out."

I didn't mind doing a detail. After all, they had all just come back from a patrol, so if something needed doing it was certainly my turn. But there was something about the way Ron said, "you'll find out," that bothered me. Chico's and Mike's suspicious smiles didn't help much either.

After I left the bunker, I felt better. Gene-the-medic was a little, skinny guy with long blond hair, blue eyes and a drooping, blond, past-regulation-length mustache. He stood on a box in front of the big oil-drum, which had been pulled out from under the potty. He looked down on the contents, which were burning with a bluish flame. A hand-lettered sign reading, "OUT OF ORDER" stretched across the steps leading up to the white enamel seat. As I watched, he dipped a wooden oar into the mess and gave it a stir.

He looked up and saw me watching. "You gotta stir it occasionally or it won't burn completely."

"I never knew it burned," I said.

"Yeah, isn't it amazing? I couldn't believe it either till I first saw it. You have to keep adding diesel fuel to it though." He stuck out his hand. "My name's Gene. I'm the company doc."

"Hi," I said, "Carl Melcher. They sent me up to help you out." I liked this guy. I didn't know why.

"Listen," he said, "this ain't a bad job. Some guys get all worked up over it, but Jees, somebody's got to do it or we'd be up to our armpits in it by now. I'd do it myself but I have to go over and check on a guy in the Fourth platoon."

"What's the matter?" I said, wondering if maybe there had been some action last night that I hadn't heard about.

Gene shook his head and stopped stirring. "Sounds like he may have malaria." He stared sadly into the blue flames. "If these guys would just take their damn malaria pills . . ."

He gave me a sudden piercing look. "You're new in country. Did they give you enough malaria pills?"

"A couple of weeks' worth."

He lay the paddle down carefully and began rummaging through a green vinyl flight bag full of vials, dressings and tubes of ointment. He pulled out two bottles and handed them to me.

"Do you need any water purification tablets?" he said, holding out a blue bottle.

I took them.

"How're your feet doing? There's a nasty fungus you get out here if you don't wash and powder your feet every day."

I told him my feet were fine and he seemed pleased. He closed his bag and stirred the drum. "Some of these guys razz me about this stuff, I know. But they'll appreciate it in the long run."

I didn't say anything.

He sat down across from me and lit a cigarette. "Did you meet the Captain yet?"

I nodded. "He seems like a pretty decent guy."

"He is. He really cares about the men."

"Really?"

"Yeah. You know, he served in World War II and in Korea, but he doesn't believe in this war."

"How do you know that?" I asked.

"You hear things around the CP. I don't believe in the war either. It's tearing the country apart."

"So why'd you come?" I said.

He smiled at me. "I'm not going to sit this thing out in Canada or prison, man. It's too important. It's history." He took a long pull at his cigarette. "I thought about it a lot. I meditated on it." He exhaled noisily. "I went through a lot of changes." He stepped on his cigarette butt. "When I realized I could come here and help people, not harm them . . . that was when everything came together for me."

"Wow," I said, trying to sound enthusiastic. He seemed to be so much more mature than me. He thought deeper, did things after he thought about them, meditated. I wanted to be like that, but I knew I wasn't. Things just happen to me, as if I have no say, and then I react.

"How do you like being in Papa's squad?" he said.

"I'm not sure yet. Papa's okay. Mike's kind of odd, though. All he ever says is 'Dig it,' or 'I'm hip.' "

Gene laughed. "He's extremely shy and quiet. But a nice guy."

I nodded. "Things're kind of uptight now. Ron and Lee got in an argument the other day."

Gene frowned. "I heard about that. Lee's got a lot of emotional problems."

"It's not just Lee. I think that guy Ron's got some problems too. I don't think he likes Glock or me."

Gene smiled. "Ron's a little grouchy," he said, "but he's okay. You'll get used to him. Did you know he joined the Army?"

"You're kidding!"

"No. He thought he could get a good deal out of it. Things must've been pretty tough where he came from. He's trying to make some rank. Then when he gets back to the world, he wants to go to drill instructor's school."

I remembered my drill instructor, or DI, with his Mountie hat, his reddened face inches from mine as he screamed at me for some infraction of the rules, spittle flying from his lips. There had only been one black DI in the battalion. One night I met some guys from his company in the beer hall. They all said they hated his guts. But, just like us with our DI, when the eight weeks of Basic were over, they bought him a watch and a bottle of whiskey and waited in line to tell him how much they appreciated him.

"Well," I said, "he's got the lungs of a DI, that's for sure."

Gene laughed. He got up and threw another cup of diesel on the flames. As he stirred the big black tub, his longish hair moving in a slight breeze, he looked like some kind of sorcerer or alchemist. He gave me a long look, like he was trying to figure me out or something. "What do you want?" he said.

"Huh?"

"I mean, Ron wants to be a DI, what do you want?"

I had to laugh. All I wanted was to get back to the world in one piece. The sooner the better.

"I don't want anything."

"Good," he said, laughing, "then you won't be disappointed out here. You know Papa's DEROS is coming up?" He sat down again.

"I know." DEROS was army-speak for when you returned home. It meant, "Date of Estimated Return from Over Seas."

Gene had a heavenly look on his face. "Next month. Man, that's really short."

"Short" meant you had a short time left to serve in Vietnam. I'd noticed that when the subject of Papa's DEROS had come up before, everybody had broken out in big smiles. I think they were thinking about their own DEROS, too. I was glad for Papa, but I didn't dare think of my own DEROS. I had too long to go.

"How long have you been in-country?" he said.

"Almost a month and a half. How about you?"

"Six months."

"Seen any action?" I said. As soon as I said it I smiled. I felt like I was speaking lines from an old war movie.

He stopped stirring and looked at me thoughtfully. "Some . . . Munson over in the fourth platoon almost chopped his toe off clearing fields-of-fire with a machete; Ted got sun poison on the chopper pad one day; Jennings burnt his hand with a smoke grenade." He smiled. "I took care of all of them right here."

He started stirring again. "Have you been out on a hump yet?"

"No." A hump was a hike or a patrol down into the jungle.

"Well, when you go, see me. You need any vitamins?"

"No."

"Oh, well." He lay the paddle down. "You know what to do." He smiled and left.

It wasn't a bad detail. I sat upwind and smoked cigarettes and read the newspaper:

> *U.S. B-52 jets, operating from Guam, were still bombing North Vietnam. The Soviet Army had taken over Czechoslovakia in a swift, surprise attack. Bill Cosby, co-star of three successful seasons of* I Spy, *had been nominated by an LA paper as, "The Most Influential Negro." With only 173 Americans soldiers killed and 818 wounded, the last week in August had been the lowest casualty week for any week in 1968.*

They were playing cards when I came back to the bunker. It was starting to get dark, and they had a candle burning, but Ron still had his sunglasses on. Without looking up from his hand he said, "You already got mail, Melcher. I put it on your bunk."

I wondered who it was from. "Thanks," I said.

Mike looked up at me as he shuffled the deck of cards. "You want to play, Carl?"

"No, I'm not much of a card player." Actually, I was just tired. I wanted to read the letter and go to bed.

"How was that detail?" Chico asked.

I watched for telltale smirks, but there were none. "Not bad. I got to sit around and read the paper."

"It ain't as tiring as working the chopper pad," Ron said.

"Dig it," Mike added.

"And it sure ain't as bad as going out on patrol," Chico went on. "I'd burn that stuff every day till my DEROS if I could stay up here inside the wire."

"Well, there ain't that much stuff on the mountain, so don't worry about it."

Everybody got a good laugh out of Ron's remark and I relaxed a little.

"Hey Carl," Ron said, "did you know Gene-the-doc is a CO?"

"No, what's a CO?"

"A conscientious objector. That means he won't fight or kill another human being."

"Really? He didn't say anything about it."

"Well, he is. He don't carry an M-16 or a pistol."

I sat down on the lower bunk and took the pill vials that Gene had given me out of my pockets.

Ron smiled. "I can see you made his day."

"I guess," I said, not wanting to join in on any ridiculing of the guy; he seemed okay, and after all, I was new on the hill.

"He's seen some action too, hasn't he?" Mike commented.

"Yeah," Ron said. "That was before I came in-country, but I heard about it."

"What happened?" I asked.

"They got ambushed and they say he was running all over the place, checking on the wounded when everybody else was pinned down. He even won some kind of medal for it."

"Wow," said Mike admiringly.

"Hey, Carl." Chico looked up from his cards. "Gene is cuckoo, huh?"

I shrugged. "A little too enthusiastic perhaps. But I was running low on malaria pills anyway."

Chico rolled his eyes. "You're cuckoo, too."

"What do you mean?" I said.

"I mean, catching malaria is not as bad as being out here in the boondocks."

"Chico's right," Ron said patiently. "If you catch malaria they send you back to the rear and while you're recuperating you get a chance to have a little R&R."

R&R meant rest and recreation.

"Vaquerro! You can say that again." Chico wriggled his eyebrows.

The others laughed.

Chico looked at me. "Carl, I saw a little mosquito in the bunker last night, but she got away. I'm going to make a sign and hang it on the wall. It'll say, 'Attention Mosquitos! For some delicious, sweet blood, try Chico, middle bunk on your left.' "

They laughed again.

I climbed up to my bunk to read my letters. One was from my parents. It was good to hear from them. They told me what was going on in the neighborhood and what some of my friends were up to. The other letter was from Ellie, my first steady girl. As I said, we broke up the summer after graduation, but we were still on good terms. I had known her during high school but had never made a move on her till senior year. Instead I had my eye on her girlfriends, Jill and Colleen, who were both better looking. Then one day I got tired of getting nowhere with them, and I asked Ellie to go with me on a double date with Wayne and his girl to the drive-in. We went in Wayne's big Chevy Impala and Ellie and I had a really good time. She and I were together all the time after that. We went to parties, movies and to our family's homes. Man, oh, man, we really liked each other. She was quite a kisser, too.

I took Ellie to my senior prom. We were both good dancers. I can still see us dancing and laughing as we looked into each other's eyes. We didn't care what we did or what we looked like, and after a while the whole dance floor opened up for us, everybody watching us move. Our picture made it into the yearbook—our eyes, zombie-like, the sweat glistening on our faces as we danced and circled each other. I got a nick name out of it too. Under the picture was the caption, "Carl Melcher, a.k.a. The Rubberman, gives a rug-cutting demonstration to his fellow classmates."

We lost touch senior summer and around February I heard she had a new boyfriend and was engaged. In her letter, she said they had just broken up. She didn't sound too upset about it. It was good hearing from her and knowing everything was okay for her, but at the same time the news made me feel far away from everyone and everything, as if I no longer mattered.

In the morning, Mike showed me how to heat my coffee using C-4 plastic explosive. The stuff looked like Ivory soap and had the consistency of putty. It burned with an intense white flame. I sat across from him, the little tin can of coffee warming my hand. He said he'd gotten the C-4 out of an old Claymore mine. It really was something the way these guys made do. They had fixed up the bunker with odds and ends they'd found around the hill. They made little tables, stools, and bunks out of old ammo boxwood. They'd even started paneling one of the dirt walls but had run out of wood. The bunker had the look and feel of the secret clubhouses we used to build when we were kids.

Mike and I went out into the trench to disconnect the Claymore mines. Then it would be safe to go down into the barbed wire and check on the flares and trip wires. This was something they did every morning, he told me. At dusk, the mines would be reconnected for the night.

The morning sun was a big, orange blob; the air, cool and crisp. Mike and I moved carefully through the barbed wire, checking that the thin, steel wires running from the trip flares were intact. We worked quietly, inspecting the flares hidden in the elephant grass. Gene-the-medic was right. Mike really was a very shy person. I tended to be on the quiet side too, but I wasn't as closemouthed as he was.

Ron appeared in the trench above us. "You guys almost finished?"

"Dig it," Mike said.

"Come on up then." His black face disappeared back over the sand-bagged trench wall. Mike quickly finished wiring up a flare he'd been working on. As I watched him, I could see how much he wanted to please Ron. It wasn't because Ron was second-in-command, but rather that Ron had a big-brother kind of influence over him.

Ron told us to get our weapons. He wanted to go down the hill and find a tree to use as an additional support column in the bunker. He told the guy in the next bunker that we were going out through the wire.

They had what they called an OP, or Observation Post, on both sides of the hill. Each OP was simply four guys with a radio lying around down by the trail, playing cards all day. They were supposed to provide advanced warning of an enemy approach, and a first line of defense. At night they called it an LP, or Listening Post, because when it was dark you couldn't observe your hand in front of your face even if your life depended on it.

Ron grabbed a machete and a canteen from the bunker. Mike carried his M-16 slung over his shoulder. We started down. Fifty feet down the trail we came upon the OP guys. They were stretched out on their poncho blankets, some of them still eating their C-ration breakfasts. They nodded as we passed. We went down the trail another couple hundred feet till Ron found the tree he wanted.

The sounds of the firebase were gone now, and other than an occasional solitary voice drifting down from the OP, there was only the gentle quiet of the jungle. It was weird. I had always expected the jungle to be full of strange noises. But it wasn't like that. It was just beautifully quiet and peaceful. At first I was nervous and looked around a lot. Ron told me that wasn't necessary and to just relax because we'd hear someone long before they got to within thirty feet of us. Neither he nor Mike seemed the least bit worried, and so I finally did relax.

Mike started chopping. Nobody was saying much. I tried to get a conversation going. As Mike worked, I asked him what he did for a living back in New York City before the army.

"I worked for the Genser Carton Company," he said, pausing between chops. "They make shipping cartons, you know, cardboard boxes."

"Really? How long were you there?" I said, trying to sound interested.

"Three years. I should've made third-shift boss, but they gave it to somebody else, you dig." Mike threw a look at Ron who smiled slightly in understanding. "They didn't pay anything anyway," he went on. "I was angry and disappointed so I joined the army."

"And now you're finally making big money, right?" Ron said.

"That's right, and learning a trade, too." They both laughed.

"Forestry, right?" I said.

"Dig it," Mike said.

"What about you, Ron," I said. "What were you doing before the army?"

"I was a pants presser."

"Uh-uh, Carl, he was a robber." Mike laughed mischievously.

"Now what are you going and telling him that for?" Ron scolded good-naturedly. "Next thing you know he'll be dropping a dime on me."

I had heard that expression from one of the black guys in my basic training unit. It meant to put a dime in the pay phone to call the police on someone.

I wondered if Ron really had been a robber. I'd never known anybody who'd done anything like that. But I figured I better not bug him about it. "What do you guys think about the Paris Peace talks?" I said.

Mike said nothing and continued whacking at the tree. "Not too much," Ron answered for both of them. "What do you think?"

"Something could come of it. It's possible they could solve this thing before my tour is up."

Ron laughed cynically. "Right, you better start looking out for your own self and forget about them Paris Peace Talks. Them dudes don't care about us. Right Mike?"

"Dig it, brother."

Ron looked at me. "You just stick with me and Mike. We'll show you what's going on." He turned to Mike. "We'll show him how to get along, won't we?"

Mike paused in his chopping and wiped his brow. He smiled sheepishly. "Dig it." He went back to his chopping.

We grew quiet, and the jungle continued its silent observation of us. There was only the steady whack of Mike's machete echoing out as he chopped a sideways V into the tree. Ron started whistling that song by Bobby Love and the Valentines, "I'll Kiss Away Your Tears."

"Okay, Carl," Ron said after a while, "why don't you take over and give Mike a break?"

It was fun. I hadn't chopped a tree down since summer camp when I was a kid. Using a machete was slow going, but with the three of us taking turns it wasn't too tiring.

"So," Ron said as I chopped, "what do you think about bein' in Vietnam so far, Carl?"

"It's not so bad," I said.

Ron laughed.

It really wasn't. So far it had been like some crazy, drawn-out camping trip, nothing like I'd imagined. If it stayed this way, I could grow to like it. I was starting to like these guys, too. "I'm serious. I kind of like it."

"Wow," Ron said, laughing. "I wouldn't go that far."

"Me neither," Mike said.

I continued chopping and then realized how much noise it was making. "Do you think there are any enemy down in the valley?" I said.

Ron smiled shyly. "Probably. But they stay away from us."

"Dig it," Mike said.

"Why?" I asked.

"They're smart, that's why. They want to bring all their heavy stuff south so they can make trouble down there. They don't give a damn about this mountain. There's nothing here they want."

I silently thanked my lucky stars for having ended up here instead of down south in a rice paddy with people taking pot shots at me all the time.

"However," Ron said slowly, "if we ever get in their way, then we're gonna have to kick their butts or get outta town."

"Dig it," Mike said.

"It don't have to get to that point though," said Ron, "if everybody's cool about things."

I chopped easier, making less noise, waiting for him to go on. "What do you mean, 'cool' about things?" I asked.

Ron smiled. "Oh, just being cool, that's all. You'll find out in time, right, Mike?"

"Dig it."

"Take a break, Carl," Ron said. "It's my turn."

Ron was strong. He was built like a boxer, not skinny like Mike or me. The muscles in his arm bulged as he swung the machete, grim determination on his face.

Ron looked over at me as he chopped. "How long have you known McLoughlin and that new rebel dude?" he asked.

"I went through Basic Training and Advanced Infantry Training with Glock. We both met Beobee at Fort Lewis, Washington."

"Is that right? McLoughlin's one bad dude, ain't he, Mike? You seen him in that black beret before he went out?"

"Dig it. He looks like John Wayne."

Ron laughed. "Don't he now? John Wayne. He was goin' out there to get himself a Charley!"

"Charley" came from Victor Charles, which the U.S. Army alpha-identifier for VC, which was short for Viet Cong. Ever since basic training they'd been telling us about "Charley." It was "Charley this" and "Charley that," until Charley seemed like some familiar character in a TV show or a comic strip; he was a clever, little guy, dangerous, but not totally unlikable.

Ron and Mike laughed. "Get him a Charley . . ." continued Ron.

"McLoughlin's a little gung ho," I said, "but he's okay."

They both continued to laugh.

Ron delivered the last few fatal chops to the tree and it finally fell over. Getting it into the bunker was easier than I thought and we finished before they closed down the chow line. Back in the cool bunker, Mike broke out three Cokes he'd been saving and we drank these with our lunch. We talked about music—Motown, Rock, Psychedelic, all of it. The soul brothers called these lengthy discussions "rapping," and that's what we did for a couple of hours before we got tired. We rapped. It was nice.

CHAPTER 4

In the darkness, Ron, Mike and Chico stood on the bunker roof talking to Beobee, who had evidently come looking for me. As I came up through the trench line, Beobee was telling Ron how we met at Fort Lewis.

"Is that right?" Ron said, trying to sound interested.

Beobee saw me. "Carl! There's gonna be an arc light out there in about five minutes."

"An arc light?" I said.

"A B-52 air strike," Ron said.

"Dig it," Mike said.

We sat and waited like moviegoers for the curtain to rise. In the distance a sudden, intense, blue light rippled across the horizon like the flash from a welder's torch. "There it goes," Beobee said.

A steady rumbling reached us. Like an earthquake, you could feel it in your gut. We watched wordlessly for about a minute.

"God Almighty," said Ron, his face grave in the dim moonlight, "I'm glad they're on our side."

"Dig it," Mike said solemnly.

"They're dropping fifteen-hundred pounders now," Beobee explained. "Used to be only thousand pounders."

It went on for another five minutes. I tried to imagine what it was like to be bombed like that. They say that even if you aren't close enough to be hit by the shrapnel, the concussions could still kill you, or at least burst your eardrums.

After a while Beobee wandered off and I went back into the bunker. Ron, Mike and Chico sat around the ammo-crate table in the flickering light of two big candles. Ron was shuffling his playing cards as Mike's radio played softly.

Chico smiled. "Now we can play some poker."

Ron put his sunglasses on. "Sit down, Carl."

I had planned on reading before I slept, but I pulled over one of the machine-gun ammo-cans they used for seats and sat.

"Where are the Cokes?" Mike asked.

"Where they always are, under Chico's bunk," Ron said testily.

Mike's face wore a look of surprise and mild hurt. "Really? Since when?"

"Really, since when?" Chico mimicked. "Just shut up and play. I need some more of your money for when I go into Pleiku to get my tooth fixed."

They laughed and Mike's smile returned.

We played five-card poker, using matches for twenty-five-cent chips. While Mike shuffled, Ron took out a pipe and started loading it with some green stuff that looked like dried weeds and bird seed. He saw me watching and smiled.

"You smoke marijuana, don't you, Melcher?" he said.

I was scared, but I didn't want to sound like a square. "Yeah, every now and then," I lied.

Ron laughed.

So that's what it was . . . marijuana . . . grass. I remembered seeing it once before. My brother Jack and I shared a bedroom. One day while looking for some cuff links I found a plastic vial of his, filled with what looked like finely-chopped lawn clippings.

Jack had just returned from his year in Vietnam with the Marines. He would come home on weekends and spend most of his time sprawled on the rug in front of the stereo, his eyes closed, the music blasting. My Mom and Dad would sit on the couch as if everything was normal, hoping, I guess, that he'd get over it soon, whatever phase it was that he was going through. He must've been smoking grass then. It was sad because I had really wanted to talk with him then, but even though he was physically there, he really wasn't there.

Ron put a match to the pipe and started puffing furiously. The stuff crackled and popped.

My heart was beating fast. I was scared to smoke it, but I didn't want to appear unfriendly. After all, I'd be spending the next year with them. The pipe came to me. They all waited, watching me expectantly.

I liked these guys, but no way was I going to smoke marijuana. So, I pretended to take a puff of it and passed the pipe to Chico.

"Pretty good, huh?" Ron said to me as he strained to keep the smoke in his lungs. He smiled his peculiar, sad smile and I nodded, hoping they wouldn't see that I wasn't really taking in the smoke. Fortunately, the candles didn't put out much light. When the pipe came to me again I took another quick, phony puff. We talked some more and I began to relax. No one had noticed my fake smoking and I now felt comfortable around these guys. They were really okay.

"Wow," I said like they did. They smiled and their smiles were genuine. The radio played one of my favorite songs by Steem Masheen called "Ornithopter Ride." I looked out the aperture at the black valley below.

Mike handed me something. "Put one of these in your mouth, brother." It was a Blasto mint.

I did and he watched me expectantly. The mint was really strong and the air of the bunker entered like a freezing winter wind. "Wow, that's dynamite!" I said.

"Dig it," Mike said.

"Far out," Chico said.

"Right on," Ron said.

We laughed. We played a few hands and I pictured an enemy crawling up through the darkness. I glanced at my rifle to make sure it was still there.

Chico smiled at me. "Don't worry, Carl. There's guards out there."

"Dig," Ron said.

I calmed down again. They were all so relaxed.

Mike turned to me. "My friend, Blakey said that some GIs even smoked grass with Charley."

"Really?" It sounded implausible to me.

Mike nodded and turned to Ron. "They bumped into each other out there on the trail, you dig, a squad of GIs and a squad of enemy, and they just lay their weapons down and smoked some grass together."

"Yeah," said Ron slowly, throwing Chico and me a look, "I heard that, too. Then they all got married and now they're living happily ever after over in Bangkok."

Ron and Chico laughed so I laughed, too. Mike looked hurt. He turned to Chico. "I swear! That's what Blakey told me."

Chico was slowly and dramatically shaking his head in disbelief when suddenly there was a loud explosion and the bunker shuddered, dirt and dust rattling down on us. I crouched on the earthen floor. They looked over at me.

"Outgoing mail, Melcher," said Ron. "The Artillery boys got a fire mission, that's all. You'll get to know the sound."

"Wow," said Chico, "those big guns done went and ruined the party for Carl."

They laughed.

The guns stopped firing and Ron took out his pipe. "You want some more, Carl" he said.

I lied again and told them I'd had enough.

"No more for me," Chico said.

"Dig it," Mike said.

We played some more cards. I felt as if I'd been whisked away to a small cave on a distant planet. Along the way, my fears about the war had shrunk to the size of dust motes and disappeared. Nothing existed anywhere except us, drinking Cokes, joking and talking as we played cards in the little, quivering circle of candlelight, as if we'd been friends forever.

Ron woke me for guard. His shift was over but he decided to stay awake and we stood in the pitch dark of the trench, saying nothing as we tried to shake off the damp morning chill. Excepting the artillery fire mission of the night before, things had been really quiet on the hill.

Lately I had come up with a theory. When I was alone and bored, I honed it, anticipating any arguments someone might have and adding the necessary details to reinforce it. I didn't really believe it myself, but no one could disprove it, at least none of the guys on the hill could. I hadn't told anybody about it yet; they'd think I was crazy. Anyway, here's how it went. There was no war in Vietnam. That's right. It was all just a giant hoax, a realistic training exercise rigged up by the intelligence community. Everybody knows they train the Green Berets in Guatemala. Well, that's where we were, Guatemala. That's right. That was my theory. They could have flown our plane in circles at thirty thousand feet for a couple of hours, and then landed in Guatemala. They could have already had about three hundred Vietnamese actors there for realism. After all, they had lots of Vietnamese back at Fort Polk, Louisiana; they were supposedly training them there. The machine-gun tracers, artillery flashes, flares, and distant rumblings in the night would be no problem for the army's pyrotechnic people. They could easily put on a show like that. Just about everything I'd seen since I'd been here could be explained this way. I knew that it was silly, like a *Twilight Zone* story, but it was a lot of fun to speculate.

Ron stared off at the purple haze in the eastern sky.

"What do you think about being here in Vietnam?" I said.

He laughed derisively. The purple haze had turned cherry red now and we could just about see each other. He took out his pipe.

"Want to smoke some?"

"No thanks," I said. "I never smoke in the daytime."

He laughed and put his pipe away. "Well, we're just here for business, business as usual."

"What do you mean?"

"I mean that this war is just a business deal, that's all. The big boys got together and said, 'Look, the economy isn't doing so hot and we got all these extra people walking around with no jobs, just causing trouble, so why don't we have us a little drawn-out war. That way we can get rid of the excess population and pump up the economy at the same time."

I smiled. My theory about us not really being here was strange, but Ron's was really weird. "C'mon, you're trying to tell me that this whole war was cooked up to boost the economy?" I said.

"That's right, and it has, too."

"The American, maybe, but not the Vietnamese. I just can't see them sacrificing thousands of their people."

"Life is cheap over here."

"No, I don't believe it."

"Why do you think there's so much trash in the company?"

I felt uncomfortable answering a question like that. "What do you mean?" I said.

"C'mon, Carl. About a third of the men on this hill are black trash and the rest are all poor white trash."

I laughed. I had never thought of myself as "white trash," or Art, Glock, Lee, or Ted for that matter.

Ron spoke like a teacher giving a lecture. "You see, the rich man in America struck a deal with the Communist bosses in Asia because they both had something to gain. The Asians have a population way in excess of what their lands can support, and America has an excess of trash."

I laughed again. I didn't want to but I couldn't help it. I didn't know if he was pulling my leg or what. He looked at me, real serious. "It's true, Carl. You laugh. Hell, trash is a class of people. It's all economics. In any society in the world, all you gotta do is look on the bottom of the economic heap and that's where you'll find the trash—black trash, brown trash, yellow trash, white trash—throwaways. It don't matter what color they are."

"I don't know, Ron."

The sun was up now. In the next bunker, we could hear some of the guys stirring.

"Pretty sunrise, isn't it?" Ron said.

"Sure is."

Ron sighed noisily. "Yeah, the only reason the war's lasted as long as it has is because it's all baloney and everybody knows it. And that's why the troops ain't taking no chances. Why should you get yourself killed when them senators' and businessmen's sons are laying up at some Ivy League college studying poli-sci or history of art or something like that, and gettin' all the girls they want! Jees. You think they give a damn about us?"

"Well, there've been a lot of demonstrations against the war."

Ron laughed a low chuckle. "You know why the hippies are growing their hair long and carrying on like that?"

I didn't know what to say. He was probably leading up to something just as crazy as the reasons he gave for the war. "No, why?"

"To get back at mommy and daddy."

He said "mommy and daddy" the way a spoiled child would.

"Really? I don't know."

He laughed again, then his smile faded. "Do you really think that twenty-five years from now anybody's gonna give a damn if some black trash from New York named Ron Jakes, or some white trash from Philly named Carl Melcher died over here? Huh?"

"Maybe."

"Dag! I thought you were smart, man. You're always reading them books. Let me tell you, Carl. The world'll go on turning and there ain't nobody gonna give a damn except maybe your mama, and your girlfriend, if you got one, and that's about it."

I didn't say anything. The thought of nobody caring was starting to bring me down. It wasn't true though. People cared. At least I thought they did.

"Now, what do *you* think about being here?" Ron asked.

"Who says we're here?" I said.

"Huh?"

"What if I told you we really weren't in Vietnam? What would you say to that?" I said.

"I'd say maybe you were smoking too much grass."

"No, really." I told him my theory and he cracked up and almost fell to the bottom of the trench.

"Dag, man. You don't really believe that? C'mon, why do you really think they sent us here? Be serious now."

"Well, the South Vietnamese asked us here. We have to honor our commitments."

"Dag, man. You read the papers too much."

As we gathered our gear together, I didn't say anything. It was getting too depressing.

Ron sighed heavily. "There's only one solution for us, Carl."

"What's that?"

"We just gotta keep our heads down, stick together, and do our time. Don't take any unnecessary chances, and we'll get back to the world in one piece, you dig?"

The way he talked it was totally up to you. You could just do certain things, like keeping your head down and so forth, and 365 days later when your DEROS came around, you'd go home. I really wanted to look at it that way but I had too many days ahead of me. I thought of the Paris Peace Talks. Maybe there'd be a breakthrough soon. When I got short like Papa, with only a month left to my tour, then maybe I could look at it Ron's way, but not now.

Ron started singing in falsetto, imitating the soul singer, Bobby Love, making the words up as he went along. *"Get on back and live, brother."* He did a few steps like the Valentines. *"Get on back to that beautiful world and live, live, live!"*

He had such a bad voice I cracked up. "Dig it," I said.

I was glad when Papa and the others came back. Ron and Mike were beginning to get on my nerves. They had started an ambitious, home-remodeling program for the bunker. I could understand improvements up to a point, but a bunker is just a hole in the ground, hardly worth the time and trouble. Reading my books was more important to me than paneling the dirt walls. Besides, I didn't want to cover them up; I liked them. I'd never lived in a hole before and it was neat. I suspected Chico would agree with me, that is, if he could be found. He'd disappeared shortly after Ron and Mike had announced their plans that morning. That's what I should've done.

We were carrying some ammo crates back when we saw Papa, Glock and Lee standing around in front of the bunker. Lee glowered when he saw us and walked off. Papa greeted us warmly. He asked me how it was going and I told him what I'd been up to. Then he went to the CP to be debriefed and I went into the bunker. Glock was sitting on his bunk, his M-16 apart, cleaning the trigger mechanism with an old toothbrush. On the other side of the bunker, Ron and Mike were making a panel of sorts from lots of small boards. Glock gave me a friendly look.

"Hi, how'd it go out there?" I said.

"Ah, no big deal. We saw some kind of a monkey and did a lot of hiking. Actually it was kind of boring."

I remembered Ron's crack about Glock being John Wayne. I guess some people might consider him a braggart, but I don't think he really meant to sound that way. I glanced over at Ron and Mike who were on their knees hammering. Ron had a slight smile on his face and I knew he'd been listening to us. I opened my book and started reading.

After a while Glock put his rifle down and went over to Ron and Mike. "You know, Mike, there's a better way to do that."

Mike stopped hammering and looked at Glock, a good-natured expression on his face.

"Don't stop!" said Ron. "Nail the board on there, will you?"

Mike lowered his head and resumed his hammering.

Glock frowned. "I was just trying to help. I can save you guys some work."

Ron smiled thinly up at him. "Oh, we like to work, man. Don't we like to work, Mike?"

"Dig it," Mike said, keeping his eyes lowered. Ron looked over at me. "Even old Carl over there can testify to that. He's seen us work."

Glock threw me a "what's-with-them?" look. I didn't say anything. Why were they trying to get me to take sides? I didn't want to. Neither did Mike. I went outside.

Firebase 29 was a busy place. Battalion's officers buzzed in regularly in the little Light Observation Helicopters, LOH, or loaches, we called them, to consult with the artillery people. Every day, patrols of three to twenty men, loaded down with provisions and ammo like mule trains, left the perimeter. I'd stand on the bunker roof and watch them make their way down through the maze of wire and into the trees. They looked like scuba divers disappearing beneath the water. I'd already asked Papa when I'd be going out. I wasn't looking forward to going, but not knowing when bothered me.

I didn't have a lot of free time to read and relax, but it was probably just as well. Glock and Ron weren't exactly the best of friends, and hanging around the bunker with them there wasn't any fun.

There were plenty of details. The cook had a corrugated tin roof to keep the sun off him while he cooked at his propane stoves, and I pulled KP with him lots of times. The two-dozen 105 Howitzer cannons on the hill fired on and off around the clock in support of patrols down in the valley and in the surrounding hills, and I must've carried thousands of shells from the chopper pad to the ammo pits. The flares and claymore mines had to be inspected every day too, and sometimes I helped Mike with that. Ron and Glock continued to bang heads over the slightest little things. Their animosity came to a head over the beer issue. Ron had divided the beer ration, and Glock felt he'd been cheated. He told me that one morning as I was coming in the bunker. Later that afternoon I was eating lunch with Ron on the bunker roof when Glock showed up. He scowled at Ron. "You cheated me out of a beer!"

"The hell I did."

"You're a liar."

They rushed at each other and I grabbed my plate and got out of the way. Ron hunched in a fighter's crouch and feinted left then threw a right jab at Glock's jaw. Glock blocked it and, after dodging sideways, rushed in and delivered a combination that Ron only partially managed to block. I could hear Glock's blows landing on Ron's arms and side. Glock's face was expressionless, no anger, no smile; he was a machine. I'd seen him box in Basic Training and he was good. He was one of the few white guys in the company that really knew how to box.

Ron charged, an angry curse hissing from his lips. In vain, he tried to land one on Glock, who danced and wove agilely, avoiding the blows. Ron rushed in too far and Glock caught him on the ear. Ron cursed furiously, throwing Glock off guard, and managed to punch Glock's nose. It started to bleed. They broke apart and rushed at each other again. Ron tried to land another punch, but Glock continued the business of boxing, backing Ron up skillfully.

Papa and Ted approached carrying their drooping paper plates of hot chow. Ted pointed. Papa dropped his plate and came running. "That's enough, guys. Stop! That's enough!" He rushed between them. "I said that's enough, fellas, now cut it out!"

Smack! Ron's last, poorly-aimed blow landed against the side of Papa's head.

Papa winced in pain, holding his ear. "Damn it, Ron, now look what you've done!"

Ron glared at Glock, and kept his hands at the ready. He was moving toward Glock when Papa pushed him back. "Ron, so help me God, if you don't cool off I'm going to report this to the Captain. You hear me?"

Ron continued toward Glock. Papa, who outweighed Ron by at least fifty pounds, wrapped his arms around him and half-carried, half-pushed him back. Glock kept his hands up, ready to repel the next charge. Mike showed up, and, along with Papa, managed to pull Ron away and down into the trench.

I went over to Glock. He seemed a little shaken now that it was over. "You okay?" I said.

He nodded, but said nothing. I felt sorry for him and Ron. They were both decent guys, but they were like fire and ice. They were both glad the fight had been broken up, though. They would never admit it, but I could tell.

CHAPTER 5

The day Papa told me I'd be a part of the next patrol, my stomach dropped. I hoped it would be as uneventful as Glock's had been, as they all had been since I'd arrived on the hill.

Papa, Ron, Mike and Glock would be going. I figured it would be Papa's last patrol; he was getting awfully short. Nobody talked about it, as if that would bring bad luck, so I didn't say anything.

I took the garbage over to the sump on the other side of the hill. The sump looked like those old bible paintings of hell—a large, black, smoke-filled pit, with fires going here and there, ashes rising in the hot, acrid air. Two guys raked wearily like lost souls as a dim red sun fell slowly toward the hills across the valley like a shrinking helium party balloon. I tossed the bag in the pit. All I could think about was the patrol, and I had to talk to somebody about it. I went looking for Gene. I knew he wouldn't lie to me about what to expect, and I always felt like I learned something when I talked with him.

I found him up by the Mess tent and we sat on the bunker roof. Down in the valley, the jungle green was turning brown fast in the dying light. It was getting cool. Tomorrow evening at this time, I'd be down there somewhere, getting ready to go to sleep. I turned to Gene. He was one of those people who could go on forever without saying a word. It's not that they're rude; it's just that they're deep thinkers. "I'm going out on my first patrol tomorrow," I said.

"That right?" He grew quiet again, like it was no big deal. Then he said, "Are you afraid?"

"Of course not. But I'm not exactly thrilled about it either."

He looked at me. "So, you're normal. Congratulations." He laughed. "Lighten up, Carl. It hasn't been too bad out here. You could've done a lot worse and gotten yourself stationed somewhere down in the Delta."

"Yeah, you're right." I laughed. "I wish I was invisible."

Gene smiled. "Hmm. That certainly would increase your odds." He lit another cigarette and offered me one. "You know, a buddy of mine came pretty close to being invisible once when we were in medic school."

"What do you mean?"

"I mean he became 'persona non grata.' That's Latin for a 'non-person.' They had lost his 201 file and so he was essentially invisible to the army."

"Why's that?"

"Well, you've heard the old saying that an army runs on its stomach?"

"Uh huh."

"Well, the army really runs on paperwork. Every man has a 201 file. Every piece of information there is on him resides there. If they're going to promote him, they need the 201 file, if they're going to bust him, they need the 201 file. They can't do anything without their stupid 201 files. In my buddy's case, they couldn't graduate him from school because they'd lost his file. They couldn't pay him either. I was keeping him in gum and movies. When I left on leave before coming here they still hadn't found his 201 file, and for all I know, he's probably still there."

"Wow, is it good time?" I asked. "I mean, will he have to make that time up?"

"Heck, yeah, it's good time. He's right there where he's supposed to be. It's the army's fault, not his. So for him the clock is still ticking."

"Wow." I wished things like that happened to me.

"Don't worry too much about this patrol. Everybody's a little scared their first time out, and the guys that act real cool are probably scared the most."

I nodded. The more I thought about it, the better I felt. It really was normal to be afraid when the stakes were this high. If you weren't, you must be crazy or something.

The sky grew purple as the last of the sunlight faded. For a few moments we said nothing.

"I heard you were in an ambush when you first got in-country?" I said.

"Yeah," he sighed. "A lot of guys got hurt bad on that one."

"How did it feel? I mean, did you actually think you'd die when the shooting started?"

He turned and looked at me. He had a gleam in his eye and a wild smile. He shook his head and spoke slowly. "I think if you are spiritually in tune with the universe, then you're somehow protected. Some guys would say you're in God's hands." He looked away and laughed nervously. "I don't know. It was a crazy experience, that's all."

Out across the valley a green flare rose up in the sky. A white one followed. They both hung there for a while, bright pinpoints of light. To a lot of people Gene was an oddball, but I thought he was really cool and had more sense than most of the people on the hill. I hoped that if I ever got caught in a firefight I'd feel the same thing he had felt.

"That's pretty far out," I said.

We stared into the darkness waiting for another flare to go up across the way.

"Yeah, that's me, far out."

We both laughed. I stood up and stretched. "Well, I better get going."

As we got ready for the patrol, they told me I'd be carrying the radio and that got me to worrying again. Supposedly the enemy tried to kill the radio man first, cutting off the patrol from any outside help. As I watched the others pull on their rucksacks, I tried to put the thought out of my mind. After I tied the radio to my rucksack and pulled it on, I realized that just carrying everything was going to be a challenge. My gear must've weighed sixty pounds. We went up to the CP. Papa and Ron sat against the CP bunker wall to study a map sheathed in acetate. Papa had been preparing Ron to take over the squad. He was always teaching him different things and giving him more and more authority in the squad.

I took my ruck off and sat down. Glock dumped his ruck and walked over to look over Papa's and Ron's shoulders. Ted came out of the CP with Beobee. Beobee was X-ed with belted machine gun ammo and carried his M-60 by the barrel. He had an M-16 slung over his shoulder. Ron looked surprised.

Ted nodded at us. "Good morning, fellas." He turned to Papa and Ron. "This is one of the new men. His name's B-O-B. He'll be your machine gunner on the patrol."

Papa reached out and shook Beobee's hand. Ron nodded curtly. He turned to Papa, frown lines etching into his brown forehead. "They're giving us three 'cruits for a six-man patrol? You think that's right?"

Papa's face reddened. "Look Ron, you're not squad leader yet, not until I go home, okay? And they don't pay us to think either. This is the infantry, not the damn Pentagon."

Ted nodded in agreement. "That's right, Ron. And besides, Beobee's not a 'cruit. He already served a tour of duty with the 1st Air Cavalry down in Cu Chi."

Ron's voice rose in pitch. "I don't care, Ted. That don't make him no expert up here! Dag!" He turned and looked off into the distance in frustration.

Beobee casually daubed his face with his handkerchief during the exchange. He didn't seem to take any offense.

Papa looked hurt as he tried to reassert control of the situation. "Look, Ron, just take it easy." He moved closer to Ron. "Let's not get all bent out of shape over this, okay?"

Ron smiled thinly. "All right. It's your patrol, man."

Ron squatted down and unfolded the map and started studying it again. He said nothing, and with his sunglasses on, there was no telling what he was thinking. Mike approached and took off his steel pot. He smiled at everybody, having missed the angry exchange of a moment before.

Ted smiled and shook his head. "Good. That's settled." His face became stern. "Be careful fellas." He patted Papa on the back. "You got a real short-timer here to take care of."

Ron walked point as we descended the hill on the main trail. The guys talked softly and joked till we passed the OP and then we grew as quiet as the jungle. Tall, thick trees cut us off from the sun's light. On the valley floor the vegetation grew thick and the trail thinned. Our rucks caught on the vines and bushes which crowded together, fighting for the available light. Ron's course took us off the trail and we had to almost tunnel through a tangled mass of vines and elephant grass. It was rough going and both Beobee and Glock wondered aloud a couple of times if maybe we had gotten off course. Ron said nothing, ignoring their questions, as did Papa, not wanting to take sides. Mike was second in the file and angrily threw himself against the tall grass, mashing it down with all his strength as if sacrificing himself for any mistakes Ron might have made.

It was very hot. Every now and then someone would knock into a tree, and the bullhead ants nesting high inside it would drop onto our faces and down the backs of our shirts and bite stingingly like bees. The going got rougher and slower. I thought we were making too much noise, but nobody else seemed to care, so I relaxed a little. After an hour or so of fighting the brush, just getting out of it seemed more important than how much noise we were making. I relieved Mike as the "masher-downer" and after twenty minutes I was so exhausted I could hardly stand. Finally we burst out onto a trail.

Ron knelt to consult his map. Mike and I flopped on the ground to rest, quickly breaking out our canteens. I was carrying five of them, and I drank half of one in a long swallow. Beobee came over behind Ron and peered over his shoulder at the map. Beobee pointed at some wavy lines of elevation. "You see, Ron, these here ridges all have trails. We could've taken this one to here, picked this one up, and been here nearly half an hour ago."

Ron turned his sweat-beaded face to him. "We're here, ain't we?" he said in a voice more exhausted than angry.

Beobee pulled out his handkerchief and ran it quickly over his face. "Yeah. Well, suit yourself. I was just tryin' to help, that's all." He moved away and sat down.

We moved out again. Glock took my place behind Ron and I went back to the middle of the file with Papa. They were keeping him in the middle to provide him a little extra protection. We humped along the trail without incident for another hour and then Ron's course again took us off the trail and into some more thick brush. We were bulling our way through that when Glock grabbed Ron from behind. Ron turned to him angrily. "What the heck's with you?" he hissed in a loud whisper.

Glock spoke softly. "Don't move, Ron. See that vine around your ankle? Booby trap! Don't move."

Ron froze. He looked like a statue carved from ebony wood. Papa, Mike and I backed away from him a little as Glock and Beobee inspected the bushes. Ron said nothing. He turned slowly round to look at us, his face sweaty and pained.

Glock and Beobee squatted down to look at something. I tried to see it but couldn't. I continued to stare and then it was just there, the way those optical illusions they have in the Academy of Science are suddenly "just there," after you've stared at them for several seconds. It was a big, ugly crossbow with a barbed arrow about five feet long, aimed right at Ron's gut. It looked like it could've skewered all six of us at once.

"Ron?" Glock said softly.

"Yeah?"

"Move to the side real slow. The trip wire's already engaged so there's no telling when it'll fire."

"What? When what'll fire? Dag!"

Papa, Mike and I watched, holding our breath, as Ron slowly leaned sideways. He suddenly dove to the ground.

Nothing happened.

"It go off?" Ron asked.

"No," said Beobee. "You all come up and see this thing."

We pushed carefully through the brush and vines. It was made of wood and vines and looked like a 17th century crossbow you'd see in the museum of history, only it was huge.

"Let's see what it does," Glock said. He poked his knife into the trigger mechanism and the machine jerked, the arrow shooting down the track. It traveled about twenty feet and dug a foot or so into the ground. We all laughed.

"That would've given you a hell of a bellyache, Ron," Beobee said.

"Dig it," Ron said, "it almost gave me a heart attack!"

We laughed again and I looked around, wondering if we were making too much noise.

"You know," Papa said, "the enemy have brought down choppers with these things."

"I know it," Ron said, smiling. He turned and looked straight at Glock. "You're all right, man, you know that?"

Glock blushed and shrugged his shoulders.

Ron turned to Mike and me. "He's all right, ain't he?"

"Yeah," I said. "He has good eyes."

"Dig it," Mike said, "like a hawk."

Beobee turned to me. "You know, Carl, we had so many of them down south you got to where you could spot them a mile away."

"Really?" I refrained from asking him why he hadn't spotted it.

"Don't worry," Papa said. "That's the first one I've seen in my whole tour. Up here the enemy don't usually bother with them."

"Is that so?" said Beobee? "Well, lordy, lordy."

The great trees and vines blotted out the sun and sky so completely it was like being in a sauna. I was really angry as we humped along. Papa had to get the patrol to our night location, which was eight kilometers, or "klicks" as the guys said, from the firebase, by five o'clock, and so we were practically running down the trail. With the weight of the radio and everything else, I was having a heck of a time keeping up. It wasn't very safe either. By the time we slowed down my clothes were soaked through and sweat was burning into my eyes. Suddenly Ron stopped and I almost bumped into him. He turned his black, sweaty face to mine and put his finger to his lips. I tried to see what Papa and the others were doing, but they were out of sight around a bend in the trail. Maybe Glock or Beobee had spotted another booby trap, or maybe they'd discovered we were going in the wrong direction—again! That wouldn't have surprised me.

It was very quiet. Even though it was Papa's last patrol and everybody wanted him to get home safe and sound, I wished something would happen. Nothing dangerous of course, but something, like finding another booby trap, or maybe a deserted tunnel complex. Or, better yet, I wished we would just set up for the night. Then I could read my book before it got too dark.

Bored, I stared into the tangled jungle. A single shot rang out and Ron and I hit the ground, pointing our weapons out. We waited, watching intently. Everything was quiet for a few minutes and then Mike came crashing through the bushes. He had a hurried, whispered conference with Ron.

My God, I thought, Mike makes as much noise as a herd of elephants and then he whispers in Ron's ear so the enemy won't hear him. You've heard of the "Keystone Cops?" Well, we were the "Keystone Army."

Ron whispered to me to watch the rear while he went forward. I sat and watched, but nothing happened. Maybe Glock's or Mike's weapon had gone off accidentally. That sort of thing happened.

The rucksack dug into my shoulders and I leaned back, using it as a backrest. I took a swig of water. This hump was beginning to seem like it would go on forever. I only weighed a hundred and twenty, but I was carrying just as much as everybody else and the radio, too.

Earlier I'd thought of asking somebody else to carry the radio, but I decided against it. Watching Mike had changed my mind. Skinny as a rail, he kept on going, never complaining. I could never live it down if I fell out. I'd rather have my heart burst and keel over right there on the trail than fall out. I was angry though. Why did they have to go so fast?

A fly buzzed my face, made a quick turn, then landed on my right hand that was balancing the canteen on my thigh. It stuck its straw-like snout into a drop of sweat and started drinking. I thought about slapping it, but luckily for it, I was too tired. It sucked that sweat drop down to half its size and flew off. I almost had to laugh as I realized that even flies had luck, good and bad. Luck was what the Buddhists called karma, and this fly had good karma. Ron came down the trail and motioned me to my feet.

In a little clearing, Beobee and Glock were whispering excitedly to Ron and Papa. Beobee's helmet was off and his bald head shone with sweat. "It was damn near the easiest shot I've ever made, Ron," he said, pausing to daub his sweaty face. Beobee had a way of wiping his face that never failed to amaze me. He made a production out of it, the way some guys packed a pipe. He'd pull out his big, olive-drab-colored hanky, snap it smartly against his pant leg to loosen it up, and then fluff it and somehow work it up into this large, green puff which wriggled across his face and head, sucking up the sweat as if it had a life of its own.

I looked around to see what they were talking about and saw some guy laying on the ground. Beobee returned his handkerchief to his pocket and continued. "I just waited till he was about a hundred feet away and let him have it. Just squeezed a round off."

Ron listened, his eyes and feelings hidden behind his sunglasses. I'd swear he was born with sunglasses.

Papa nervously rubbed his dark smudgy beard and looked over at Glock who was on his knees beside the enemy guy, going through his pockets.

"He didn't try and run?" said Papa.

"Hell, no," said Beobee. "With me behind all this brush here, there was no way in hell he could see me."

I moved away from them to see the dead guy. His skin looked clean, almost scrubbed, and his fine, black, oriental hair was cut nicely, not long and matted with dirt like mine. His fatigues were clean, too. He didn't look dead, but then I'd never seen anybody who'd just died. The only dead people I'd ever seen had already been to the undertakers and looked horrible, like wax figures. This guy looked like he was asleep and might wake up any second.

"Are you sure he's dead?" I asked.

Ron cursed and Papa gave me a sad, understanding look.

Beobee came over and knelt beside Glock and me. "Look at the entry hole if you don't believe me, Carl." He yanked the dead boy's shirt clear up to his armpits, popping the buttons off and exposing his belly and chest. Then he turned him a bit and pulled the shirt back over his arms and tossed it aside. I didn't think it was right to treat him that roughly.

"See!" Beobee pointed below the rib cage to a small, pink hole, like a birthmark.

"Let's turn him over," Beobee said to Glock. "I want to see if the bullet exited."

They rolled him over like a sack of potatoes. There were no marks on his back. The bullet was evidently still inside him. From this angle you could see how distended his belly was, as if he were pregnant. Ron said it was because of all the internal bleeding the round had caused when it ricocheted off his ribs, whipping his insides to jelly. Then I noticed the blood. Like a thin red line of gleaming nail polish, it coursed from his wound, down his tan belly, and onto the brown earth. It reminded me of the way I felt about two years earlier, when my cousin Bobby and I had been over at my friend Lou's house. Bobby and I were boxing around, and I backed up into a table and knocked a lamp onto the floor, breaking it. It was Lou's mother's favorite lamp, an irreplaceable antique. I felt terrible because I knew that no matter what I did I could never make amends. I had the same feeling now, a panicky feeling of never being able to make something right again, no matter what you did. I looked at the others and wondered if they felt it too.

Beobee came over with an AK-47 rifle. He lovingly ran his hand up and down the wooden stock. "This here's one of the best fighting rifles made, Carl," he said softly.

Glock looked at it. "Let me see it, will you?"

Beobee handed it to Glock and he brought it to his cheek smartly, sighting along the barrel. "Pretty nice," he said. He handed it back.

"Sure it is," said Beobee. "It's a damn sight better'n that plastic M-16 they give us. The AK's all wood and steel, got a good weight and balance, and it don't hardly ever jam." He smiled suddenly and turned to the others. "I'm sending it home to my daddy to shoot squirrels with."

Papa tried to smile, but couldn't. Ron hid his feelings behind his sunglasses. Beobee hefted the AK over his head triumphantly and smiled at me. Just meeting his look was all the encouragement he needed and he continued bragging.

"You shoulda' seen it, Carl. He was comin' down the trail with his eyes on the ground. He had his rifle slung over his shoulder like he was on leave in Hanoi or something."

I listened to him for a while and then he went over to the dead soldier's ruck and started going through it.

Papa watched him. "I think he's NVA regular forces," he said. "They usually carry nice equipment like that."

"Is that right?" said Ron.

Beobee looked up. "Papa's right, Ron. He's NVA all right. He was a medic too. Just look at this equipment; it's all made in Czechoslovakia." Beobee laid out the shiny, stainless steel tools—scalpels, scissors and clamps. They looked odd against the dust of the trail. There were vials of pills, letters, and papers with official-looking stamps.

I had the radio in my ruck and Papa motioned me over. He called in to the CP and told them what had happened. I couldn't hear what they said to him. After a moment Papa put the handset back. He turned to the others. "Pack the tools and letters up and let's get moving. He may've been lost, but I doubt it. Chances are his unit is close by and that's why he was so careless."

The other guys quickly put their rucks on. The boy looked so cold lying there in the shade. I picked up his shirt and laid it over him. As I put on my ruck, Beobee and Glock dragged him by his arms and legs into the bushes and hid him. As we started down the trail, I kept looking back, half expecting him to get up and run away.

CHAPTER 6

We sat in a circle on the ground, playing cards. As we studied our hands, we talked about Papa's imminent departure. Papa said his wife and kids already had their tickets to fly out to the West Coast to meet him. Then they'd rent a car and drive cross-country to see the sights. Suddenly Beobee put his finger to his lips. We put down our cards and slowly reached for our weapons. Looking around, we listened carefully for a minute and the silence was broken by a small click of sound as a stone or something landed in our midst. In a flash we were all lying in the prone, pointing our weapons out.

"What is it?" Mike asked.

"Yeah," Ron said, "that could've been a grenade."

"Nah," Beobee scoffed, "if it were enemy, it would've been one, believe me."

I looked at the others; they were as mystified as I was. Leaves rustled high overhead. A large, black-faced monkey with a fringe of yellow hair hanging from his arms and chest, swung slowly and lazily from one branch to another, watching us with that comical, almost-human look monkeys have. Then he was gone. A dead leaf floated slowly down.

"What was that?" Mike asked.

"Rock ape," Beobee said.

We sat up and lay our rifles down again. Ron and Papa laughed nervously.

I quit the game and tried to read. The others sat in a circle, talking quietly as they played cards. They looked like a bunch of people having a picnic, but we were smack dab in the middle of the jungle. Earlier there had been a lot of radio traffic, with different people from the CP calling every so often to ask about the dead NVA, and what we'd found in his rucksack. They'd told Papa that there was probably a battalion of NVA in our area and to be careful. Everyone was a little uptight. I kept thinking about that medic. I pictured him suddenly sitting up and yawning. He got to his feet and put on his shirt. His face grew worried and he quickly walked off.

The hike back the next day was all uphill. Carrying the radio was killing me. I wondered if we'd stop and look at the medic. I wasn't so sure he'd be there. When we came to the place where they'd hidden him in the bushes, a noisy cloud of flies swarmed us. We waved them away as we passed, nobody saying anything. That feeling of paybacks came over me again. I still couldn't believe it. The others rushed on as if the jungle itself would close in and swallow us up. I had to run to keep up with them or they would have left me behind.

Back inside the wire, Ron and Mike embraced Papa and congratulated him. He wouldn't have to go outside the wire again and now he was safe. Mike started crying. Beobee and Glock shook Papa's hand and told him how happy they were for him. Now all he had to do for the next week or so was to count the days.

Papa looked haggard and pale. When I shook his hand, I choked up. "I'm gonna miss you, man."

He smiled sadly. "I know, Carl. I'll miss you too."

Ron, Glock and the others came closer. Papa looked around at us. "You guys stick together and you'll be alright, you hear?"

We nodded.

"Seriously, guys," Papa said. His eyes were glazed. "I want you all to stick together."

"Like glue," Ron said.

"You bet," Glock said.

"Dig it," Mike said.

I nodded.

Ron and Papa went up to the CP to be debriefed. I went looking for Gene, but I couldn't find him. I was coming back past the CP when I saw Captain Harris shaking Papa's hand. Then, another Captain I had never seen before came out of the CP. He had a stiff military bearing about him, acne scars, and a little reddish mustache.

The next day, Ron, Mike and I worked chopper pad detail. We got back to the bunker around noon and Gene was inside, wrapping a bandage around Chico's foot

"Hello, turkeys," Chico said. He pointed up at my bunk. "You got a letter, Carl."

It was from Linda, the girl I'd been seeing at State who broke up with me. I put it in my pocket.

"What happened to you?" Ron asked Chico as Gene cut the bandage with a pair of surgical scissors.

"I was helping Marco cut down a tree and cut myself on the foot with the machete. That's all."

"That's all?" Gene said, turning to Ron and shaking his scissors angrily. "He cut himself almost to the bone. I had to sterilize his wound and put two stitches in it, not to mention a tetanus shot . . . That's all!" Gene directed a look of mild reproach at Chico, paused a moment, then returned to his work, putting a pin in the bandage.

"Well," Ron said, turning to smile at us, "do you think they'll have to send him back to McGernity?"

"Oh, no," Gene said, not taking his eyes off his task and missing the pun. "He'll just have to pull light duty for a couple of days, that's all." Gene stood and started putting his things away. "I guess you guys heard about Captain Harris?"

"Heard what?" Glock asked.

"He's been relieved of his command. His replacement is here already."

I remembered the Captain I'd seen at the CP bunker.

"You're kidding!" Ron said. "I saw some captain up by the CP, but I didn't know he was Harris's replacement."

"Well, he is," Gene said. "Division HQ thinks Harris hasn't been aggressive enough. He'll be leaving for Dak-To tomorrow."

I looked at Gene. "Does the Captain have a small red mustache?"
Gene nodded.

"He looks like a tough son-of-a-gun," I said. "I think we're going to miss Harris."

"He can't be that bad," Glock said.

Gene shook his head. "Yes he can, fellas."

We fell silent.

Gene's hair was getting long and he had started wearing an Aussie bush hat. He almost looked like a hippie. He looked at Ron. "Don't let Chico go out walking on that leg today, will ya?"

"We'll keep an eye on him," Ron said, "won't we, guys?"

"Sure we will," Glock said.

"Dig it," Mike said.

Gene grabbed his bag and left.

"He's a good man," Ron said after a moment.

Glock smiled mischievously. "A little weird, though."

"Yeah," Chico said, "a little cuckoo in the head, but a damned good medic." Chico turned to Mike. "Mike, do me a favor, will you? See if he's still out there?"

Mike went outside; he came back in and shook his head. Chico got up. He used a board as a crutch as he made his way to the aperture.

"Chico?" I said, "where are you going?"

"To see Marco and Jonesy and play some cards. Why?"

"After Gene told you not to walk on it?"

"I won't let him see me."

Ron stepped in front of Chico. "Yeah, the dude won't see you cause you ain't goin' anywhere."

Ron and Chico stared at each other, locked into a Mexican standoff of sorts.

"Aha," said Chico. He turned to Glock, Mike and me, and nodded his head slowly, as if having just glimpsed some deep truth. "You see what is happening here, guys? I just now begin to see it. When Papa leaves us, Ron will be the squad leader. Already he is pulling rank on us."

Ron went into a boxer's stance and threw a flurry of fake blows at Chico. Chico hopped backwards, laughing and waving his board-crutch defensively. He fell back onto his bunk and they both burst out laughing. It was the first time I'd seen Ron have a real belly laugh and it gave me a good feeling. Chico and Ron were very close, like brothers.

I went up to the giant potty to read Linda's letter. She told me about the new Steem Masheen record she couldn't stop playing, about her girlfriend's abortion, the antiwar demonstration she went to, a party she had where she smoked marijuana and passed out. I don't know why she bothered to write. Linda was the one who wanted to break up. After our first date, she had started chasing me. She called me on the phone all the time, and sent me notes on these little cards she drew scenes on. She was an Arts Major and could draw really well. I wasn't in love with her yet, but one night something kind of magical happened. She came to my house during a snowstorm. Her brother, Johnny, had driven her over. We walked down to the corner and talked under the light of a street lamp. The thick, falling snow swirled around us and it was like we were suddenly in one of those little crystal ball-encased winter scenes that you shake up, and her brother was on the outside somewhere. She wore bright, yellow mittens and a matching yellow, knit hat, and her cheeks were red. As I looked into her eyes, I could actually hear the snowflakes clinking like tiny shards of glass as they struck the car and the icy street. I watched snowflakes stick in her hair and melt on her red cheeks and then I looked into her eyes and it seemed as if time stopped. She asked me to go skiing with her the next day and I said I would. All of a sudden her brother was saying that they had to go and the spell was broken.

The next day Papa came in carrying a package. He set it on his bunk. Taking off his rucksack, he sat down tiredly at the ammo table. Ron, Glock and Mike smiled broadly.

"Hey, short-timer," Chico said.

Papa smiled as he began unpacking his rucksack. "Did you all hear about Harris?"

"Yeah," Ron said. "Gene was telling us." Ron started shuffling his cards, getting ready for a game. Glock sat down at the table with him.

Papa looked at me suddenly and indicated the package on his bunk. "Oh, I almost forgot, Carl. That's your package. Ted must've overlooked it when he sorted the mail."

It was from my parents. Papa and the others watched as I opened it and took out a neat-looking paperback novel about Indians, a loaf of stateside white bread, the fluffy kind like foam rubber, two big cans of Sloppy Joe mix, a bottle of Worcestershire sauce, and a small manila envelope. I opened it up and found a Saint Christopher medal on a silver chain. I put it on.

I held up the cans of Sloppy Joe mix. "What do you say we have this now? We can open up both cans in Papa's honor."

"Yeah," Ron said. "We'll have a going-home party for Papa."

Papa blushed again. "C'mon, Ron," he said. "You guys don't have to do this."

"Aw, be quiet," Ron said, "we're gonna have a party for you whether you want one or not."

I got a pot from the cook's shed and brought it back to the bunker. When I got there, Ted, the company clerk, and Beobee, were in the bunker. Gene, the doc, and Lee, showed up next. I heated up the Sloppy Joe mix and served it on paper plates. The small talk died as everybody ate. A moment later Papa scraped his plate with his spoon and looked at me. "That was pretty good, Carl. When I get home I'm going to have it again."

Beobee pointed his spoon at Papa. "What's the story on the dead enemy medic?"

Papa paused to wipe his lips with a napkin. "Believe it or not, they think he was deserting his unit. Military Intelligence flew in a man from Pleiku to go through his things. He's up there right now with the new CO. Ain't that right, Ted?"

Ted nodded.

"What's the new Commanding Officer like?" Beobee asked Papa.

Papa turned to him. "Well, let me put it this way. If I had to spend one day more than the fifteen I got left, in his company, I'd re-enlist for four years and get out of the field."

"He's that bad?" Ron asked.

Papa frowned. "Badder. He was Colonel Carp's favorite back at Camp McGernity."

Colonel Carp had recently made the newspapers back home for threatening to ship out to an Infantry line company, any base camp soldiers who failed an inspection, or who failed to salute an officer. My parents had written me, warning me about him. I had to laugh when I read it, since they didn't realize I was already in an Infantry line company.

Mike turned to Ted. "Is that right, Ted? Is he bad news?"

"I guess," Ted said. "That's what everybody says." He put down his paper plate and cleared his throat. "And, while we're on the subject of bad news, fellas. When I heard about Carl's package, I was already on my way over here to give you some. You have another patrol to run."

"You're kidding," Papa said. Everyone looked at Ted angrily.

"Didn't you tell him we just got back?" Mike asked.

"Yeah," Chico said, an angry glow suffusing his face.

Ted held up his hand. "Whooa now, fellas. Don't gang up on me. Of course I did, but we got ten patrols going out." Ted shook his head in exasperation. "Things are going to be very busy on the hill from here on out."

"What about Papa?" Lee asked. "He ain't gonna send him out, is he?"

Ted nodded. "I'm afraid so."

"Dag," Ron said. "Papa ain't got but two weeks left!"

I looked at Papa. He didn't look worried about it.

"I know, I know," Ted said, sighing. "Listen, fellas, this new Captain, DeVoors, is tough. You'd better get used to that. Things have been pretty smooth under Harris, but that's all over now. This is all part of DeVoors' new policy. You better get used to the idea of more details, too. He said the hill's not going to be an R&R center anymore."

Everybody chuckled.

"Harris would never pull that sort of thing," Lee said as the candlelight flickered across his pale face. "If I was Papa, I'd refuse to go out."

Papa laughed. "Yeah, Lee, like I'm gonna take a chance on getting court-martialed with two weeks left."

Everybody fell silent for a moment.

"Hey, Ted," Glock asked, "is Captain DeVoors up there now?"

"Yeah."

Glock turned to Ron and nodded toward the aperture. They got up.

"Where are you guys going?" Ted asked.

"We're gonna go up and talk to him."

Papa's voice rose in exasperation. "C'mon, fellas, that's not necessary."

"We know it," Ron said, "but we're gonna try it anyway."

"No," Papa said. "Ron! Come back here!"

They left. Mike got up and put on his steel pot. Papa grabbed him. "Oh no, you don't."

Mike laughed and sat back down.

I had to go to the latrine so I walked Ted back up through the dark trenches toward the top of the hill. He paused outside the CP bunker.

"Carl, did you know Lee is trying to transfer out of the squad?"

"I figured as much."

He was silent for a few moments. "Carl, you're not smoking any of that stuff, are you?"

"You mean marijuana?"

"Yeah."

"No. I just fake it. I don't inhale."

Ted frowned. "I hope not. They say some of that stuff has been doctored up by the enemy."

"Don't worry," I said, wishing he'd believe me, "I don't smoke it."

The poncho covering the aperture of the CP suddenly flapped open and Captain DeVoors came out. In the light that escaped from the CP, I could see his tailored fatigues and the sharp creases in his pants. He glared at us and walked toward the trench line.

Ted turned to me with concern on his face. "Things are changing around here, Carl. You better be careful."

"I will."

Later I climbed the steps to the latrine and sat. Above me among the stars, a tiny pinpoint of light moved across the black sky. It was too high for a plane or a helicopter, and if I had never seen a satellite, I probably would've thought I'd spotted a UFO. I remembered the first satellite I'd seen. I must've been in 5th or 6th grade. I was out in the front yard with my parents when Mister Beatty from across the street walked over and told us that Sputnik, the Russian satellite, was due over in a few minutes. My dad yelled in to my brother Jack, the one who went to Vietnam before I did. Jack was in the kitchen making himself a sandwich, and he yelled back that he'd be right out. Sure enough, in another minute, Mister Beatty pointed to Sputnik as it moved across the night sky. "Hurry," my dad yelled in to Jack.

We watched in awe as Sputnik sailed silently and invincibly over our heads. At the very moment it disappeared over the horizon, the screen door banged open and Jack came bounding down the steps, a triple-decker sandwich in one hand and a glass of iced tea in the other. He tripped and fell flat on his face, chipping his tooth. He still had that little chip in it the last time I saw him.

CHAPTER 7

*I sat in my bunk reading a book Gene had given me by an American mys-*tic named Edger Cayce. Cayce could remember all his past lives. It was fascinating. I wondered if maybe someday somebody would remember being a Private in Vietnam named Carl Melcher. Probably not. If I were a General they might, though. Everybody who can recall their past lives seems to have been Pharaoh, or a High Priest. Nobody remembers being a poor common slob, pushing granite blocks up a greased incline.

At the little table below, Mike and Chico were playing pinochle. Glock and Papa had gone off to visit somebody on the other side of the hill. I didn't know where Lee was. We hadn't seen much of him lately.

Ron came in the bunker. He had a big smile on his face. "Dig this," he said, "the Captain's gonna let Papa stay inside the wire."

"All right!" Chico said.

"Dig it," Ron said. "But the Captain's gonna make him work the sump detail for the next week or so instead."

"That ain't bad detail," Mike said.

"Dig," Ron said.

"So, who takes out the patrol?" I said

"I do," Ron said.

"Right on!" Mike said emphatically.

I was glad for Ron. I knew he really wanted to lead the patrol. Glock, Mike and I would be going.

Ron took the patrol across the valley floor about five klicks from the hill. Then we took our first break on the trail. I sat across from Mike and leaned back on my rucksack to rest. I heard Ron's voice shift into an angry, high pitch; he and Glock were arguing. Mike and I tried to see what was going on.

"No, we set up now," Ron said, "right in that clearing over there."

"Wait a minute," Glock said, "according to the map we got another five klicks to go."

"I don't care what the map says! I say we're staying here."

Glock frowned at Mike and I and shook his head. "You're the hancho on this one," he said bitterly.

Ron mimicked him.

"Go to hell!" Glock said, and then the both of them laughed. They had become really close, best friends. I felt a little left out, but only a little, because Gene and I were good buddies. We had a lot in common, like philosophy and books. I looked over at Mike who was staring blankly into the bushes and I felt sorry for him. He had become the odd man out. He and Ron were still close, but it was different now. It was as if Ron and Glock were up on one level, and Mike and I were on the next one down. I didn't care, but Mike wanted to be on the same level with Ron. Overall, though, I think the new development was a good thing. Ron and Glock's friendship balanced things out in the squad and lent a good feeling.

Ron looked over at us. "Well, what are you two waiting for?" His voice was playful. "Get them claymore mines out."

I started unpacking the mines. Mike moved slowly. Besides having been pushed down a tier by Glock, I sensed there was something else bothering him.

After we got set up, the rain came. From the high, thick jungle canopy, a steady drizzle started, as if some technician had turned on a fire-sprinkler system hidden up there among the branches of the trees. I realized it was the beginning of the monsoons and thought of Papa back at the firebase. When I'd first come in-country, he had told me he'd be going home when the rains came, and, sure enough, here they were and he was already packing his things.

We built a hootch, even though we weren't supposed to. Actually, a half-tent would be a more accurate description. It was just a vinyl poncho stretched taut like a canopy, and camouflaged with leaves and vines. The rain put a sheen on everything. The poncho-liner blankets got damp, but fortunately they were made of a synthetic material that kept in body heat. With the liner-blankets wrapped around us, we sat around under the hootch, staring into the brush. For the first couple hours it was okay. The rain was warm after having dripped off the sun-warmed leaves overhead, and everything around us had a clean wet look. I watched the leaves tremble with the drops that hit them.

After a while, however, the rain grew cold and I could see my breath. We played poker for about an hour, then stopped. We talked for a while, but eventually the steady downpour reduced our conversation to vague, mumbled longings and complaints. Finally the rain slowed to a light drizzle.

Ron set up the guard shifts as we sat quietly in the growing gloom of dusk. For some strange reason, every time I shut my eyes I imagined myself back at my parent's house. It was hot and dry, like the summer before I went away to State. Back then, evenings were my favorite time. Since I was soon leaving for school, my parents more or less gave me the run of the house. I usually came home around eleven and they were already upstairs in bed. After I shut and locked the door, my mother always called down in this semi-worried voice and said, "Carl, is that you?" It didn't really bother me though; it just struck me as funny. A couple of times I was tempted to call up to her and say, "No, it's Jack the Ripper. I'll be right up." But I always resisted. My parents treated me more like an equal than a kid then, and I really liked it. We got along great.

I'd go in the kitchen and get a piece of pie, or a dish of ice cream. Then I'd sit on the recliner in front of the TV. The weatherman had become like an old friend. I can still see his face as he jabbed his pointer at a half dozen of those little, plastic, magnetized snowflakes sticking to a map of Pennsylvania. Knocking one down, he'd laugh and quickly point to the little cloud over Jersey which is weeping a few tears of rain. After the weather I'd watch an old movie on the Late Show. God, how I loved that house and that recliner and TV.

Someone shook me. I blinked my eyes. Everything was black fuzz. I tried to go back to sleep, but again, someone shook me as if trying to tell me something. I shivered in the cool air and then I realized it was Glock. He'd had first guard and now it was my turn. The others were sleeping on the ground around me. A pale luminescence floated in front of my face— the phosphor-painted face of Glock's watch. I patted him on the back, signaling that I was now awake.

Tiny insect sounds filled the night. Occasionally I heard a rustle as one of the sleepers shifted position. One of the guys—I couldn't tell which one—cried out, a soft childlike cry. I wondered what horror was at this very moment stalking him through his dreams. As I sat quietly in total blackness, I seemed to be disembodied and floating, capable of moving vast distances. I could be in Vietnam or in Guatemala. I could be on a distant planet. I could be anywhere. There really was no way of telling. I couldn't see anything except for the phosphor face of the watch. Then I heard a tiny voice. "Bullet four, this is Bullet one. Sitrep, over?"

I was on the floor of the ocean in a diving bell.

"Bullet four, sitrep, over?" it repeated.

Millions of tons of black water pressed down on me and they wanted to know if I was alive. The little voice came again, an angry urgency in it, and I suddenly remembered the handset and the procedure Ron had explained to me earlier. "Sitrep" meant "situation report." They wanted to know how we were. A squeeze of the talk button on the handset would produce a click in their set back on the hill. I grabbed the handset and squeezed the button.

"Roger," the voice said. "Have a good night."

I remembered some of my favorite songs in my head to keep my mind occupied. That got me to thinking about the dances back in Philly. Record Hops, Bandstand—it had all started in Philly. The Bandstand TV station was only six blocks from where I went to high school, down on Forty-fifth near Market. I used to watch the older guys and girls from school dancing on TV, and trying to look cool whenever the camera panned by them. By the time I got to my teens, Bandstand had already moved out to Hollywood, but there were still kids from the neighborhood who would actually fly out to California to try and get on.

When I was in high school, we went to the dance at Chez Vous Ballroom, out at Sixty-ninth Street. The place was huge, a roller-skating rink six nights a week, but on Fridays it was ours, packed thick with guys and girls. When you walked past the bouncers and through the doors, the thumping rhythms of drums and bass washed over you like waves on a beach. I thought about that place and that music, and I was somehow suddenly there, up in the rafters somewhere. That Bobby Love and the Valentine's tune, "Parachute," with the slinky, funky beat, was blasting through the speakers. A line of boys faced a line of girls, moving back and forth under the dance floor lights to the base and booming beat. Undulating like happy zombies, they slipped and slid, herky-jerky on the hardwood. The guys sneered and snapped their fingers as they tried to look cool and tough (Parachute! Float to me, hon-ney) and the girls rolled their hips and shook (jump with me, bay-bee) as they stared straight ahead blankly and chewed their gum like cuds. All the while Bobby's brassy sax screamed and swooped through the rafters around me like a bird of prey.

There was another sound now, not in my head, but out there in the jungle blackness somewhere—a gentle rustle of movement. It was getting closer and louder. I quickly shook the closest guy awake, Glock I think, and in a moment they were all up. I found my rifle as someone grabbed my shoulder. Ron whispered in my ear, "take your safety off, but don't shoot unless I give the order."

The sound increased in volume, becoming distinct; leaves swished and branches and bamboo crackled and popped. It grew louder and I heard Glock whisper to Ron that he better call in artillery on them.

Ron's voice hissed in the darkness. "And have a whole company of enemy looking for us? Dag! We're only four dudes, man!"

"Dig it," Mike whispered.

I didn't say anything; I wasn't so sure it was enemy. All this time we hadn't heard one human voice, hadn't seen one flashlight, and whatever was out there must've been big because it was making an awful racket. Finally, when it couldn't have been more than thirty feet from us, it veered off to the side and slowly moved away. A half hour later we settled down again.

In the morning we looked for traces of whoever or whatever had made all the noise. The way the branches were broken and flattened left no doubt that something had passed. But what? The others didn't seem to care, but the mystery intrigued me.

The jungle was a strange place but I really liked it. The light was soft and greenish, the air, still. All around there was wildlife, but you hardly ever saw it. Its sounds were soft and slight, residual sounds—the click of falling fronds, knocked loose perhaps by some monkey trapeze artist, the flutter of a pair of wings as a colorful bird swooped between the branches of the trees, the passing hum of a large flying insect. There were tigers and giant pythons, too. They all gave us wide berth, but I knew they were there.

Ron and the others bent intently over their cards, seemingly unaware of it all. Maybe they were merely used to it. As Ron shuffled the cards, I took out a book Gene had lent me, *Siddhartha,* by Herman Hesse. I'd been reading it for a week now. It was the only book that hadn't gotten wet. Gene said he'd gotten a lot out of it. It was the story of a young man named Siddhartha who was seeking enlightenment. When I read this book I found myself in the forest with Siddhartha and his friend Govinda, listening in as they talked of their search for happiness and chanted the sacred Ohmmm. Siddhartha was very independent, but also very spiritual. He didn't follow people, not even the Buddha when he came to the village and talked to the people. Instead, Siddhartha listened to his own "inner voice." When he was faced with some great decision he would think and meditate and struggle and eventually his inner voice would speak.

I put the book down and stared into the bushes. I really wanted to be like that but I knew I wasn't. Not yet, anyway. Some things I did because I had to, like going into the Army, and going to Vietnam, but a lot of other things I just did, for no particular reason. And the closest thing I had to an inner voice was the growling in my stomach when I was hungry.

Ron looked up from his cards. "You want in the game, Carl?"

"No," I said, wanting to read a little while longer.

Glock turned to Ron. "How many do you think there were?"

Ron smiled as he studied his cards. "A company or better."

"Are you sure it was enemies?" I said.

Ron turned to me. "Well, suppose you tell us what it was."

"I don't know," I said, "maybe some animal."

"Dig," said Mike. "There are some big animals out here, like tigers."

Ron laughed. "No tiger makes that much noise."

"Maybe not," I said, "but there must be other animals out here that make a lot of noise when they move around."

"Maybe it was little green men from Mars," Glock said. "Their flying saucer ran out of gas."

"Yeah," Ron said, "they were carrying 5-gallon cans and looking for a filling station."

Mike smiled softly, as if apologizing for Ron. "You read too many of them books, Carl," he said.

I was angry, but I didn't say anything. It probably had been the enemy, but they couldn't prove it; that was my point. It was like my theory . . . I couldn't prove that either, but it was possible.

Ten minutes later it started raining again—hard. It broke up the game and put us all in a foul mood. That night the rain came down in a torrent, but at least there was no movement in the bush.

As we started up the hill to the firebase, the rain settled into a bone-chilling drizzle. Coming up through the wire, we saw Papa on his sump detail about fifty meters to our left. He was leaning on a rake while he supervised a couple of 'cruits. A mist of steam rose from the burning trash and moved about their feet as they worked. Ron waved to Papa and he smiled his warm smile and waved back. We were almost to the trench line when we heard an explosion. As we hit the dirt I saw Papa stagger and fall, a small gray cloud slowly drifting away from him. The two 'cruits were running for the edge of the sump. We waited for a few seconds but nothing further happened.

"C'mon," said Ron. "Let's go."

Papa lay sprawled on his back. The two 'cruits had returned and now stood over him, holding their rakes dumbly. Glock and Ron knelt quickly beside Papa. His eyes were closed. Ron tapped one of the 'cruits on the leg. "Don't just stand there . . . go get the medic. Hurry!"

The guy took off running. Mike was shaking his head slowly.

"How is he?" Glock said to Ron.

"How do I know?" Ron turned to me. "Carl, go find Gene, will you?"

Just as I turned to go, I saw them coming down the hill. Gene led the way, his bag flapping noisily against his leg. Lee was with him, his eyes wild-looking. Gene skidded into us like a ballplayer sliding into home plate. He immediately put his ear to Papa's chest. "Tsk, tsk," he said, shaking his head grimly. I looked closely but couldn't see any marks on Papa and his fatigues seemed to be intact.

Gene turned to Ron. "Give me your bedroll. Let's prop his head up."

"What was it?" I said, "a mortar? What happened?"

"It wasn't a mortar," Ron said. "I think it was something in the sump, maybe a booby trap or something."

Gene lifted Papa's head momentarily, then gently put it down again. He slid his hand out and it was covered with dark, gelatinous blood. Lee started saying, "oh no" over and over in a low moan. Gene stole a quick look at him then returned his attention to Papa. He wiped his hands on his pants and, rummaging noisily through his bag, took out a little pink, plastic, make-up mirror. Crouching over Papa's head to keep the drizzle off him, he held the mirror to his nose.

"What're you doing?" Mike asked.

"Checking to see if he's breathing. He ain't. He's gone."

Mike put his head in his hands and rocked back and forth as he sobbed. Lee's face was white as a sheet. He smacked his fist in his hand and started pacing. "Why did they do it," he chanted over and over as he continued to pound his fist. "Why couldn't they leave him alone." His voice rose to a scream. "Why did DeVoors have to put him to work? I'll get that creep!"

Lee chambered a round in his M-16. Ron and Glock blocked him. Lee tried to push past them and Mike and I grabbed him from behind. He struggled as Gene got a needle of something ready.

"It ain't the Captains's fault, Lee," Glock said, as if talking to a child. He took Lee's M-16 from him.

Tears streamed down Lee's face. "Yes, it is," he cried. "If he hadn't put him on that detail, he'd be alive now."

"That's right," Mike said.

Ron turned to them. "We ain't back in the world shooting blanks at each other at the Escape and Evasion course." Ron turned and glared at me. "This is real! You dudes better realize that."

Gene jabbed the needle into Lee's arm through his shirt. Lee looked at him, not seeming to understand what he was doing, or why. Then he suddenly fell to the ground, sobbing.

Gene began putting his stuff away. Up in the trench line a bunch of guys were watching us. Ted and the new CO pushed past them and started down through the wire. I told Ron I was going up to the bunker and walked off. I just couldn't be around anybody.

After I put my gear away in the bunker, the others began arriving. I put my poncho on and went out and sat on the roof. The rain was coming down harder now. A few minutes later Ron came out into the trench and ducked down under his poncho to smoke his pipe. He looked up and saw me. I didn't say anything and after a few minutes he went back inside. The poncho kept the rain off me, but a cold wet puddle had formed where I was sitting.

I really had thought Papa would get home. He was older, and for some reason I thought the older guys were safer. I don't know why, it was just a feeling I had. I wondered why he had to die. He was a good person, really, and it had looked like he'd make it. It didn't make any sense. He'd been so close! It was as if he couldn't leave Vietnam, as if he couldn't escape his karma. The river of life had swept him away from us, into a strong side stream and over a waterfall. It was just meant to be. I remembered a refrain from a song that had been popular a few years back.

". . . meant to be, meant to bee-ee, meant to be." They sang it in three-part harmony, with drums pounding and guitars strumming. As I looked out into the wet, gray mists, it played in my head, over and over, for a long time.

CHAPTER 8

In the damp, dimly lit bunker, Ron and Chico sat around writing letters.
Mike was cleaning his M-79 grenade launcher. It was about a month after Papa died. Up on the highest bunk, Glock pulled back on a slingshot he'd made and let it fly. "Got 'im," he said, looking down at me. As he climbed down, we heard a scurrying in the plastic tarp above as the rat he'd been aiming at made its escape.

Ron spoke without looking up from his letter writing. "Yeah, Kemosabe, you got him all right."

"Damn!"

We'd been trying to run out the rats that had invaded our bunker. It seemed as if the monsoons had driven all the rats in Pleiku Province to take shelter in the bunkers of Firebase 29. Most of them lived in the spaces between the sandbags and the plastic waterproofing in the roof. In the beginning we heard them only at night, their little feet pitter-pattering across the plastic overhead as they foraged. After a couple weeks of rain we heard them all the time. And after a month of rain they were getting into things, chewing up C-rations boxes and cans. One night we woke to a horrible scream. We lit a candle and Mike was standing anxiously in the center of the bunker, clutching his M-16. He told us how he had awakened to find a rat the size of a cat sitting on his chest, looking at him with little, glowing eyes. He spent the rest of the night seated at the table, staring into the quivering light of a candle.

According to Ted, the CP had ordered rat poison a month ago.

Glock watched as Ron packed his pipe. "You're smoking more since you got the squad," he said.

Ron smiled. "No more than when Papa was squad leader."

"Dig it," Mike said.

Glock shook his head. "Well, with all due respect, hancho, you ought to cut back on it."

I kind of agreed with Glock, but I didn't say anything.

Glock frowned and grabbed his slingshot. "I'm going to try and pick off some rats from outside."

I opened my book. We'd all been uptight since Papa's death. I put my book down and got up.

"Where you going?" Ron asked. "It's raining out there."

I grabbed the sandbag full of trash. "I'm going to the sump."

Glock wasn't outside. I took the long way to the sump, walking all the way around the hill in the trenches. The valley below was a stormy, gray sea and the sky above a vast, gray sponge. The rain had finally washed the color out of everything. It fell in a mist, with drops the size of dust motes. They whirled around and up with the slightest movement of your hand. Just last night it had come down in a torrent, dumping about an inch of water on the bunker floor. Most of the time though it was everything in between these two extremes. But, it never stopped raining.

The sergeant in charge at the sump had me dump the bag out on the ground. Then he poked through it with a rake. They inspected everything now, since they'd discovered it was one of our own grenades that had killed Papa. Some idiot had accidently thrown a grenade out with his trash, and it had laid there cooking in the heat until Papa tapped it with his rake, setting it off.

Up at the Giant Potty, someone had left a New York paper in the rack. I read a story about the Paris Peace Talks. They were deadlocked. There was a difference of opinion as to whether they should seat the four parties at four separate sides of the table, or if instead, the North Vietnamese and the Viet Cong should be seated on one side and the Americans and the South Vietnamese on the other. So much for the peacemakers.

When I came back to the bunker, Beobee was there.

"Well, look who it is," he said. He was seated on an ammo can, smoking a bowl of what smelled like Half and Half. Across from him Ron, Mike and Chico were playing poker.

Beobee turned back to Ron. "So tell me, Ron, how in the world did you manage to get such a dry bunker?"

Ron smiled. "This bunker would be just as wet as the rest of them, except that me and Mike fixed that roof two months ago with some plastic we found up at the mess tent."

"Is that right?" Beobee asked Mike.

"Dig it," Mike said proudly.

"Well," Beobee drawled slowly. "I hope you consider yourselves lucky, cause just about every damned bunker on this here hill 'cept yours is leaking like a damned sieve."

"I'm hip," Mike said, as he studied his hand.

"How's Lee doing, Beobee?" I asked, as I pulled up an ammo can and sat. Lee had been transferred to Beobee's squad as an assistant machine gunner. I think Ron had something to do with it.

"I don't rightly know," Beobee said. He took off his steel pot and ran his fingers over his bald spot. "I ain't no psychologist. But he ain't doing me no good. That much I do know."

Ron opened up a chocolate bar and took a big bite. "What do you mean?"

"Oh, he just mopes around and sleeps all the time. The chaplain's been out to talk with him and is supposed to come out again." Beobee sighed dramatically. "I'll tell you one thing. DeVoors may have put Lee in my squad, but until he shapes up he ain't going out on no patrol with me."

"Really?" I said, knowing Beobee wanted to elaborate.

He looked at me with mock indignation. "I'll take a court-martial first! I don't want him on my machine gun if I run into some stuff out there."

Chico jumped suddenly to his feet. "Four eights?" he said incredulously. "Vacquero!"

"Who had four eights?" said Beobee.

Ron smiled as he pulled the pile of matches we used for chips toward him. His gold, ruby-studded pinky ring gleamed triumphantly in the dim light.

"Who do you think?" said Mike sadly, shaking his head in awe.

Ron took out his little black book and opened it. "How much do you owe me now, brother?" he said to Mike.

"Twenty bucks," Mike said sadly.

The poncho flapped back and Ted came in. He was carrying the red mail sack. He reached inside it. "Here you go, Carl." He handed me a rain-dampened letter from my parents. I put it in my pocket. Ron got a letter and so did Mike. It was only the second letter I'd seen Mike get since I'd been in the squad. Ron and Mike started opening theirs. Ted gave Beobee a stack of letters for his squad and the two of them left together.

Chico got up and went rooting through the CP bag. I spotted a pack of Blastos he'd overlooked and made a mental note to get them later. The bunker shuddered suddenly as the big guns fired half a dozen rounds in quick succession.

A cackle of laughter escaped Ron as he read his letter. Everybody was watching him except Mike who was still reading his own letter, a serious look on his face as his lips moved haltingly. Ron continued his cackly laughing, "Oh, this is a trip!"

"What is?" Chico asked.

"Here." Ron passed the letter to him and I couldn't help but see it over his shoulder. It was printed in big, block letters on lined, yellow notepad paper. Chico smiled as he read it over.

"What's it say?" I said.

Chico flipped the letter over to read the other side. Finding nothing there he asked Ron for the envelope. Ron passed it to him and Chico read the return address. "It's from Quentin Colby Elementary School in Eustace, Virginia. It's a Christmas wish."

"It's also a little early," I said.

"Dig it," said Ron, "a full month."

Mike was still staring fixedly at his letter, not paying any attention to us.

Chico read aloud. "Hi, my name is William Hoffman and my teacher said we should write you a Christmas letter of cheer. I'm seven years old and in second grade. Will you have a turkey for Christmas or a ham? My mom says we're having ham. Thank you for your sacrifice so far away from home and I hope you don't die. Sincerely, your friend, William Hoffman."

We all laughed. Mike seemed troubled as he looked round at us. He folded his letter, got to his feet, and walked out.

"What's with him?" said Chico.

Ron frowned. He put on his poncho and followed Mike out into the trench.

I got the Blastos out of the CP bag, popped a cherry one in my mouth and read my parents' letter. They wanted to know if they could send me anything special for Christmas. God, I thought, not really. All I wanted was to get home safe, and there was no way they could arrange that. If my father was a congressman or something it might be a different story, but he wasn't.

Ron returned after a few minutes and took off his poncho.

"Did you talk to Mike," Chico asked.

"Yeah. It's his wife."

"What about her?"

"She's divorcing him."

"Carajo!" Chico exclaimed. "Where's he now?"

Ron hung up his poncho. "Up at the mortar pit, under the tarp. He'll be all right." Ron sat back down at the table and started packing his pipe. I went back to my book. I felt sorry for Mike because I knew how it felt. Linda had made me feel that way a long time ago. It was like a sucker punch to the gut. It takes all the wind out of you and leaves you real lowdown.

For the next week Mike became more withdrawn. He didn't talk to anybody, not even Ron. Then Glock was told to take out his first patrol. I was going, along with Mike, Beobee, and a new, skinny, tobacco-chewing reb guy from Beobee's squad, named Arley.

It hadn't rained in four days and I was becoming reacquainted with the sun, spending time up on the bunker roof under its warm, healing rays. My hands were finally losing the dead-looking, white wrinkles they'd acquired over the weeks of wet.

"Well," Glock said with a smile as we started down through the concertina wire, "I hope you guys are up for a walk, 'cause we have a lot of ground to cover."

Glock held open a taut strand of barbed wire for Mike. After he'd squeezed through, Mike said, "How far we going?"

"Fifteen klicks."

Mike stopped suddenly "Fifteen klicks! That's crazy."

Glock looked at him for a moment, mild amusement on his face. He turned and continued walking.

"Don't look at it that way, Mike," Beobee said, as we followed along behind, "just think of it as a little vacation away from the firebase."

Mike turned to him quickly. "Don't tell me what to think." Then Mike threw me an angry, warning look.

Beobee frowned. "Well now, don't go getting yourself all riled up, Mike. I was just making a little joke, that's all."

Arley, the new reb guy, watched the exchange closely as we humped carefully down the steep slope, his Adam's apple bobbing up and down. We entered the dappled darkness of the jungle and Glock called down to the guys at the OP. When we came upon them, they were playing cards. We left them behind and humped for an hour at a good clip, finally reaching the flat, valley floor. Down there, it was another world. The light that made it through the triple canopy of trees was greenish and anemic. Gone was the whirr and whine of the choppers as they came and went, the ground-shaking explosions of the 105 Howitzer fire missions, the constant buzz of the little gasoline electric-generators. All were lost to us now as we moved deeper and deeper into the churchy quiet of the jungle. A familiar gentle sadness settled over me. It was the soul of the jungle, I think. There was only the soft rustle of our boots on the papyrus-like bamboo husks which littered the trail like sawdust in a hamster's cage, and the occasionally mournful creak of the taller bamboos as they moved slightly to an unfelt breeze high overhead.

I thought of the enemy doctor laying back in his shady resting place. He'd been there a long time now. I tried to turn my mind to other thoughts. Glock found a trail that went in the direction he wanted and we humped for three long hours before we finally broke for lunch.

Not one minute after we'd finished eating, Glock was on his feet again. He folded the map and put it in his pocket. "We'd better get going," he said. "We still have a long way to go."

Mike angrily pulled on his ruck and glared at Glock's back.

Glock took the point and we humped along at a fast clip. Glock really was gung ho. And I wasn't the only one who thought so, either. According to Ted, the new Captain had his eye on Glock as a potential squad leader. That was all fine and dandy with me, as long as they didn't put me in his squad. That's probably not the way it would work out, though. Those things that you want the least, well, they're usually the ones the army gives you. You can forget about everything else.

We were all soaked with sweat like somebody'd turned a hose on us. We came to the bottom of a hill and discovered a small trail that ran parallel with a muddy stream about four feet wide. We had only gone a hundred yards when Beobee spotted some baskets filled with rice. They were sitting on a foundation of piled rocks, off the trail a bit. Beobee and Arley knelt to inspect them. We grew quiet and everyone began walking in that careful, cartoonish way, as if they were walking on eggs. We went another fifty feet down the trail and came upon some half-finished bamboo hootches. In front of them, six footstool-sized rocks were arranged in a circle. "Barber shop," Arley mouthed to Mike and me, as he pointed at the clippings of long, black hair that lay all over the ground.

Seeing this stuff all at once was weird. It was like walking into somebody's house just after they'd run out the back door, and finding their TV still on, a beer on the arm of the easy chair, and their dinner in the oven. It reminded me of the VC villages they'd constructed back at Fort Polk. They had props planted here and there and guys dressed in black pajamas and conical straw hats hiding in spider holes, ready to jump out at you.

You could've heard a fly fart as we stared into the bushes around us. Glock and Beobee held a whispered conference as Arley looked on. I thought of my theory again and it still couldn't be disproved. All we'd seen so far were props like the ones back in Fort Polk. And even if there were NVA in the area, I don't think they'd been around here for at least a couple of days. It was way too quiet. I heard a "pssst, pssst," and turned. Glock was waving Mike and me over to a clump of bushes. We walked over.

"C'mon," Glock said in a whisper. "We're going down the trail some. So be extra careful."

Mike looked at him angrily. "You're crazy," he hissed. "You didn't have to take us this far . . . You're just trying to make rank, that's all. You'll get us all killed."

"You're full of it," Glock hissed. "We still haven't reached our night position."

Mike swung at Glock. Glock stepped in to him, clipping him on the jaw and sending him sprawling on the ground. Mike was crying quietly and trying to get to his feet.

"I told you," Glock hissed as he leaned over him, "you can't pull that stuff out here, you can't . . ."

Beobee suddenly clamped his hand over Glock's mouth. Arley knelt to Mike, holding his finger to his lips for silence. We all turned. "Enemy," Beobee mouthed silently. We squatted down behind the bushes. I looked around but saw nothing.

"Where are they?" whispered Glock.

Beobee pointed in the direction we'd been heading in. He and Glock peeked through the bushes. "Jees," Glock said, "about ten of them."

"Yeah," Beobee said in a whisper, "ten you can see. About a half dozen of them just walked off to the left there."

"Jees," Glock said.

I slowly raised myself up to see, but someone pushed down on my helmet and I couldn't move.

"See the one in the pith helmet?" Arley said.

"Yeah," Glock said, "he's coming this way. We better move back."

We moved backwards clumsily, in one big clump, no one wanting to put himself between them and us. When we came to the trail, we ran. Five minutes later we stopped. Everybody was out of breath. Glock and Beobee quickly called in the coordinates of the place for the 105 howitzers back on the firebase.

We took off running again and soon we could hear the rounds rippling high overhead and exploding in the distance. Beobee took rear security and we settled down to a swift walk. Two hours later we set up for the night. Mike wouldn't say a word to anybody. I played 500 Rummy with Arley for a while. When it grew dark, I lay under the canopy of trees, the whole day's events seeming unreal and dreamy. In some ways it was like the time four years ago in my neighborhood when the UFO came. It sounds crazy, I know, but it had supposedly appeared over Golden Cross Cemetery every night for a week. My brother saw it. My mother saw it. Gary and Ray, the two cashiers at the Shop'N'Save, saw it. By the time I went down to see it, the cemetery wall was lined with kids like a flock of crows on the telephone line. I joined them and waited patiently but nothing much happened that night. Once, a helicopter approached and half the people ran, but no UFO.

Now, if someone were to ask me if I believed in UFOs, I'd tell them I thought it was possible, but that I personally didn't believe because I personally hadn't seen one. I'd have to see one to believe they existed. I know everybody believed the enemy was real and dangerous, and I'm sure he was. The thing was, though, I still hadn't seen one alive and my theory still held water.

When we got back to the hill, I went straight to the mess tent and ate out in the sun by myself. When I came back to the bunker, Chico was standing between Glock and Beobee on one side, and Ron and Mike on the other, trying to keep them apart.

"He slugged me," Mike said to Ron.

Ron turned to Glock. "Did you hit him?"

"Damn right I did, after he swung at me."

"That's the truth, Ron," drawled Beobee, "so help me God."

Ron glared angrily at Mike. "Look, when the patrol leader tells you to do something, that's his job. You dig? And your job is to do it and keep your big mouth shut."

Mike's jaw hung open.

Beobee moved toward Ron. "I'm sorry about all this, Ron, but Mike brought it on hisself."

"This ain't any of your business now," Ron said, "dig?"

Beobee put on his steel pot. "Well, if you feel that way about it." He walked off.

Glock shook his head. "Sorry, Ron. I wasn't trying to get on Mike's case or anything, but he ain't been worth much since his wife dumped him."

Ron shook his head angrily. "Don't give me that stuff. You probably took that patrol halfway through Cambodia."

"You're full of it. I do what I'm told to do. That's all."

Ron kicked an ammo can out of his way and ran at Glock. Chico and I ran between them. They cursed and threatened each other, and it was all we could do to keep them apart.

CHAPTER 9

I was reading Siddhartha again. He had just apprenticed himself to a ferryman and the two of them sat on the bank of a broad, peaceful river. I was with them, gazing at the slow, rippling black water, when Ron called me.

"Carl, you ready? We got an LP to do tonight."

Captain DeVoors had put additional Listening Posts out. The one down the hill between our bunker and the next bunker was ours and their responsibility. It worked out to one LP or OP detail per man approximately every other day, and it was getting to be a real burden. Add to that the extra patrols we were running, and DeVoors' insistence on clean-up sweeps, and things were getting real busy.

I put my book in my ditty bag. Books had become my only pleasure, my only diversion. I grabbed my weapon and went out into the trench. The setting sun cast a reddish glow across the sky. "Who's doing LP with us?" I asked Ron as we climbed the hill.

"How do I know?" he glared at me. "They didn't give me a crystal ball when they made me squad leader."

"Dig it," I said. Ron was still angry at Glock. And Glock was angry at him. And Mike was angry at Ron and Glock. And the whole company was angry with Captain DeVoors. What an angry, stupid place this had turned into. One of the last things Papa had said to us was that if we stuck together we'd make it. I really believed that. When Ron and Glock got along, so did everybody else, and the days went smoothly and quickly. Not now, though. Yin and Yang were out of balance, and the little universe that was our bunker was no longer a happy place.

Ted waited outside the CP with the other two members of our LP—Chick Rendy, the skinny, blond Californian, and Charley Slade, the short, chubby black guy from Georgia. I don't think Charley'd been on the hill a week.

Ron and I nodded a greeting at them. I didn't know Chick well, but

89

I'd worked chopper pad detail with him once. Ron and him were pretty chummy; I'd seen them rapping a couple of times. I don't think Ron had ever met Charley, though. Charley talked slowly, with a thick southern accent.

"Ron," Ted said, "here's your men."

"Is that what they are?" Ron said jokingly.

Chick laughed heartily. Charley smiled broadly. We stood there awkwardly for a moment.

Ron turned. "Let's get down there before it gets too dark."

Down in the trees, we arranged our bedrolls pointing out, like the spokes of a wheel. In the hub, we put the radio, canteens and the weapons. We pulled straws to see who got which guard. Ron had already claimed first for himself. I got last, which is what I wanted, and Chick and Charley would have second and third.

Ron said to Charley, "you know how to work this radio?"

Charley shook his head.

"Well, when were you going to ask me, after I'm asleep?"

Charley winced. "Sorry."

"Look," Ron said, pulling the radio close, "here's how it works. Each guy pulls a two-and-a-half-hour shift. The radio's turned down real low, dig, and every fifteen minutes or so, the hill will call down asking for a 'sitrep.' That's a situation report. Then you just squeeze the talk button on the handset."

Charley frowned. "What's that do?"

"That makes a clicking noise in their receiver back on the hill, dig? That way you don't have to talk. Now if they don't get that click, they know that either the enemy got you, or else you're asleep. Either way, you're in big trouble."

When Ron finished with Charley, we got ready to sleep. I stared into the tangled branches and vines. The sad, greenish light was fading and the air was becoming nice and cool. I descended into sleep.

I awoke and sat upright. It was pitch black, cool and damp. Crickets and other insects chirped and buzzed and I suddenly remembered that I was on the LP, way down below the bunkers. I could tell that everyone else was asleep, but no one had awakened me. A sound had . . . a tiny sound out there in the jungle! I'd heard that sound before—the swishing of leaves, tiny clicks and snaps—movement! I quickly shook Ron awake. "We got movement out there," I whispered.

A moment later everybody was sitting up. Crack! A big bamboo snapped not twenty meters away and I almost jumped out of my skin.

"Lock and load," Ron whispered to us. "Put your weapons on automatic and fire when I tell you."

The swishing of leaves and crackling of bamboo was distinct and clear and whatever was doing it couldn't have been more than ten meters away from us. My heart beat so loudly I thought for sure they'd be able to hear it. Ron hissed, "Fire!" and we opened up, each of us spraying a full clip of rounds in the direction of the sound. After that all hell broke loose as the guys up on the hill began shooting up the night. A grenade boomed above.

Ron grabbed me roughly. "Face out, face out," he shouted. The others shifted their positions. Ron spoke on the radio as I looked intently into the blackness. I didn't see or hear anything as the other guys fired sporadically. Maybe the enemy had snuck past us and were already on their way up to the hill. I'd heard they either try to sneak past the LP, or put them out of commission. Ron shouted to hold our fire. We listened and a great relief came over me. It seemed to be over. As Ron spoke to the CP, the sound of sporadic firing reached us. It was distant, from the other side of the firebase.

"They must've disengaged," Ron said into the horn.

All of us stayed awake for the next hour or so and then Ron took a shift of guard and we tried to get some sleep. I lay in the blackness and wondered who had fallen asleep on guard, Chick or Charley? One of them had.

I awoke to pale, cold light filtering down from above. Ron was sitting in the gloom, deep in thought. The others slept. Ron hadn't awakened me and had, instead, taken my shift of guard. "You awake now, Carl?"

He sounded troubled. "Yeah."

"Good. Keep an eye on these two guys. I'm going up the hill to find out what happened."

"Okay."

Ron called the perimeter guards on the radio and then he left. Soon Chick and Charley were up and we heated some C's for breakfast. Not two words passed between us. Again I wondered which of them had fallen asleep. Somebody did, or the enemy wouldn't have been able to sneak up on us like that. After an hour or so Ron still hadn't come back and I called the CP. They told us to pack it up and come on in.

Just on the inside of the wire we passed a body. I could tell it was one of ours by the looks on everybody's faces. It was just laying there on the ground, the jungle boots sticking out from under the poncho they'd covered it with.

Ron sat by himself. His sunglasses were on and below them his face was wet with tears. Ted motioned me over and told me what had happened. Mike was dead. He had evidently left the wire and walked down the path last night; they weren't sure why yet, and he was the one we had heard. He had approached our position and we had shot him to death. Ron had found the body.

I turned. Glock was comforting Ron as he sobbed spastically. I headed up to the giant potty. For a moment I wondered if any of my rounds had hit Mike and I threw up. The next day they interviewed us, one by one, for their investigation, but most of the guys on the hill had already figured it out. Someone had fallen asleep on guard. It happened every now and then. It didn't have to happen, though. If someone on guard couldn't stay awake, they were supposed to wake somebody and tell them, not just go to sleep.

I could picture in my mind how it had happened. Mike had stood in the dim starlight of the trench, looking anxiously down into the blackness below. He spoke softly into the mouthpiece of the radio, "Goldstar three, this is Diamond one. Sitrep, over."

There was no reply, no click. He knew that someone must have fallen asleep on guard. He would have paced nervously. For a long time he paced, and still he couldn't get a response. Somebody was definitely asleep on their guard. It happened. He knew that if he went up to the CP and told them, Ron would get in trouble, big trouble, with DeVoors now in charge.

Mike climbed to the top of the bunker and tossed a rock down, hoping someone would hear it and wake up, hoping maybe to get real lucky and crack the sleeping guard in the head. It would serve him right. He went back down into the trench and tried the radio again. Nothing. He got an idea. They were only fifty meters down the trail. He would go down and wake them. He knew his way through the wire; he'd been through it a million times in the daylight. He disconnected the claymores. He would go down and wake them; it was the only way. His face pinched with worry and concern, he slung his M-16 over his shoulder and started down the trail.

Ron and Glock patched their differences up. But despite their renewed friendship, Mike's death cast a pall over the squad. Then Lee had a nervous breakdown. Up at the CP, he'd threatened to shoot the payroll officer and they had sent him back to the hospital at Cam Ranh Bay. I inherited Mike's M-79 grenade launcher. A vest with about fifty pockets came with it. Each pocket held a big, golden-tipped grenade round. I really missed Mike. He never had a lot to say, but he was good company. Like me, he'd had some bad luck with the girls, but he tried hard to get over it. After he died, images of the old Keystone Cops silent movies kept working their way into my dreams. I'd see them on a fire truck racing away, some of them holding on for dear life. They'd get off for some reason or other and the next thing you knew the empty fire truck was chasing them. One night I sat straight up in my bunk as I suddenly realized why I kept dreaming that stuff. That was us! Things were always backfiring on us, and we were blowing each other up and shooting each other to death, and the comic stupidity of it all made it even more horrible.

Nowadays we were going out just about every two or three days on what Captain DeVoors called "ambush patrols." There were a lot of rumors going around about the enemy building up for another big Tet offensive. Everybody was worried and beat from all the patrols and a delegation of about ten patrol leaders, Ron included, had gone to Captain DeVoors to try and get him to slow things down a bit. Glock and Beobee had been asked to join the delegation, but had declined. When the delegation came to him, DeVoors had really blown his top. He had Ted take everybody's name and rank and sent them back with a warning that he wasn't going to put up with any shirkers. There was talk of going over DeVoors' head to the Inspector General. I don't think there was really much that anybody could do, though, except to just make the best of a bad situation. That's the approach that most people seemed to be taking.

Glock took out his second patrol. I stayed behind this time. Ron had already taken out a patrol the day before and was still out there somewhere. I worked chopper pad detail till I thought I'd drop. Then I came back and read some more of Siddhartha. His wife, Kamala had just died and their son, whom she had raised alone, and who didn't want to live with Siddhartha, had run away. This broke Siddhartha's heart. He suffered long and hard with this and had finally found the key in acceptance. He just simply accepted his lot. I guess I'd accepted a few things lately too, like the fact that the Paris Peace talks would be going on long after I'd done my 365 days. Gene helped me a lot. He kept telling me I'd do my time, no sweat. He always had an encouraging word for me. I'd been reading for a half hour or so when someone came in the bunker. It was Ted.

"Glock's in big trouble, Carl."

"What do you mean?"

"There were three or four patrols that set up short on the next hill," Ted said. "Glock's was one of them."

"Really? That doesn't sound like Glock."

"I know. But he's involved. You know they had half the 105's on the hill aimed at them. They thought they were enemy. Most of the guys on the firebase were up on the bunker roofs trying to get a good view before the barrage began."

"Wow," I said.

Ted gave me a funny look. "What were you doing in here?"

"Reading."

Ted shook is head. "Really? Well, I just thought I'd tell you what was happening."

Glock came back and just dumped his stuff on his bunk. He sat and said nothing.

"What happened?" I said.

He looked at me and shook his head sadly. "Damn it, Carl. I let my-self get talked into something dumb. Real dumb." He shook his head again and went out. I went out to take a walk and bumped into Gene up at the giant potty.

"Boy, those guys were lucky," he said as I approached.

"That's what I hear."

He had the big drum off to the side and was pouring diesel into it, getting ready to do a burn. He lit a piece of newspaper and dropped it in. Soon flames were licking over the side and smudgy smoke drifting off. We got upwind of it.

"How many guys were out there?" I said.

"More than twenty-four."

"God, are you serious?"

"Yeah. There were six patrols setting up short out there." Gene shook his head in amazement. "Captain DeVoors is gonna have Glock's head on a plate for this."

"Why is he coming down so hard on Glock?" I said.

"He really liked Glock's stuff, had plans for him. Now he's really dis-appointed, and angry." Gene grabbed his paddle and gave the mess in the can a stir. He sat back down again. "You know, if enough stuff like this happens maybe the leaders of this country will finally get the mes-sage that the war isn't working. The troops just plain don't know what they're fighting for, don't know why they're here."

"I know. I once had this really crazy rap with Ron. He said the whole war was arranged by both sides so they could get rid of their excess population."

Gene laughed. "He's funny."

"I know. But, I think he really believes that."

"Come on."

I told him everything Ron had told me, about the rich, old men and the Communist bosses seated around a table in a smoke-filled room somewhere, deciding that there were too many undesirables.

Gene shook his head, then looked at me calmly. "Well, I don't know if I'd go as far as that. But I do agree with Ron about one thing."

"What's that?"

"That a lot of good people are being thrown away on this war, sacrificed on the altar of stupidity and ego."

A week passed before Captain DeVoors finally passed judgment on Glock. We were all in the bunker playing cards when Glock came back from the CP. He hung up his steel pot, pulled over an ammo crate and sat down at the table. Saying nothing, he watched Ron shuffle the cards.

"So, what happened?" Ron said.

Glock looked at him and cleared his throat. "You want the good news or the bad?"

"Vaquero," said Chico, his eyes flashing, "stop being John Wayne, please, and tell us what the Captain is going to do to you."

"They're busting me a grade and fining me a month's salary."

"Is that all?" Ron said. He turned to Chico. "I thought for sure DeVoors was gonna have him shot at dawn."

"So did I," I said, laughing.

Glock just looked at us sadly.

"So you ain't gonna make General after all?" Chico said. "Tsk, tsk, tsk."

Glock tried to smile. "I don't know how to break the news to El about the month's pay."

"Just tell her, that's all," Ron said. "If you need money we can lend you some, right, Carl? Chico?"

"Yes," said Chico.

"Sure," I said.

Ron started some of his fancy, one-handed card shuffling, his gold pinkie ring twinkling in the dim candlelight. "So, what's the good news?"

Glock's eyebrows rose. "I saw Ted up at the CP."

Ron rolled his eyes. "Yeah. I've seen him up there a few times myself. I think he works up there. But that's hardly good news."

Glock smiled feebly. "He said they're flying us off the hill in a couple of days for a Christmas stand-down at Dak-To."

"Seriously?"

Glock nodded.

Ron slammed the cards face down on the table. "Right on!" he said. Chico slapped him five. I'd heard about Dak-To. It wasn't as big as Pleiku, but compared to being out in the boonies, it was New York City. There were roads and trucks, wooden barracks, electric lights, a movie bunker, a barber shop and PX; they were supposedly getting flush toilets, too.

"DeVoors is doing that?" Chico asked. "Is he cuckoo now, too?"

Glock shook his head. "It don't have anything to do with him. It's Battalion's decision."

"This calls for a celebration," Ron said.

"Before you start celebrating," Glock said, "remember . . . DeVoors will be going with us."

Ron smiled and shook his head. "It don't mean nothing. In Dak-To we can still have us some powerful good times, DeVoors or no DeVoors."

"Dig it," Chico said.

Ron held out his two hands. "Take my hands," he said to us. We all joined hands, making a circle around the table.

"Now," Ron intoned slowly with an air of great solemnity, "everything is as it should be. We are finally headed for some good times, and we are together."

In the distance the approaching choppers were tiny and insect-like. Ron, Glock, Chico and I were hunched over at the waist from the weight of our rucks. Everything we owned was in them, and all our ammo and field gear to boot. A lot of guys lay back against the bunker walls like overturned turtles as we waited. As the first chopper landed, Glock and I exchanged a smile.

Our replacements emerged from the dust storm at the pad and filed past us in the trench. In one way I envied them. Firebase 29 might be the boondocks, but at least the enemy didn't seem to be interested in it, and I'd managed to do more than four months of my tour here. I wouldn't have minded staying here for the remaining eight. In fact, I would've preferred it. Give me a known over an unknown any day.

I remembered from some of my readings on philosophy what the Taoists said about life being like a river, and that all you had to do was just trust and go along with the flow. I really wanted to trust and relax, but I couldn't. I was too uptight. There were hidden whirlpools and waterfalls, like the ones that had killed Papa and Mike, and who really knew what their karma was and what might happen tomorrow.

CHAPTER 10

Dak-To was situated on a broad plain of reddish dirt. The mountains that we had lived and humped on, were now just a low dark smudge on the horizon. On the morning of our first day in Dak-To, they sent all the guys with bad teeth over to the dentist, one at a time. When my turn came, Gene told me to report first to Battalion Headquarters to get the proper paperwork.

When I got to the HQ, they were in the process of moving to another building. Three 5-ton trucks were lined up on the dirt street, and inside, boxes were stacked everywhere and people rushed around carrying things. I found the guy I was supposed to report to, a skinny Specialist Fourth Class, with a bad case of acne, wearing starched and pressed jungle fatigues. He frowned at me. "Another cavity for the dentist! Don't you guys ever floss?"

"Yeah," I lied. "My company doc said to report to you."

"Name?"

"PFC Carl Melcher."

"Have a seat." He swiveled in his chair and pulled open a file drawer. He turned to me. "Serial number?"

"US52912846."

He took a manila folder from the file and set it on his desk. Sniffling from a cold or something, he jammed a preprinted form in an old Royal typewriter and started typing with his index fingers. A few minutes later, two guys in green tee shirts came by and started wrestling his file cabinet onto a hand truck.

"Whoa!" he said. "Where you goin' with that?"

The bigger of the two guys smirked. "Go cry on Sergeant Vicker's shoulder, Chucky boy. He said everything's gotta be out of here by ten hundred hours."

The clerk watched them in angry astonishment as they took his file cabinet away. He sighed and went on typing. When he was through, he yanked the form from the typewriter and handed it to me. "Give this to the dentist."

I started to get up.

"Wait," he said. He gave me the manila folder. "I'm not gonna be here an hour from now. You better bring your 201 file with you. When they finish with your teeth, take it to building seven on Colonel Childer's Avenue. You got that?"

"Yeah. Where is that?"

He drew me a little map on a sheet of paper and I went outside.

The dentist, a Captain, was a fat, baldheaded guy with glasses so thick that his eyes looked the size of silver dollars. He was your typical Army officer, a sadist. He gave me a needle, but when he started drilling, I felt like he'd plugged a one hundred and twenty volt outlet into my tooth. I pushed him away.

"What's the matter, son?" he said. He was smiling.

"I can feel every revolution of the damn drill!"

"Okay, okay, we can fix that up. Relax now."

He gave me another shot, but a minute later I was out of the chair. He apologized and I decided to give him one more chance. I got back in the torture chair.

I had cavities in three of my front teeth. He had to give me four shots, numbing my entire face from my hairline to my chin, from ear to ear. After he finished, I felt like I didn't have a face anymore. I went into the latrine to make sure it was still there. Then, I went outside.

It was a beautiful day. The sky was blue and cloudless, the air full of smells—diesel fumes from the occasional truck rumbling by, the smell of asphalt from a road they were laying nearby. These were the smells of civilization, of men working outside unafraid. Like the smell of bread baking, or a freshly opened can of ground coffee. These were smells I hadn't smelled in a long time, and I breathed them deep into my lungs.

I walked down the wooden sidewalk. Free of my heavy rucksack, I felt strong and light as air, as if I could walk forever. I was four blocks from the new Battalion Headquarters when I turned a corner and came upon the scene of an accident. A five-ton water-tank truck had evidently broken its water valve clean off when it backed up into another truck.

Water gushed from the valve like the flow from a fire hydrant, turning the dirt street into a sea of chocolate pudding. Just then a jeep turned the corner and started down. I knew he wouldn't make it through that mess and I stopped to watch from the sidewalk. The jeep driver tried to maneuver past the two trucks and got stuck up to his axles. He rocked the jeep back and forth, the whine of the engine barely covering the angry curses of the only passenger, a big-bellied Captain dressed in starched and pressed jungle fatigues. The Captain divided his efforts between leaning over the side to frown at the spinning wheels and yelling angrily at the driver. The tanker-truck driver was gone. Perhaps he'd gone off to report the accident.

The Captain looked around and spotted me. He waved. "You! Come over here."

I tiptoed over, managing to not dirty my pants. I stood in muck up to my boot tops, looking at him.

"Well," he said angrily, "don't just stand there, push!"

I pushed as hard as I could, synchronizing my pushes with the rocking of the jeep. The wheels threw mud, coating my pants from the waist down.

The Captain turned and frowned at me. "What the heck's that in your hand?"

I'd been holding onto the manila folder containing my 201 file with one hand, and pushing with the other. Over the screaming of the engine, I tried to tell him it was my 201 file, but my lips were still numb from the shots and my words came out something like, "Bish my tudor on fire."

"Speak English, soldier."

I tried to explain a second time, louder.

He shook his head and looked at me like I was crazy. "Put that down and push, soldier. That's an order!"

"Yes, Sir." I put the file behind the driver's seat and leaned against the jeep, pushing as hard as I could. After a few minutes of rocking back and forth, the jeep quieted. The jeep's springs creaked as the driver stepped down into the muddy soup and came around back to stand beside me. The jeep's springs creaked again as the Captain climbed behind the wheel. "Now, push, damn it!" he encouraged us. "Push! Push!"

With the reduced weight and the added muscle, the jeep began moving slowly forward, spraying us with buckets of mud and filling the air with clouds of blue exhaust.

"Keep pushing," the Captain shouted over the noise. "Keep pushing!" Suddenly the jeep's front wheels grabbed dry land and the jeep lurched forward, pulling me flat onto my face in the mud. I looked up to see the driver climbing aboard. Without a look behind, they drive off, bouncing and fishtailing down the street.

"Wait! My papers!" I yelled at them, but they were already turning the corner.

"Fat son-of-a . . . !"

Unheard by anyone but me, my words hung in the hot, dry air. Fear chilled the pit of my stomach. My 201 file was gone! I walked over to the tank truck and washed my face and hands from the trickle that now issued from the broken-off valve. I tried to think of what to do as I rubbed mud from my shirt.

I started walking toward Battalion. Then I stopped. What could I tell them? If I told them what had really happened they probably wouldn't believe me. I turned and headed back toward the line bunkers. I would get cleaned up and try to think up a good story.

I had just walked up to our bunker when Ted pulled up in a little jeep towing a trailer. Some big guy about six feet, with red hair sat beside him in the passenger seat.

Ted called to me. "Don't bother going in, Carl. You guys won't be staying there anyway. Is Ron there?"

I yelled in. Ron, Glock and Chico came out and greeted Ted and the big stranger.

"Fellas," Ted said, "I want you to meet your new squad member, Bubba Hampton."

"Howdy," Bubba said, with a twangy, western accent. "I'm glad to meet y'all."

"Welcome to the squad," Ron said. Glock, Chico and I nodded a greeting.

"Ron," Ted said slowly, "you and your guys aren't going to be staying here."

"We ain't?"

We all looked at Ted, waiting for him to say he was only joking.

"That's right. You guys are going to have to pull bridge guard for the next couple of weeks."

"Aren't you a little early?" Glock said.

"Huh?" Ted said. "What do you mean?"

"Well," Glock said, "we still have a few more things to unpack and stow in the bunker. Aren't you supposed to hide somewhere and wait till we're all moved in before you tell us this?"

Ted laughed sheepishly. He knew we were all angry. "Well, you guys should know by now that the Army works in mysterious ways. Ours is not to reason why, ours is but to do or die."

"Skip it," Ron said angrily. "We gotta leave now?"

"Yeah. Sorry."

Ron headed for the bunker. He stopped and turned to us. "You heard what the man said. Get your gear together."

As we loaded everything into the trailer, a cloud of disgust settled over us. Nobody spoke. We'd all been looking forward to Dak-To. They were planning a big turkey dinner for us next week on Christmas day. We climbed into the jeep. Strangely, though, our anger began to ebb almost as soon as the wheels of the jeep started turning. A cool breeze washed over us as we bounced along past fields and huts. After months of carrying rucksacks up jungle hills in the heat with the damned bullhead ants biting your face and the vines pulling you back and wearing you down, the effortless movement of the jeep ride worked a wonderful magic on us.

We drove through a lot of open, brush-filled country that stretched out to the Highlands. It was deserted and I guess if there'd been any enemy around it would've been a good place to ambush us. But Ted said the area had been secured for years. Indeed, after the boonies, it seemed as safe as New Jersey. I tried to speak with Bubba, but the whine of the jeep's engine and the rush of the wind made it impossible. From the bits of conversation he shouted at me I gathered he was from North Dakota, cowboy country. He really looked it, too. All he needed was the boots, hat and a horse.

The asphalt came to an end and we bounced along on a dirt track, raising clouds of dust. We drove through a small village Ron named "Tin Can City" because of the corrugated roofs on the houses. It was a strange place. Everything in the village was the same dull, tan color—the houses, fences, the leaves on the trees, even the children who lined the streets begging for C-rations and cigarettes—all coated with the flour-like dust from the road. Ted said that when the convoy from Pleiku, about fifty trucks, jeeps and tanks in all, raced through here, it raised so much dust it took a whole day to settle.

At the edge of the village, a group of little boys, their skinny legs jutting out of their shorts like chopsticks, waved and yelled at us. Realizing that we weren't going to give them anything, they threw some rocks at us.

The river was only another mile or so down the road. I had pictured something like the Delaware River between Philly and Camden, about a mile wide with big oil tankers anchored there and ferries moving back and forth. This was different. About fifty feet across at its widest point, it was more like a creek, but it ran swift and looked to be about twenty feet deep. The bridge was temporary, made of steel plates hinged together, and floating on these big, black, rubber pontoons. Downstream the concrete supports of the permanent bridge they had been building rose out of the water, bristling with rusting reinforcement rods. For some reason or other they'd stopped working on it.

Our compound was small, just a ratty-looking bunker surrounded by a chest-high jumble of concertina wire. A huge, solitary Chinese Banyan tree rose from the sandy bank across the river, its branches hanging almost to the water. And across the street was an old, French fort with timber walls and watch towers. It looked like a Hollywood set for a Western movie. It was occupied by ARVN soldiers.

We went in our bunker. It was poorly constructed, the walls being only one sandbag thick.

"This would never stop an RPG," Glock said. An RPG was a rocket-propelled grenade.

"How do you know?" Ron asked.

Glock ignored the question.

Bubba put his hands on his hips decisively. "I'll start us a new bunker, Ron."

Ron smiled. "Okay, but first we got to get started on a hootch to sleep in."

We used our ponchos to begin building a big lean-to sleeping hootch against the old bunker. Bubba started digging the new bunker. As we worked, a crowd of onlookers gathered. The old women, who were called mamasans, were black-toothed from chewing betel nuts. Despite the shade from their conical hats, their faces were weathered and tanned. They sold Cokes, beers and black-market cigarettes out of nylon, fish net bags. Small, trim ARVN soldiers stood singly or in pairs. Some smoked as they watched us, others stood with their hands behind their backs, smiling occasionally, a gold tooth or two flashing in the sun. Around and under the adults, a bunch of happy, raggedy-dressed children ran and played, yelling and raising a dusty din. I took a break and bought a drippy-cold can of Coke from one of the old mamasans.

Someone tapped me on the leg. A little boy of five or six, wearing a tattered, blue, rayon playsuit held up a black leather case. "You buy?" he asked me. Inside was a nice pair of Japanese binoculars.

"Maybe," I said, "let me see." I walked back to the compound. He anxiously followed me to the wire. "Wait a minute," I said. I left him there and climbed up onto the bunker roof. I put the binoculars to my eyes. Across the street, an ARVN guard in the corner tower picked his nose. I swept the binoculars over to the bridge. The Engineer who maintained it pulled a cigarette from a pack, Kools. The binoculars were quite powerful. The engineer lit his cigarette and crawled down into one of the pontoons with a wrench to fix something. Out in the street Ron and Glock were talking to two teenage Vietnamese boys and a teenage girl.

I turned the glasses back in the direction of Tin Can City and saw a beautiful, young, redheaded girl walking down the road. I had never seen a girl this beautiful. She was wearing black pajama pants and a white blouse. As she got closer that Steem Masheen song, "Pretty Girl," was playing from a radio or in my head, I couldn't tell which, and I projected the two of us into a sort-of movie together, me standing out there on the road as she approached, winking at her, and then her giving me a

look as Turk sang, "shimmy show and shimmy shake, naughty girl you
make me ache," and then she throws a look at me and I wave her over
and we start to dance right there in the dust to those driving guitars and
that rapping beat. I'm swinging her around and around, looking in her
eyes and singing, ". . . do you boogie just like me?" and we just laugh
like crazy.

She went into the Engineer's hootch and my little movie jammed in
the projector and the house lights came on. Dag!

I climbed down from the bunker. The little boy walked up to me.

"You like?" he said.

"Yeah," I said, looking back at the bridge, "I like a lot."

"Twenty dollar," he said.

I gave him the money and he gave me the binoculars.

Out in the street, Ron and Glock were still talking to the Vietnamese
teenagers. I went over to join them. The bigger boy was about fourteen
and wore thick glasses. "What's your name?" Glock was asking him.

"Kennedy," the boy said.

"That's not his name," the other boy said.

"Yes, it is," Kennedy said.

Ron looked at Kennedy. "Where are the boom-boom girls?"

I had heard of the boom-boom girls. They would dance and hang out
with soldiers for money.

Kennedy turned to the other boy and the two of them huddled for a
moment. "I'll find out for you," Kennedy said after a moment or two.
"I'll bring them."

"When?" Glock asked.

"Tonight."

Satisfied, Ron and Glock went back to the compound to unpack.

I borrowed Kennedy's bicycle for awhile. The first couple times I
rode by the Engineer's hootch, the redheaded girl didn't see me, but the
third time she did, and she laughed and clapped. I guess she'd never
seen anybody riding no-hands before.

I got a real good look at her. She had pretty brown eyes and these lips
that were permanently puckered, like she was about to give you a kiss.
She was the most beautiful girl I'd ever seen in my life. That afternoon I

kept hoping to spot her, but she spent all her time in the Engineer's hootch.

I took my first swim in the river. The water was great, but the current was very swift. Swimming as fast as I could, I barely managed to move upstream. After about ten minutes I was beat. I climbed onto the bank by the big banyan tree to rest. For the first time in a long time I felt happy. Most of the day I'd been worrying about my lost 201 file, but eventually I just forgot about it. The surroundings had a lot to do with it. It was so beautiful and peaceful here. The others probably would've preferred to stay in Dak-To, but I was glad we came.

I looked across the dark, rippling expanse of river and thought of Siddhartha. He had finally found his answers beside a river. Perhaps I would too, especially with the beautiful redheaded girl close by. I felt like there was already some connection between the two of us.

The little boy who'd sold me the binoculars came by. He sat beside me under the shade of the banyan tree. "Me Joe," he said, and I cracked up. He was a good kid, a regular Junior Chamber of Commerce type. He sold me a small Sony transistor radio, including batteries, for ten bucks. He had everything but the keys to the city.

In the morning an old papasan sold us French bread and a dozen bottles of beer. After I ate breakfast I walked by the Engineer's hootch but the girl hadn't come yet. I took a swim with Bubba and then we went for a walk to see what the surrounding area was like. I kept hoping to see the girl but she didn't show. Bubba and I found a grove of banana trees down river. They were smaller than the kind you get back home at the supermarket, but sweeter. We brought about fifty pounds of them back.

The others laid around the compound and I went for another swim. Afterward, I lay in the shade under the banyan tree. The girl arrived and began sweeping out the hootch. I could see her pretty good. After a while the Engineer started the compressor to pump up the pontoons. The girl disappeared and showed up a few minutes later in a bikini. She lay down to sunbathe. She was so beautiful I couldn't take my eyes off her. I'd stare at the back of her head as she lay there and after a moment or two she'd turn around. She knew I liked her. I was sure of it. Later I asked Kennedy about her and he told me her name was Chantal. Her father had been a French Officer who died fighting the Viet Minh. She was sixteen and was the Engineer's girl friend.

I awoke the next morning while mist still covered the river. Bubba was already at work digging the new bunker. Ron, Chico and Glock played cards in the hootch. I made myself a coffee and went down to the riverbank. The sun was just beginning to heat the air. I swam under the patches of mist and then climbed the bank to sit under the banyan and read. Chantal arrived and I put down my book. After she finished her cleaning, she changed into her bikini and lay down in the middle pontoon to sun herself.

I stared at the back of her head. She turned and her eyes met mine; a chill ran up my spine. Every now and then for the next couple of hours I'd catch her looking at me. I was so in love with her I felt dizzy.

I lowered myself into the water and swam around for a while but she didn't look. Later, though, she clapped when I did a jackknife from the bank, and another time, when I was floating on my back, she threw something into the water beside me, a coin I think. About four in the afternoon she walked back to town. As I watched her walk off, I wished I had spoken to her. I'd come close but had lost my nerve. Tomorrow I would do it, I promised myself.

Late that afternoon the boom-boom girls arrived. I spotted them first with my binoculars from up on the bunker roof. A rooster's tail of yellow dust about five klicks away showed their progress on the dirt road. Ten minutes later they pulled up in front of the compound riding on the backs of about a dozen little Honda Fifty motorcycles. Their Vietnamese drivers were all dressed like Elvis, with slicked-back hair, wearing tight jeans, sunglasses and black boots. After a few quick revs of their throttles, the guys turned the bikes off and the girls dismounted and stood in a group. The guys moved off to smoke and talk quietly by themselves.

Ron, Glock, Chico and Bubba went out into the hot street to talk to the girls. They were too loud for my taste, and wore way too much make-up. I liked Chantal, and I couldn't think of any other girl now. I stayed up on top of the bunker and napped. Later they all came in the compound.

Chico called up to me. "Hey, Carl. Why don't you come down and dance with the girls?"

"I'll pass," I said, "some other time."

"He's got his eye on that engineer fella's girl," Bubba said, "didn't you know that?"

I went back to my book. If I came down and just hung out, Chantal might get word of it and take it the wrong way. I wasn't going to take that chance.

Despite the noisy party below, I managed to read more of Siddhartha. When it began to grow dark, the Mammasan yelled to the girls and they said their good-byes to Ron and the others. They climbed on the motor-bikes behind their Elvis-like escorts. The Hondas started with little roars and they all raced off into the night.

The next morning I had a big cup of coffee, some French bread and a couple of bananas. I climbed back up onto the bunker with my binoculars and my little Sony. The radio station was playing Top 40 as the villagers walked down the road and crossed the bridge to work their fields. There were about a dozen old men, a dozen or so boys of nine or ten, and lots of women. They carried their hoes and rakes over their shoulders, their faces shaded beneath their conical hats. After they disappeared into the fields, a small herd of eight cows came by, driven by two skinny boys wielding long, thin, willow switches.

The sun was about ten o'clock high and I figured Chantal would be along shortly. I went down to the river to wait. It was hot and I lay in the shade between the smooth roots of the banyan tree and took a nap. The sputter of the Engineer's pump motor woke me. He was busy filling one of the pontoons on the far side of the bridge. Chantal's red hair spilled over the black rubber of the middle pontoon where she was napping. The shade had moved and now the sun beat down on my head. I felt dizzy.

I slipped into the water. It was warm. I swam upstream a couple hundred feet and turned on my back. Floating with closed eyes, I let the water move me. I felt peaceful and calm, the way I always felt around water. The sun disappeared and something gently bumped me. I opened my eyes. I was turning slowly in an eddy under the cool shade of the bridge. Chantal lay on the pontoon, studying my face. She said nothing as sunlight reflected off the rippling water and danced around her, like the light from one of those spinning, mirrored balls they have in the circus. I felt paralyzed.

She smiled. "I want talk to you," she said. Her eyes blinked slowly and she reached out her hand and touched my face. I was so surprised I doubled over and the swift current caught me, pulling me under. Swallowing water and coughing, I was pulled along the slimy underside of the pontoon by the black water. Surfacing on the other side, I heard her laughing and talking to someone. I swallowed half the river before I made it to the bank. When I walked back over the bridge, the Engineer was talking to her and she wouldn't look at me. I felt bad and then I realized she didn't want him to know about us, and so I didn't say anything. I was floating on air. I'd talked to her . . . and she'd touched me! She may have been his girl, but not anymore.

Back in front of the compound, Ron and Glock had stripped to the waist and were boxing playfully in front of a growing crowd of children. As the children laughed and cheered, I marveled at how much better things had gotten. The squad was happy again, as black yin moved and jabbed, while white yang wove and dodged, or was it white yin and black yang. Anyway, things were balanced now and it was good. Up in the hootch, Chico slept, his boots hanging over the edge of the cot. Bubba had dug himself happily into his hole, shovelfuls of dirt flying up, one after the other, landing in a growing mound. The Vietnamese boom-boom girls had a lot to do with it. Ron and the others liked to dance and party, and this duty had been really good for them.

The first couple of nights Ron set up guards, but after a while he didn't bother. The place really seemed secure. Every night one of our tanks rolled up and parked across the bridge for the night. And then, of course, there was a whole company of ARVNs across the street. Ron, Glock and Chico were up till eleven or twelve every night partying anyway. I spent my nights on the bunker roof where it was a little quieter. There was always a bit of a breeze and I slept dreaming of Chantal.

CHAPTER 11

Chantal was alone in the pontoon as I eased into the water. She watched wordlessly as I floated up to her. I pulled myself up onto the wet, black rubber. She wore a gold charm shaped like a spoked wheel on a gold chain around her neck.

I nodded at it. "What's that?"

She smiled at me. "It mean good luck. Buddha's luck."

"You know something?" I said.

"What?"

"You're the most beautiful woman in the world."

"You lie," she said, but I could tell she was happy. She tightened the cloth chin strap of her hat.

We looked at each other for a while. With the sun blocked by the overhang of the bridge, the water seemed to grow colder. My teeth started chattering a little.

I looked into her eyes and I felt like we were moving into each other. Somewhere in the dark under the bridge an eddy gurgled softly. "Do you want to go out?" I said.

"Go out?" she said.

"You know, go see a movie maybe, or have dinner together."

"No have movie."

"We could go for a walk," I said.

"You cold," she said.

"No," I lied, but my teeth were chattering.

"Your lips blue."

"Let's go into town."

"Engineer go away for two weeks."

"Where?"

She smiled sadly. "I waiting for you all morning."

"Really?" My heart was pounding. I really loved her.

"Wait," she said. "I get changed."

* * *

Chantal took me to a little restaurant and we ate the best meal I'd had in six months. They served us these little pieces of meat with a sweet sauce on them, rice, and salad stuff. It was delicious. But better than that, was just being with her.

After the meal I said to her, "I wanted to be with you the moment I saw you."

She smiled. "Really?" Her R's sounded like W's.

"Really." I sipped my Coke. "I want to see you often."

"I come tomorrow. We go swimming."

We spent the next day together swimming and sunning ourselves on the pontoon. I brought some C-rations over for us to eat for lunch and she prepared them on a little stove she got from the hootch. She was a great cook. Afterward we talked some more.

"I want to take a walk with you in the moonlight," I said. I thought it would be really neat.

"We get shot," she said, "all blow up!" She laughed. "You crazy guy."

"Crazy about you."

She started fixing the hair behind her ear. "I here every day, but at night I go home to mother."

"Can I walk you home?"

She smiled. "Yes. Walk home with me."

We got word there would be a big convoy coming through. I watched from the bunker roof with the binoculars and spotted it a full two hours before it arrived. It first appeared as a tan smudge on the southern horizon, like a dust storm. I adjusted the binoculars and a giant rooster's tail of dust, like the vapor trail from the big B-52's, came into focus as it rose from the road. All the vehicles except for the lead one, a jeep with a fifty-caliber machine gun on top, were invisible, obscured by the dust.

I went over to the banyan tree and sat down to wait. Little Joe joined me. After a half hour the jeep and the first big diesel trucks rumbled by. Then a whirling, roaring, reddish-brown cloud of dust engulfed us, blotting out sun and sky. Tanks and trucks rumbled and rattled across the metal bridge, not fifty feet away from us, but we could barely see them. They sank the pontoons almost completely beneath the water, sending wave after wave sloshing against the bank beneath us. I counted at least fifty trucks and tanks by the time the noise began to abate. When the last truck had gone, a quiet calm settled over us, but the dust cloud remained.

I didn't want Little Joe running around on the bridge and so I took his hand and we crossed together. There ahead of us, I thought I saw something. We approached cautiously and a thin American soldier materialized out of the cloud. Seeing us, he took out his hanky and wiped his face.

"What's happening, brother?" I said, extending my hand.

"Indeed," he said. He looked a little annoyed, but he shook my hand anyway. Joe extended his hand and that seemed to cheer him a little. He took off his camouflaged steel pot and brushed it off, uncovering a little, black, Second Lieutenant's patch stitched to it. Satisfied, he put his helmet back on and started slapping the dust from his fatigues till they were green, bright, 'cruit green. Finishing, he looked at me. "Do you know where Specialist Fourth Class Ron Jakes can be found?"

I'd never heard anyone speak as beautifully as this guy did. His voice was totally without an accent and he spoke better English than my Lit teacher at State. "Yes, Sir," I said. "He's my squad leader. We're all right over here in the compound." The compound was now becoming visible to our left.

"Hmm. What is your name, soldier, and where is your shirt?"

My stomach dropped. I wondered if he was here because of my missing 201 file. "PFC Carl Melcher, Sir. I'm having my shirt laundered by one of the locals."

He blinked some dust from his eyelids. "Don't you have a spare set of fatigues?"

"No, Sir."

He closed his eyes for a second, then snapped them back open. "Well, we'll see what we can do about that."

Relief swept over me. He didn't know anything about the 201 file. Maybe they'd already found it on the jeep and returned it. He headed toward the opening in the wire. I sent Joe home and followed him.

Ron, Glock and Chico stood at a loose form of attention before the Lieutenant. They were all bare-chested. Ron wore a handkerchief pulled tightly around his head like a pirate. Glock had his black beret on, and Chico wore a towel twisted around his head like a turban. I don't know where Bubba was.

"I'm looking for the third squad of Company B, First of the Eighth, Fourth Infantry Division," the Lieutenant said.

"You found it, Sir," Ron said.

"Really?" The Lieutenant's brow furrowed. "I thought I'd found the lost brigade of the Salvation Army."

No one said anything.

"Which one of you is Specialist Ron Jakes?"

"I am, Sir," Ron said from behind his sunglasses. The tiniest hint of a smile spread out from the corners of his mouth.

"I'm Lieutenant Goodkin, your new Platoon Leader." The Lieutenant had a soft, baby face. He was about six feet tall and he stood stiff and straight. Even in the uniform there was something about him that suggested money. I'd bet he'd joined the army. Guys like him didn't get drafted.

"Do you know you are setting a very bad example for your men, Specialist," he said.

"Yes, Sir," said Ron, tingeing his face with sadness, "I'm sorry, Sir."

The Lieutenant seemed pleased with Ron's new demeanor and relaxed somewhat. He was young, maybe four or five years younger than Ron.

"The Captain has been getting some rather strange reports about your men running around nude, about wild parties. Is there any truth to these reports?"

"Absolutely not, Sir," Ron said. "This here is about as nude as we ever get, and only because of the heat, you understand. And we don't really party any more than anybody else around here."

"I see." The Lieutenant seemed momentarily at a loss. "What is your mission here?" he said after a moment.

"We were sent here to guard the floating bridge, Sir."

"I see that it's still there. Good job."

"Thank you, Sir."

The Lieutenant moved to the edge of Bubba's hole and looked down. "How long have you been working on this bunker?"

Ron moved to his side. "Since we got here, Sir. We take turns at it, but we usually don't do anything during the late afternoon when it gets real hot like this, Sir."

Lieutenant Goodkin hooked his thumbs through his web gear and turned to watch the river. "How deep is the river?"

Ron laughed. "I don't know, Sir. I can't swim."

I looked at the bridge to see if Chantal had come. She hadn't.

"It's well over ten feet, Sir," Glock said.

"How's the current?"

"Very swift, Sir," I said. "If you swim really fast you can barely move against it."

Everybody began to relax a little. Out in the street a small crowd of boys watched quietly, trying to hear what was being said. The Lieutenant climbed up onto the roof of the bunker to look around. I heard something in the street and turned to see Ted pull up in a jeep. He beeped the horn once and waved at the Lieutenant. The Lieutenant waved back and climbed down.

"Specialist," said the Lieutenant.

"Yes, Sir?"

"I want you to use some of the time you and your men have on your hands to figure out several ways to transport a squad across a river such as that one over there."

Oh, boy, I thought, here we go. Now we'd have to play Green Berets. How would I get away to spend time with Chantal?

"Like, what kind of ways, Sir?" Ron asked.

The Lieutenant looked pleased. "That's part of the problem, Specialist. You and your men formulate some plans and put them into action. I want a full report in a week when I return. Is that understood?"

Ron smiled. "I'm not sure, Sir. You want us to actually cross, with all our gear?"

"That is correct. Come with me. I want to have a closer look at that river."

As the Lieutenant, Ron and Glock moved down to the river, Chico and I walked out into the street to see Ted.

"Hey, fellas," he said. "I hear you're having some real good times here?"

"Damn right," Chico said, "and we deserve them, too. Right, Carl?"

"Dig it," I said.

Ted raised his eyebrows. "I wish I could join you guys. You don't know how good you have it."

"Oh, we do, we do," Chico said in a loud exaggerated tone. "We know how good we got it, don't you worry about that."

Ted laughed. "I'm tellin' ya, any other guy in the company'd give a month's salary to be in your shoes here."

"Really?" I said. "I thought Dak-To was supposed to be grunt heaven compared to the boonies?"

"It would be if we didn't have Captain DeVoors on our case."

Chico's brows furrowed with concern. "Why, what did he do?"

"What didn't he do?" Ted said. "Morning, afternoon and evening formations, spit-shined jungle boots, barracks inspections, details. . . . I'm telling you, we were a lot better off on the Firebase."

"Wow," I said. We were silent for a moment.

The Lieutenant approached. Ron and Glock flanked him, listening respectfully as he gave them their orders.

Ted started the jeep. "Well, you guys better enjoy it while it lasts."

"We will," I said.

"Dig it," said Chico.

The Lieutenant paused to emphasize some point to Ron. The jeep engine ticked rhythmically. Ted shook his head, a serious look clouding his normally buoyant, boyish features. "By the way, fellas, there's been a lot of enemy movement. Supposedly they're getting ready for their big Tet offensive. Battalion's probably gonna try and hit them first. There's been all kinds of top brass flying in for meetings."

Ted's talk of "movement" and "offensives," and his concern, seemed unreal now. That was all going on out *there*. And we were *here*. I tried not to let it in. I only wanted to think about Chantal.

Chico dismissed the news with a snarl. "Eh, there's always talk of the next big offensive! And the generals will always be meeting and smoking their big cigars. So what else is new, huh? You just want us to worry because you wish you were in our boots."

Ted laughed. The Lieutenant climbed into the jeep beside him.

Ron and Glock approached. Glock held his beret respectfully in both hands. "Can we use rope, Sir?" he said.

"That's up to the Specialist," the Lieutenant said. "I would say that anything that can be carried by four men could be used."

"Thank you, Sir," Ron said.

Ted shifted into first with a gnashing of metal gears and waved as he turned the jeep around and headed north to Dak-To. As the whine of the jeep receded, Ron mimicked Glock, "Can we use rope, Sir?"

Glock laughed and went into a fighter's stance. Ron did the same. They bobbed and wove in the street for a moment, their faces dark with feigned animosity. Soon a swarm of local ragamuffins boxed playfully in the dust at their feet. We had a laugh at that and went back into the compound to talk.

The next day I spent most of the morning with the squad working on the problem of trying to get five guys safely across the river. Glock had tried swimming across in his fatigues and boots, holding his M-16 aloft. He'd almost drowned but we managed to pull him out. Chico and I had crossed safely, with Chico floating on an air mattress with our weapons and packs, and me swimming and pushing. That seemed to be the best way.

We finished around noon and I went over to the banyan tree and waited for Chantal. She arrived with a lunch of sandwiches and cold Cokes and we ate on the pontoon in the shade.

She smiled at me. "Where you from?"

"Philadelphia."

"Oh, Liberty Bell."

"You know about that?"

She nodded. "We study it in school."

"I think I love you, you know that?"

"You crazy guy."

"No, I'm serious. I really do."

"Really?"

I had to laugh again at the way she pronounced "really." I loved the way she talked.

"You know what else is in Philly?"

"Philly?"

"That's what we call Philadelphia for short."

She nodded. "What?"

"Bandstand."

"Band stand," she said tentatively.

I nodded. "You know, dancing . . . on TV. It started not too far from where I live."

"Oh, you go to dance?"

"No, I didn't go there. You have to be really good for that. They have auditions. I went to Chez Vous."

"You no go to my house," she said.

I didn't know what she meant at first. Then I remembered my high school French. *Chez Vous* meant 'your house,' and Chantal also spoke French. "No," I laughed, "the dancing place in Philly is called 'Chez Vous.' It's a big roller skating rink, but they have dances there on Friday nights."

She nodded as she listened.

"Anyway," I went on, "I don't know all of the dances, just the Mashed Potatoes, the Stomp, the Twist, the Hully Gully, and the Slop. Maybe someday I'll teach you."

"Oh," she said slowly, "I don't think so." She seemed sad all of a sudden. "You very nice," she said, folding up the paper the sandwiches had been wrapped in.

"Thank you." I wished we were back in Philly together. I pictured the two of us riding on the Market-Frankford Elevated train, the car jerking and squeaking as it roared past the black tar roofs and second-story windows of the East Philly row houses.

With my hand I swept the crumbs off the pontoon and into the river. She said she had to go and I asked her if she could come back around dinner time. She said no, that she didn't want to leave her mother alone. But she said she would come tomorrow.

The rest of the day I felt like a million dollars. I really wanted to tell the guys about her, but I didn't.

That evening a fantastic pink sky stretched as far as you could see. The boom-boom girls didn't come and Ron and the guys stayed in the hootch, rapping and playing cards. I stayed up on the roof, reading and thinking. I stared at the purple blur where the sun had been and thought of Chantal, wondering what she was doing now. I pictured her and her mom eating dinner. Their table was wooden and plain, but clean, and they had white china rice bowls. I wondered what you had to do to marry a Vietnamese. Knowing the Army, there were probably a million forms to fill out. Guys did it, though.

I woke up briefly in pitch blackness. Crickets chirped, the river sighed, and someone was singing softly. It was Ron, singing that Bobby Love song that went, "Ain't got no money, but I got you, honey." He didn't have a very good voice, but he put so much feeling into it that I found myself smiling. Before he finished, I drifted back to sleep.

I opened my eyes on the bunker roof. The sun was up, but not too high and it felt warm and good on my face. Down below, the guys were still sleeping. I made myself a cup of coffee and looked over toward the river, wondering when Chantal would come. When it started getting hot, I walked over and sat under the banyan tree. I tried to read, but couldn't. By twelve o'clock she still hadn't come and I grew worried. I went back to the compound.

Ron and the others were playing cards. I went in to get some C's for lunch. I opened up a can of hot dogs and beans but I couldn't eat. I climbed up onto the bunker and looked over at the Engineer's hootch. Why hadn't she come? Just the other day I'd been on top of the world, but now I felt like I was down in Death Valley. If only Gene were here to talk to, I would've felt better. I listened to the radio for a while and took a nap.

The next day I sat under the banyan tree all morning but Chantal never came. At noon, Ted pulled up to the compound in a jeep. I crossed the bridge to see what was up. Ron, Glock and Bubba were packing up their things.

Ted nodded when he saw me. "You better get it packed up, Carl. We're moving out."

"You're kidding," I said. I couldn't believe it.

Ted shook his head. "Movin' out, man."

That was just like the army! They would wait till you met a girl you really cared for, then move you away. I started slamming things into my ruck.

Chico slapped me on the back. "You'll be okay, Vaquerro. You'll be okay."

They went into the hootch to talk and I left the compound and started walking down the road. When I was half a block away, I started running. I didn't care. I made it to Tin Can City without seeing Ted and the others. I walked through the town asking people if they knew where Chantal was. I didn't speak Vietnamese, but I knew a few French words, and many Vietnamese spoke French. I'd touch the hair on my head and say the word, rouge, which meant "red" in French. Most of the people looked at me like I was crazy. About three I saw a jeep in the distance and ducked into a little grocery store. The jeep went by and my heart sank. Captain DeVoors sat next to the military police driver and Lieutenant Goodkin sat in the back next to another military police with a big MP painted on his helmet.

I left the grocery and walked in the opposite direction. Then I spotted her. She was talking to an old Mammasan at a vegetable stall. I started running in her direction. I heard yelling behind me. Brakes squealed. Captain DeVoors was pointing me out to the MP driver. I ran as hard as I could and reached her just as the jeep squealed to a stop behind us. She held her hand up to her eyes to block the swirling dust. There was a fine sheen of sweat on her face from the heat, but she looked beautiful.

The Lieutenant and MP approached.

"Get in the jeep, creep," said the MP. I heard the others laugh.

I turned. The MP was smiling and smacking his night stick into his open palm.

"Give him a minute," said the Lieutenant.

I turned back to Chantal. "I have to go."

"I know," she said. She took the gold, good luck charm from around her neck and gave it to me. I put it in my pocket.

"You come back," she said. "You come see me, okay?"

The MP beeped the horn.

"Say good-bye, Private," said the Lieutenant.

The Captain and MP laughed at something but I ignored them. I kissed her and walked back to the jeep. I got in the back between the Lieutenant and the big MP.

The driver ground the jeep into gear and we lurched forward. I turned and looked back, watching her beautiful face disappear behind the swirl of dust.

CHAPTER 12

We pulled off the main road at Dak-To and bounced along the dirt track beside one of the runways. The rest of the company was already there, standing around or sitting on the ground in small groups. The jeep stopped and the two MPs walked off.

Captain DeVoors turned to me. "You're lucky we found you when we did, soldier. If you'd missed this chopper ride I coulda had you for desertion."

"Yes, Sir," I said, beginning to get scared. Desertion was very serious. You could end up in Long Bien Jail for that. I'd heard horror stories about the place.

"As it stands, the best I can do for you is an Article Fifteen with all the trimmings." He glared at me as he got out of the jeep. "I'll be watching you." He walked off.

"I'm really disappointed in you," the Lieutenant said.

"Yes, Sir. Sorry, Sir." He really did seem disappointed and I felt bad. He was a nice guy, but I had had to do what I did.

"You're dismissed, soldier."

I spotted Gene off by himself. He knelt over his rucksack as he rummaged for something. I walked over.

"Hey," he said, "you're back! I heard you went AWOL over some Vietnamese girl."

"Yeah, her name's Chantal."

He smiled sadly. "Don't worry too much. I don't think it'll amount to much more than a fine."

"I don't care."

"Yeah. That must've been tough leaving her."

"Yeah."

"Ah, you'll get over it."

"No, I won't."

We were silent for a moment as we watched the others. I thought about getting over her. It was impossible. "How can I get back there to see her?"

He shook his head. "I don't really see any way, man. You might pass through Dak-To on the way to your R&R, but that would only be for a few hours while you waited on a flight. No, man. The only way you could get back there was to somehow get yourself stationed back at Dak-To and that's impossible. Unless you re-enlisted or something."

I felt a stirring of hope. Never before would I have considered re-enlisting. But now things were different. "Would re-enlisting really get me back there?"

"Maybe, for certain schools." Gene looked at me. "You should talk to Lieutenant Goodkin about it."

I found Ron, Glock and Chico. We shook hands. Ron smiled and I knew he held nothing against me.

Lieutenant Goodkin came over. He had leaves tied all over his fatigues and two antler-like branches were tucked into the sweat band of his helmet, giving him a sort-of moose look. I almost laughed. He had a huddle with Ron and Glock.

I heard choppers approaching

The Lieutenant turned and called to Ted.

"Where're we going?" I asked Chico.

Chico looked worried. "Firebase 15."

The noise from the approaching choppers grew louder. They settled down a hundred feet away, their blades kicking up the dust.

"What kind of a place is it?"

Chico shook his head. "Follow me."

We boarded the second chopper. As the chopper lifted off, the ride boosted my spirits a bit, but only a bit.

"Put a round in your weapon," Chico shouted, "but keep the safety on."

I did as he said and soon we were shimmying and bouncing through the air. Everybody was grim-faced and quiet. I looked over at Goodkin's cockeyed, camouflage, moose antlers and felt sorry for him, sorry that nobody had told him how silly he looked, not even the other officers. Our chopper swayed and shuddered over dirty green jungle for maybe half an hour and then we began descending in a very tight spiral, corkscrewing straight down to the dirty mud brown of the Firebase. All of us watched in amazed silence, hoping there would be no hostile fire.

Our chopper touched down with a slight wobble and we jumped out and ran. I saw a sandbag wall and pressed up hard against it. Nothing happened. When the dust cleared, I noticed everybody else standing around nonchalantly.

Firebase 15 was not as high a hill as 29, and it was really two hills in one, one large, one small, like the figure 8, with the main trail that came up off the valley floor bisecting the two. At this point, the lowest point of the perimeter, yellow, waist-high elephant grass ran down about a hundred meters to where the jungle started. This is where our bunker was located. There were no 105 howitzers on the hill, but instead a mortar company and their tubes. The story going around was that the hill had once been overrun by the enemy and all the GI's killed.

The first couple of days after we arrived, everybody kept telling me I'd get over Chantal. That really bothered me since I didn't want to get over her. I went to see Lieutenant Goodkin and we had a long talk. He said I'd lessened my chances for a school by going AWOL, but that he would see if there were any openings back at Dak-To. He also said he would try to find out Chantal's address.

It was growing dark, and a guy from the next bunker was already on guard out in the trench when I got back. I went inside. Bubba slept in his bunk. Chico sat in his bunk, his brows furrowed in concentration as he dug the dirt out from under his fingernails with a pocketknife. Glock sat at the table writing a letter. Across from him, Ron was reading one of the sci-fi books I'd gotten in the mail. I had to smile at the sight of Ron and Glock together. The day we'd arrived on 15, they had shaved their heads smooth. A lot of other guys in the company were now wearing weird hairdos and mustaches, even Gene. I had just started a mustache myself.

I pulled up a crate and sat down.

Ron put the book down. "Now that old, rich Carl is here, what do you say we play some poker, huh?"

"Yeah," said Glock, "we better play him now before his Article 15 kicks in."

"Dig it," I said.

As we gathered around the little table, Bubba sat up slowly and yawned. He climbed down and joined us. When we'd first arrived on the hill, everybody had been pretty uptight, but now people were mellowing out a bit. Unfortunately I had some bad news for the guys concerning their R&Rs, which were now only two weeks away.

"So," said Ron from behind his sunglasses, "was the Lieutenant able to help you?"

"Yeah," I said, hoping he'd just let the subject drop. The thought of leaving the squad to go to school suddenly saddened me. Ron dealt the cards and we played five-card draw. I was holding two jacks, two threes and an ace. Ron and Glock were talking about the possibility of every-body getting together in New York for a reunion after we all DEROS'd. They'd been talking about it a lot lately.

"I think I could get the time off," Glock said. "I could come up for a week or so."

"Yeah," Ron said, "c'mon up. Just be sure to bring your M-16. You might need it in my neighborhood."

Glock laughed. "Oh, yeah?"

I thought about getting together with these guys in New York. It would be really great. Philly was close to New York. My friends and I used to go there when I was in high school. I remembered the last time . . . on a Sunday morning. . . . My buddies and I had stayed out late the night before and they didn't want to go out. So I decided to go to the park by myself. I found my way to the subway. The train pulled in; the doors hissed open. I headed for the seat directly in front of me and al-most sat down in a pool of pink puke. I moved half a car away and sat out of range of the smell. Some old lady, dressed in fox furs for Sunday church, got on at the next stop and did the same exact thing, only she was real cool about it, as if it hadn't happened. Then some guy and his two kids, dressed for a day in the park, almost sat in it, too. The thing that really cracked me up though, was that everybody, after having al-most sat in the stuff, moved down the car and watched to see if someone getting on at the next stop would sit in it.

"Look at the smile on Carl," Glock said. He turned to me. "What were you and Bryce discussing up there in the CP?"

"Nothing." Somebody'd discovered that the Lieutenant's first name was Bryce and now everybody on the hill called him that behind his back. I discarded the ace in my hand and drew a jack, giving me the full house I needed to win the hand. I decided that this was as good a time as any to tell them about their R&R's.

"You know what he told me tonight?" I said.

"No," Ron said as he shuffled the cards, "enlighten me."

"All R&R's have been canceled until further notice."

Ron said nothing and slowly put the cards on the table.

"You're kidding?" Glock said.

They were all watching me, Bubba included.

"I'm not kidding," I said. "Canceled until further notice." I'd been angry too when I heard it, but not too much. With every passing day I cared less about R&R and more about getting back to Dak-To to see Chantal.

Glock slammed his fist on the table and turned to Ron. "Can they do that?"

"I guess so," Ron said flatly, "they just did it, didn't they?" He lit a cigarette and exhaled noisily. No one spoke. Ron and Glock had really been looking forward to their R&R. Some friend of Ron's that'd been to Bangkok was supposed to come over to the bunker tomorrow night and tell them about it.

"The thing is," Ron said after a moment, "can they make it stick? Maybe we could go over the Captain's head."

Glock got up and went over to his bunk. He brought back a can of Coke and popped the top. He took a swig and looked at me. "Did Bryce say why they were canceled?"

I shrugged. "They're still talking about a big enemy build-up, and the Tet offensive."

"Dag," Ron said, "Tet is over now, has been for the past couple of days."

"Is that right?" Glock said.

Ron nodded.

Bubba turned to Glock. "The other day I was talking to that little

Vietnamese Kit Carson scout and he was saying the same thing. Tet's over and nothing's happened. But the brass think that's only because the rains have slowed Charley down. They still think there'll be some kind of offensive."

Ron clicked the radio on, dialing through the Vietnamese stations, settling on the cool harmonies of Bobby Love and the Valentines on AFVN. "C'mon," he said. "Forget about that stuff for a while and show me your cards."

I smiled as I lay mine down. "Full house!"

Ron shook his head. "Good, Carl. Good, but not good enough. Royal Flush!" He lay down the ladies and gents, all hearts.

"Jees," I said in amazement as he pulled the chips toward him.

Ron looked at me. "So, you gonna come up to New York, too?"

"Of course," I said.

"You ever been there?" said Glock.

"Lots of times."

Ron looked at Glock. "You been there?"

"Sure, back when I was a kid." Glock looked at me. "Not only am I going up to New York, Carl, but Ron's gonna visit me in Erie."

"Really?"

Ron smiled. "Dig it. How far is Erie from New York?"

"Oh, three-fifty, four hundred miles. You can get there by train."

"Dig it," Ron said, "or the gray dog." He looked at me and chuckled. "They're gonna burn a cross on his lawn, Carl."

Glock was red-faced. He shook his head. "C'mon, man," he said. "We're talking Erie, Pennsylvania, not Selma, Alabama."

"If you say so," Ron said. He laughed. "I bring it up 'cause that's the world, man. White and black don't hang out together back there."

The poncho flapped back and the guard stuck his head in. "You guys better get out here," he said. "Something's going on down past the wire!"

We crowded out into the trench. There was no moon and you couldn't see your hand in front of your face. I could hear Lieutenant Goodkin and some others talking down by where the trail came through the wire.

There was a field-phone set up down there with a wire that ran down to the LP. I went down to hear what they were talking about.

"When did you last contact them?" Lieutenant Goodkin asked the guard.

"We got a sitrep from them a half hour ago. They said the new man heard some movement. But Brody, he's in charge, he thought that it was nerves. When we called them a half hour later, the field phone was dead. That's when I called you."

Lieutenant Goodkin didn't say anything for a minute. He called Ron.

"Yes, Sir?" Ron said.

"I want you to take a couple men down there and see if you can find out what's going on."

For a moment Ron didn't say anything. I could imagine his impassive face turned toward Goodkin. He would be thinking, "What good are only three men gonna do down there? Why don't you go down there yourself?"

"Okay, Sir," Ron said after a moment. "Glock?" he called, angrily, "where are you?"

"Over here, getting my gear ready."

"Dig it," said Ron. "Chico?"

Glock's voice came out of the darkness, "Chico went over to Kessler's squad to see his buddy, remember?"

"Right," came Ron's voice. I knew he'd call me next. I was a little scared. I wished the handset would come to life with the LP guys on the other end and then this whole thing would be over and everything would be all right. I knew I would go, though. If he called my name, I'd go. And then, just as I could almost hear my name forming in Ron's mouth, a familiar voice with a distinctive drawl said, "I'm goin' with you all, Ron." It was Beobee. For a moment I felt cheated. I had resigned myself to going, psyched myself up for it. I was ready. And then Beobee had volunteered. Now, the next time they called me, I'd have to psyche myself up all over again.

"Good," Ron said, "get your gear."

"I already got it right here."

I heard the Lieutenant talking to the Captain on the radio. "Yes, Sir, that's correct, Sir," he said. Then the Lieutenant was talking to someone close by, probably Ted. "Call the mortar platoon for some illumination rounds. Tell them to keep them coming."

Ted relayed the message.

The first flare was not long in coming. I heard the mortar guys talking up on the hill behind us. Then there was a scraping sound, like a rock sliding down the inside of a pipe, as the mortar rocket dropped into the tube, then a "thunk," followed by the mortar's hissing climb, and finally, a popping sound high overhead.

Ugly, harsh light glared down on us, casting eerie, moving shadows as the flare floated down, swinging back and forth under its little parachute. I couldn't see anything or anybody down there. I looked over at the other guys in the trench. Ron, Glock and Beobee huddled with Lieutenant Goodkin. I hoped they'd be okay. I suddenly pictured them all lying still on the ground and the image really scared me. They were my family.

The flare went out suddenly, turning everything black. About a half minute later another flare rocketed skyward and popped. You couldn't see the LP. It was down the hill about a hundred meters, past the elephant grass and in the bushes and stunted trees. The trees and bushes moved menacingly in the wriggling light of the flare as it descended. It went out, again plunging us into total darkness. They were evidently only using one mortar tube, and there was a dark gap of four or five seconds between when one flare flickered out and the next one popped on.

I went over to Ron and the others.

"You men ready?" the Lieutenant asked. In the faint glow of the radio's dial, I could make out his features. Under his slightly too-big helmet, his baby face with its dark beard-shadow struck me as funny.

"Just a minute, Sir," Ron said.

Ron and the others huddled for a moment, and then moved up toward the wire, their gear clacking noisily. Ron was at the head of the little file. "You guys ready?" he said, not turning as he stared at the bleak landscape below twitching in the ugly, stark white light.

"Yeah," they replied curtly.

"Let's go then!" Ron ran in a crouch for the jumble of wire, his rifle at the ready. Beobee and Glock bunched together right behind him.

Back in Infantry School they'd always told us not to bunch up like that. One grenade could get everyone, they'd said.

Ron and the others had just gotten into the wire, and begun stealthily negotiating the tricky little path snaking through it, when the flare blinked out and they disappeared from view. Not wanting to miss anything, I didn't move my eyes from the spot where the darkness had swallowed them up. I heard some kind of commotion there. Behind us a flare climbed, hissing, into the sky. It popped and bright, ugly light revealed Ron, Glock and Beobee writhing painfully in the tangle of barbed wire like three fat flies caught in a spider's web. I cracked up laughing. I didn't want to, but I couldn't help it. The flare went out.

"Get them out of there," came the Lieutenant's voice. He sounded embarrassed and angry. I ran up to help, but not as quickly as I could have because I had this stupid smirk on my face that I hated myself for, and that wouldn't go away.

They helped the three of them off behind the trench. Somebody said they were all right, just a few cuts. I felt horrible. God! I didn't want to laugh! But it had seemed funny to me.

I remained back where I was. All of a sudden some guy yelled, "Sir, we got movement down there. Someone's comin' up!"

Everybody looked downhill. There was a clatter of sound as everyone knelt and aimed their weapons. Then we heard the approaching figures yelling, "Friendlies! Don't shoot! Friendlies!"

"It's Brody and the LP!" someone shouted. "Don't shoot."

By the time they got to the wire they were yelling at the top of their lungs. Once inside they collapsed in the trench. I went over. Brody was breathing heavily, his mouth open like a fish's under that big droopy Fu Manchu mustache of his. The other guys sat with their backs against the dirt wall of the trench, one of them with his head in his hands. No one said anything for a while.

"Kee-riest!" said Brody finally. He coughed and gasped.

After another minute or so Lieutenant Goodkin said, "What happened down there?"

Brody looked at him, then back at his feet as he fought for breath. "They cut the field-phone wires."

"I thought so," Lieutenant Goodkin said.

"Dig it," Ron said.

I looked at the other LP guys; they were still panting, staring into space.

"By the time we realized they were there," Brody said, between gasps, "they were all around us."

"How many were there?" the Lieutenant asked.

"About forty or fifty. And they knew exactly where we were, too! They were all around us at once, so close I coulda touched one of them. And then one of them starts talking to me. He . . ."

"Huh?" said the Lieutenant.

"He starts talkin' to me. He said, 'You die soon.' Just like that. 'GI die soon.' "

Nobody said anything for a minute.

"Well, what did . . ." the Lieutenant said, fumbling for the right words.

"They didn't do anything," said Brody. "We didn't do anything. What could we do? They were all around us. I thought they'd take us prisoner, but they were going somewhere in a big hurry and that's why they didn't mess with us. They just said that, that's all."

"I'm going back to the bunker," Brody said. The other three LP guys got up to follow him. The Lieutenant didn't say anything to them, didn't tell them to stop.

The next day I worked a shift of stuff-burning detail with Gene. He didn't think there was any big attack imminent. I wanted to believe him, but I think he was just trying to put me at ease. I asked him what he thought about me re-enlisting for a school so I could be close to Chantal at Dak-To. He seemed to think it was a good idea if I could get it.

That night I read one of Gene's sci-fi books. I tried to blot out every-thing that was going on, and forget where I was, just by reading. But it was getting harder and harder to do that. Instead I found myself imagin-ing I was back at the bridge, swimming in the river with Chantal. Our time together hadn't been more than a couple weeks but it had seemed like a lifetime. I wanted to get back there more than I'd ever wanted any-thing in my life.

CHAPTER 13

I was working chopper pad detail when the big Chinook helicopter got shot down. Earlier in the afternoon, Ted had told us that the Chinook would be carrying a blivit, and that we had to dig a hole for them to set it in. I'd asked him what a blivit was, and he had said jokingly that it was a thousand pounds of stuff in a five hundred pound bag. I pressed him on that and he said it was a big rubber container they used for carrying water or fuel. We had just finished digging the hole for it when the Chinook arrived. It loomed fifty feet over us like a huge, olive-drab Greyhound bus with rotors forward and aft. The big, black cylindrical blivit of water, weighing at least a ton, hung from its drop hook. The Chinook's down draft raised a stinging dust storm as Ted used hand signals to help them set the blivit in the center of the hole so it wouldn't roll down the hill.

The big helicopter dipped lower and lower, its turbines whining ear-splittingly. I heard a faint "pock pock pock" sound.

The pilot was oblivious to it as he watched Ted carefully. I thought maybe it was an engine or transmission noise. Then Sergeant Berry rushed over yelling that the chopper was taking small arms fire. I looked up at the Chinook as the noise grew louder, a distinct rattling.

Ted waved the pilot off and he looked at us in confusion. There was another flurry of "pock pock pock" sounds and Ted and I hit the dirt. The pilot released the blivit and slowly turned the Chinook.

Ted and I ducked behind a sandbag wall as the big chopper inched sluggishly off the hill. A jet of black smoke issued from the left turbine. The Chinook sank toward the valley floor, becoming smaller and smaller until it disappeared into the sea of green. A moment later a thin column of smoke curled skyward.

Sergeant Berry called for mortar fire on the surrounding ridges as everybody ran around bent over, Groucho Marx style. There was no more firing and after a few minutes people began walking upright.

That's when I noticed the crowd of guys down at the trench line. At first I didn't know what they were doing down there and then Ted pointed out that the blivit was gone.

We ran down. They had a blanket over some guy. He was alive, but unconscious. Gene knelt beside him, patting his hand. The guy had evidently been digging in the trench when the Chinook came in and had sat down and turned away from the blast of dirt and grit. When the pilot realized he was taking fire, he had set the blivit down on the edge of the hole, instead of in the center. It had evidently started rolling like a steam roller, and had smashed the guy flat, then continued down the hill, ripping out all the concertina wire and finally tearing itself apart when it slammed into the big trees a hundred meters below.

Over the next couple weeks, most of the choppers took sniper fire. Then the mortars would saturate the surrounding ridges and a patrol would be quickly dispatched. But they never caught them. The enemy always melted back into the jungle like fish disappearing into the depths. A rumor was going around that a new enemy division had moved into our AO. Everybody was growing more uptight. Only my nights were peaceful and worry-free, filled with dreams of Chantal. Always she'd be there beside me as we drove along Woodland Avenue in a new Mustang convertible, listening to Steem Masheen, cool summer night air washing over us.

Something woke me. The bunker was black. Nearby, someone tossed in his sleep. I heard nothing further and had almost fallen back to sleep when a terrific explosion shook the bunker. I jumped out of the bunk, grabbed my weapon and web gear, and rushed out into the trench. A crescent moon shone down from a cloudless sky and you could see a little. The other guys were already there and sporadic rifle fire came from around the curve of the hill. Glock aimed his M-16 down into the darkness looking for a target, but couldn't find any. Neither could I.

"What was it?" I said.

"Heck if I know. Keep your eyes open."

The firing started up again, this time more intense. A grenade boomed around the curve of the trench line. Some guy came running down the trench from the next bunker.

"Sappers," he called out nervously. "They blew away some guys in the next bunker. We got them pinned down in the sump." He ran off.

I'd heard about Sappers. They were enemy suicide squads. They wrapped their bodies tightly like mummies so if they got shot their guts wouldn't fall out and they'd live a few minutes longer. Supposedly they smoked a lot of opium before they went on a mission so they wouldn't feel any pain if they got shot.

Ron went into the bunker and brought out a radio tuned to the command channel. There was a lot of back-and-forth chatter about enemy movement, but it didn't sound like they knew where they were yet.

A flare rocketed skyward and burst. Stark, shaky light glared down. I still couldn't see anything down there. Rifle fire and the booming thump of grenades came from around the curve of the hill, near the sump. The grenades were going off about one every minute, but none of us had even fired a shot yet.

"Ron," Glock said in a hoarse whisper, "I'm goin' over to see what's going on."

"Okay, but be cool."

"Yeah." Glock moved off down the trench.

As I watched for movement in the faint moonlight, I realized that I had never seen an enemy alive. For a moment I thought it would be exciting to see some enemy down there. But that might signal the beginning of something really bad, like a full-scale ground attack, and I hoped there would be nothing.

Ron ducked down in the trench and lit a cigarette as Bubba, Chico and I peered into the darkness.

"Still nothing down there?" Ron asked.

"No," Chico said, "nothing."

We stared into the dark for another few minutes and then Glock came back. He gave me a funny look.

"What's going on over there?" Bubba asked.

Glock shook his head. "It's just like the guy said. Sappers. They think they got them pinned down in the sump."

"Anybody get hit?" Ron asked.

"Three guys," Glock said. He turned to me. "They said Gene was one of them. He was visiting in the bunker when the sappers threw their charge in."

My insides turned to ice water. There must be a mistake, I thought. Glock moved back into the shadows of the trench and I heard him retching in the dark. Bubba went into the bunker and brought out a canteen of water.

The sporadic firing went on all night. Occasionally a grenade boomed as we peered down the hill, seeing nothing. It had evidently been just the one team of Sappers. I still couldn't believe Gene was dead, even after Ron went and confirmed it. It seemed impossible and crazy. Only this morning I had sat and had a cup of coffee with him.

Shortly after daybreak we heard that they'd found the Sappers dead in the sump. Ron and Glock stayed on guard in the trench, and Chico, Bubba and I went up to the top of the hill. I saw the body bags containing Gene and the other two guys up at the chopper pad, but I didn't go near them. The guys that wanted to look at the dead enemies had formed a line. Just like at a regular funeral, it stretched all the way down to the sump. I went back to the bunker and tried to sleep, but I couldn't. Every time I was about to fall asleep I'd imagine Sappers sneaking up through the wire with their bombs.

Lieutenant Goodkin took the whole platoon with him on his first patrol. There had been so much enemy contact lately, we knew we'd be extremely lucky not to see any action. For that reason, everybody packed plenty of ammo. I was carrying the M-79 grenade launcher and about fifty rounds. But it would only be a one-day sweep and we wouldn't have to carry three or four days worth of food and water. So we could move fast if we had to.

Goodkin had our squad take the lead and he stayed right behind us. Ron put Chico on point. We started down the trail and about five minutes later were enveloped in thick heat and humidity, and that sad, jungle half-light. Immediately everyone began sweating heavily. For about an hour we followed the main trail down to the valley floor and then Goodkin called a halt.

The Lieutenant's face was flushed as he crouched down and studied the map with Ron and Chico. A drop of sweat jiggled at the end of the Lieutenant's long, thin nose. A line of guys stretched up the trail behind us.

We began moving again. The giant trees rose all around us like huge columns, and I noticed that the jungle was not as thick here as it was back at Firebase 29. Instead of dense bamboo groves and elephant grass there were small bushes and ferns, and we could move faster, making less noise. Everybody was very quiet as they watched the dark undergrowth with big eyes. We covered a lot of ground without seeing anything.

As I searched the shadows, I kept thinking that the farther we went without anything happening, the greater the chances that something would. Finally, Chico signaled a halt. Glock crept forward to talk to him, and together they checked out what looked like some kind of structure.

While the column was stopped, I moved closer to see it. It was a ruin of some kind. An overturned column lay on a stone foundation, and there was lots of stone rubble on the ground. Ron found a fragment of a statue, the left side of a head. It looked like it had been sliced neatly in half with a knife. The ear was long and the lips kind of big. I thought it might have been made by the Montagnards, the aborigines who lived here in the Highlands.

The Lieutenant disappeared into the bushes and emerged a moment later dragging a big, stone jar. It must've weighed sixty pounds. He took off his ruck and waved us over. "Ron," he said, "go on down the line and tell them to break for lunch."

"Okay, Lieutenant."

Lieutenant Goodkin turned to me. "Come with me."

I followed him as he placed some guards in a perimeter. Finally he turned to me. "I haven't had any luck finding the girl yet."

I nodded. "Do you really think we can contact her through the mail?"

"Maybe. Do you still want to go to that school?"

Hope flooded through me. "Sure."

"All right. I'll see what I can do. The Captain has to sign off on it, though. So you better keep your nose clean."

"Yes, Sir. Thank you, Sir."

All I could think about was the bridge and Chantal. If I was stationed in Dak-To I'd be able to get down to Tin Can City a couple of times a week for sure. It would be great.

They were eating when we got back. The Lieutenant sat across from us and opened a can of C-rations. He looked at me. "So, Private Melcher, what was your major at State?"

"I didn't have one. I was only there for one semester."

Glock laughed and looked over at the Lieutenant. "He was taking up time and space."

The Lieutenant laughed.

"There are a lot of dudes back in the world doing that," Ron said, "so they can get out of coming here."

"Yeah," Chico said, "send them over here to take my place and I'll go home and study outer space or something."

The Lieutenant hungrily spooned down some Scrambled Eggs'n' Ham. Scrambled Eggs'n'Ham was the most disgusting C ration there was, the one that nobody wanted. It was pasty gray with flecks of pink, and had the texture of day-old oatmeal. If you were unlucky enough to get it, you couldn't trade it and had to throw it away. He looked over at us.

"What about the rest of you, did any of you go to college?"

Ron smiled from behind his glasses. "The school of hard knocks in New York."

The other guys laughed and shook their heads.

"Hey, Lieutenant," Glock said, "are you planning on carrying that vase back up to the perimeter?"

"Sure, why do you ask?"

Glock smiled wryly. "Well, it's kind of heavy."

"And it's a long way up, too," Chico said.

Under the pale, green light, we laughed nervously. We were beginning to feel a little better now that we had food in our bellies.

"What do you think that thing weighs, Lieutenant?" Ron asked.

Lieutenant Goodkin looked at him. "Oh, maybe fifty, sixty pounds."

"Why do you want that thing, Lieutenant?" Chico asked.

"Well," Lieutenant Goodkin said slowly, "my mother collects antiques. I don't know what I have here, but I think she'd really appreciate it."

"Oh," Chico said, "a present for your momma. I see." The others smiled.

Lieutenant Goodkin knelt to tie the jar to his ruck. He smiled when he looked up and saw the smirks on the men's faces.

"Ten dollars he doesn't make it," I heard Glock say behind me. Ron said something in return. I walked off. I didn't want the Lieutenant to think I was betting on whether or not he'd make it. I was pretty sure he would. He was a good guy for an officer, nothing like DeVoors.

I watched with the others as he tried unsuccessfully to swing the ruck up onto his back. Then he sat down in front of it and put his arms through the straps, the way I did when I had too much to carry. The rest of the Platoon sat around watching him, hoping he'd take another twenty minutes to repack the thing so they could rest some more.

We moved out and Lieutenant Goodkin put the fourth squad in the lead. We moved into the center of the column. I hiked along behind the Lieutenant. A couple of times he turned sideways to negotiate some obstacle and I saw how the straps of the ruck were cutting into his shoulders. I knew what that felt like. It decreased the blood and made your arms numb from your shoulders to your fingertips. Every so often Goodkin would lean over and hoist the ruck up higher on his back to take the tension off his shoulders and arms.

We made good time across the sparsely forested floor of the valley and started climbing our hill. I figured we'd be back inside the perimeter in another hour.

Goodkin stopped suddenly and raised his arm, signaling a halt. His face was beet red and he was panting. He was too winded to speak.

The light was beginning to fade. We probably had only another forty-five minutes before it would be too dark to move.

"Take ten," the Lieutenant said in a hoarse whisper.

We sat down and watched the bush. I thought about all the deaths and about how strange it had all been. I used to think that good people would somehow be safe. But I knew now that that wasn't how it worked. Papa, Mike and Gene were good people, the best, and they had gotten killed. It seemed to boil down to being in the wrong place at the wrong time. That's all there was to it. Dumb luck. So far I'd been lucky. I prayed my luck would hold until I got out of the field.

After ten minutes of rest, Goodkin's breathing had evened out. He sat still and looked straight ahead, evidently exhausted. Glock nudged Ron to take a look at him.

Goodkin looked over. He knew we'd been watching him. He got on his knees. Then he grabbed onto a tree trunk to slowly pull himself up. "Pass the word," he said. "Move out!"

We went another klick or so and Goodkin stopped suddenly and leaned against a tree, breathing heavily. His weapon fell from his hands and clattered onto the ground as he slid slowly down into a sitting position. The guys behind us were eager to get back, and annoyed at the many stops. They craned their necks to see what the holdup was. Ron held up one finger indicating that we'd be moving in just one minute. "Are you okay, Sir?" he asked, his face beaded with sweat.

The Lieutenant nodded weakly.

"You want me to carry that for a while, Sir?" Glock asked.

The Lieutenant shook his head and struggled to get up, but couldn't. He might as well have been nailed to the tree.

Ron and I pulled him to his feet. His face and eyes were blank. He staggered forward. "Let's go."

We moved on and the light grew more anemic. I realized that if we didn't get to the hill within a half hour or so we'd either have to hike in the dark or else set up outside the wire. We came to the part of the trail where we'd had to climb over two fallen trees. You had to kind of slide over the first one, the bigger one, and then step up onto the smaller one and step down.

The Lieutenant slid slowly over the first log and stepped up onto the second. When he went to step off, the log wobbled and his knees buckled. The weight of the vase snapped him backwards and he fell between the logs. As I leaned over to help him, rifle fire erupted all around us. I dove between two logs and heard the cries and curses of the guys caught in the fire. My insides turned to ice as the mad firing roared around us.

Somebody pounded on my boot heel and I turned and looked into Lieutenant Goodkin's eyes. He was jamming a clip in his rifle. "Put some fire out there," he yelled. He peeked over the log then raised his weapon and fired a quick burst.

Ron passed the radio up to him and yelled that they had a casualty up forward and several wounded. I took the safety off the M-79, popped my head up quickly, and fired a round into some hedges across the way. I heard the boom of the explosion as I ducked back down. I hoped it did some good, but doubted it. I hadn't seen anything out there and didn't know where the heck they were.

"We need those mortars, Sir!" Ron yelled to the Lieutenant.

The Lieutenant's face was red as a beet as he nodded. He yelled hoarsely into the radio as the wounded screamed and cursed, and the firing roared around us. A mortar round crashed down through the trees. Two guys in the bushes to our left got to their feet and rushed up the hill. I started to get up when a hand grabbed my boot and pulled me down. The Lieutenant's face was in front of mine as he yelled into the radio. I realized the mortar fire was ours and he was directing it. "When it stops, we go," he yelled at me. "Pass it along."

The barrage lasted about a minute. When it was over, people were getting up and spraying the bush with their weapons as they ran up the trail. I was afraid I'd be left behind. I got up and ran as fast as I could. I looked back and ran into something, banging my head so hard my eyes started tearing.

It was Ron; he'd been helping some guy hobble along. "Grab hold of his other arm and let's go," he yelled. It was almost too dark to see where we were going and we followed along behind the others. Finally we came out from under the trees into the light of some flares. We wound our way through the wire on the hill as people yelled and directed us. A medic ran over to look at the guy Ron and I were carrying. The guy's arm was so tight around my neck, I could hardly breathe.

"Get him in the trench," the medic ordered. We hurried the guy over and I noticed that the toe of his boot dripped blood like water from a bad faucet.

I saw the Lieutenant sprawled in the trench. He looked exhausted and spent, but uninjured. His stone jar was beside him.

CHAPTER 14

*Under a beautiful, blue sky, I held a sandbag open for Bubba as he shov-*eled dirt into it. We were putting another layer of sandbags on the bunker roof. I looked out over the jungle valley, wondering where the enemy that had ambushed us was now. I wondered if we'd killed any of them. Glock swore he'd shot four of them, but that was Glock. I hadn't even seen one. I asked Bubba if he'd hit any.

He paused, his foot resting on the shovel. "I don't rightly know, Carl. I saw something in the bushes and I think I hit it, but I can't say for sure. They were hid pretty darn good."

"I know."

Beobee and Ted approached. "Hi, fellas," said Ted. He had a look of wonder on his face. "You guys gave a good account of yourselves last night. That's what your Lieutenant says."

Bubba laughed. "Is that right?"

"Yeah," said Ted. "They estimate it was a company-size force of enemy."

"Wow," I said. I'd thought there were a lot of them. It was hard to say how many though, because they were so well hidden. Thinking about it bothered me though because we'd have to go out there again. I tried to change the subject.

"What's the latest on the R&R's, Ted? Any possibility they'll be unfrozen?"

Ted shook his head. "Nothing happening there, pal. Especially now that they've found out about the road. Nobody's going anywhere till it's taken out."

"The road?" I said.

"I thought I heard somebody talking about a road," Beobee chimed in. "Where is it?"

Ted shrugged his shoulders. "Beats me. All I know is, the Green Berets interviewed a couple of Montagnards who claim they were blindfolded by the enemy and taken out to the middle of the jungle to work on a big road. It's supposed to be big enough to bring in tanks and trucks."

I looked out over that sea of dirty green and wondered where it could possibly be. Beneath that thick jungle it would be more a tunnel than a road.

I spent an hour alone in the bunker trying to nap but I couldn't get to sleep. I went up to the top of the hill and there were a couple dozen guys hanging out in small groups. I saw my friend Willet and stood around with him while he smoked a cigarette. The Captain came out of the CP and every head turned. Then people went back to their conversations, acting like they hadn't seen him. Captain DeVoors looked around and laughed like he'd just remembered a good joke. He started walking in our direction. As he came closer, I realized he was headed straight for us. DeVoors stopped in front of Willet and said, "I want to have a word with this soldier here."

"Yes, Sir," Willet said, walking off.

The Captain looked at me coldly. "There seems to be a problem with your paperwork at Battalion. Did you know that, Melcher?"

"No, Sir." For a moment I didn't know what the heck he was talking about.

His eyes bore into mine. "You don't happen to have any peon clerks as friends back there in McGernity, do you?"

"No, Sir," I said. That's when it dawned on me. My 201 file must be missing. It was probably still in the back of that jeep, covered with mud and muck. That was why they still had not processed my Article 15 for going AWOL. I couldn't help smiling at my good luck.

DeVoor's blushed angrily. "You better wipe that smile off your face, soldier. My men are tigers. They're not allowed to smile. You got that?"

"Yes, Sir."

He scowled as he brushed past me. As soon as he was out of earshot people came up to me, asking me what had happened. "Nothing," I said, not wanting to be the center of attention. I went back to the bunker.

I was out in the darkness of the trench on first guard when firing erupted just below the tree line. The *pop—pop—popping* quickly mushroomed in volume and then grenades began booming ominously, one after another. The rest of the squad ran out with their gear, Ron carrying the radio, as a report crackled over the command channel. The Second Platoon had been ambushed on their way back up the hill! It sounded like they were getting it worse than we had. Already they had eight casualties.

I aimed my weapon down into the darkness. The firing was sporadic, grenades booming dully. Surely the enemy'd be coming up for us. If not tonight, then some other night. But soon. We seemed to be a threat to them now.

"Pop a flare," Glock said suddenly. "I think I see something."

Ron fired one aloft with a hiss. It popped and glared down cold, white light. We saw nothing.

"I swear I saw something," said Glock.

The firing continued down below the tree line. From the little rise above us I could hear the mortar rounds thunking out of the tubes. They crashed down into the trees below. Radio reports indicated that the second platoon was pinned down so badly they couldn't break away. They needed help bad, but to send men down into that would be horrible, with everybody shooting at everybody else. That's what the enemy wanted us to do, of course. They were very clever.

It went on all night. I think everybody on the hill felt guilty about not being down there helping them; I knew I did.

We took turns guarding and sleeping in the trench. About an hour before sunup Ted came by and told us to get our gear together. A platoon-sized force would be sent down at first light. Just when we were ready to go, the enemy disengaged and the Second Platoon and the rescue team began to straggle in.

They'd been worked over really bad. Someone said there'd been nine killed and seven wounded. I thought it was more than that. As the morning sun inched over the horizon, Bubba and I helped the medics carry the wounded up to the chopper pad. Later someone brought over a big jug of coffee and some Styrofoam cups. Bubba and I were sitting and sipping when Beobee came by.

"Howdy, Carl, Bubba," he said. "Did you all hear about the parachute yet?"

"Huh?"

"What parachute?" Bubba asked.

Beobee put his hands on his hips. "Well, it seems the enemy dropped something, or somebody, into that valley over yonder by parachute last night."

"You're kidding," Bubba said.

"I swear to God. Come on and I'll show you the dang thing."

We followed Beobee to the top of the hill and climbed onto a bunker. Sure enough, in the distance, a tiny spot of white lay upon the green canopy of jungle trees.

"Are you sure it's a parachute?" Bubba asked.

"No," Beobee said, "but what else in heaven's name could it be?"

"Maybe it's one of our parachutes," I said, "from a flare."

"Maybe," Beobee said, "but the brass up in the CP don't think so."

The more I thought about it, though, the more it looked too big to be a flare parachute. I didn't think you could see a flare parachute from this distance. As we looked out over the green valley one of the gasoline generators behind the bunker coughed and came to life with a muffled drone.

"I'll tell you one thing," Beobee said solemnly, "there's something big going on down there. Charley's up to something and we're gonna find out real soon what it is."

I was coming back from the mess tent, carrying a drooping paper plate of hot chow, when I saw Ron and Beobee over at the next bunker. Beobee waved me over.

"They have proof there's a road, Carl," he said.

"What proof?"

"A spotter plane got shot down," Ron said. "He spotted smoke and flew through it, said it smelled like diesel fumes, then they shot him down."

"That's right, Carl," Beobee said. "Me and a bunch of artillery guys saw him go down."

"Dig," Ron said. "They sent a reconnaissance team in to get him and they confirmed there's a road down there. We're goin' out to destroy it."

Well, I guess it was bound to happen. I couldn't expect to get through my whole tour in Vietnam without having to go out on something really dangerous. But that didn't make me feel any better about it. I thought of Chantal and wished I could see her before I went. And boy, oh, boy, what I would have given to be able to talk to Papa or Gene. I went back to the bunker.

It was supposed to be a quick operation and we only packed a day's worth of water and C's. There were some combat engineers going with us, and in addition to our own gear, we had to help them carry the dynamite charges. There were two different kinds of charges. The shape charges resembled TV picture tubes, and would be used to blow narrow holes in the ground. Then the cratering charges, big, green tubes about eight inches in diameter and four feet long, would be lowered in the holes. When they blew, they would make holes the size of houses, making the road impassable.

Each platoon had to carry one of the charges. Lieutenant Goodkin gave our squad one of the cratering charges, and Ron gave it to me. It looked like a big, fat, fifty-pound stick of TNT. As I tied it to my ruck I wondered if a rifle round could set it off. I asked an Engineer who was walking by.

He seemed surprised at the question. "I don't think so."

"Well, what about one of my M-79 grenade rounds? What if one of them went off?" I was carrying seventy HE, or high explosive grenade rounds in my vest and in my ruck.

He sighed. "Maybe. I don't know." He walked off. I sat down and pulled the ruck on. It was your typical army logic—if a rifle round wouldn't explode the thing, and only another explosion would, why not give it to the guy carrying seventy little rounds of high explosive? It made perfect army sense.

I tried to put it all out of my head, but this image of the cartoon character, Wylie E. Coyote kept crowding in. He had a huge red rocket strapped to his back with a fuse dangling down. He lit a match to it and, of course, it immediately blew up.

We went through the wire and started down the steepest part of the trail. Soon I was worrying less about blowing up and more about keeping up. It was the heaviest load I'd ever carried and the column was moving fast. I hoped nothing would happen until I got rid of it. Fortunately we reached the valley floor without incident.

The pace picked up. The others were hiking super-light-weight rucks and were practically running! I felt like screaming at them to stop. All the weight I was carrying was killing me, and for the first time in my life I thought I might have to fall out. Fortunately, though, they called a halt and I flopped on the ground. My legs were like rubber and my arms and shoulders numb.

Lieutenant Goodkin walked over, swigging from a canteen. "How are you doing with that?"

"I'm all right." As soon as I said it I hated myself for lying. Fortunately the Lieutenant didn't believe me. He asked Glock to carry it the rest of the way.

They gave our squad the point and I was behind Chico. The triple canopy of trees blotted out all direct sunlight and the foliage on the ground was sparse, mostly ferns, and small waist-high bushes. We hiked another hour or so, warily scanning the jungle floor. Chico stopped abruptly and pointed. There, among the brown of earth and the green and gray of leaves and vines, ran a thin, bright, yellow, land phone line across the ground—a yellow wire! It crossed our path, stretching away in either direction.

Lieutenant Goodkin came forward with Bubba, who was packing the radio. They knelt to inspect it. I followed the wire to where it disappeared and imagined it leading to some enemy Captain in a pith helmet. He was squatting down on his haunches, talking into a field phone.

The Lieutenant finished his whispered conversation and turned to us. "Who has a pocket knife?"

Bubba took out his Barlow, opened it and handed it to him.

They were going to cut it! "No, don't!" I said in a harsh whisper, not really meaning to.

Everybody looked at me like I was crazy as the Lieutenant cut the wire.

"Sorry," I said. I felt like a fool, but I thought it would've been smarter not to let them know we were here. I had a sudden sick feeling, as if everything had suddenly gone wrong and every bit of my luck had just run out. I looked at the cut wire and imagined the enemy Captain staring into his handset, wondering why it had gone dead. Realization formed on his face.

Hunkered down, with our weapons pointed out, we waited while Lieutenant Goodkin studied his map. Then we moved out.

We went another kilometer and came to one of those bombed-out, defoliated areas. It was a relief to see the sky. The open ground was covered with a lot of tan-colored, crackly deadfall.

Lieutenant Goodkin got word over the radio that the Second Platoon was to take the point from here on. We waited on the side of the trail as most of the company filed by and across the open space. Then it was our turn and we crossed quickly, making an awful racket in the dry brush.

We re-entered the jungle and moved along quick and quiet, nervously scanning the dark shadows on either side of the trail. Nothing happened for a while and I began to feel a little better, except for the heat. The jungle canopy kept it in like an oven and it drew the energy out of you. I'd emptied three of the four canteens I was carrying, and some guys were already bumming water, guys that had either been too stupid or too lazy to pack enough. Fortunately, though, we didn't encounter any enemy and we finally found the road.

When they reached the road, the file just stopped. We stood around for about ten minutes while the Captain and his people inspected it. Then they brought up the rest of us. We pushed through some thick bushes and vines and then we kind of stumbled out into it. It was like we entered something, like a room. As big as a two-lane country road, and made of packed earth, it was covered by the roof-like, thick canopy of jungle.

Small groups of guys stood around on the tamped red earth, talking softly, while others climbed up into the jungle on either side and poked around. Everyone was walking stiffly and awkwardly, not wanting to put their feet down too noisily or too hard, or in the wrong place.

I saw Ron and the others and went over. Glock had the cratering charge sitting on the road beside him. Lieutenant Goodkin and an engineer carried a shape charge. The other guys had disappeared around the curve of the road to plant their charges.

The Engineer looked at Glock. "Take that thing back up there about thirty feet for now, will you?" Glock and Goodkin carried off the cratering charge. The Engineer turned to me. "Give me a hand."

The two of us quickly dug a small hole about a foot deep. We laid the shape charge in and he wired it up to a blasting cap.

"Go over there," he said, indicating where the Lieutenant and the others were. He started tamping the dirt down around the charge.

I joined Glock and Ron in the bushes as one of the shape charges went off around the corner, shaking the ground slightly. Another one boomed. The Engineer climbed up onto the bank of the road, uncoiling some thick white wire from a spool as he went. We heard small arms fire from around the bend. Goodkin got on the radio. A drop of sweat dangled from the tip of his pointy nose. The engineer blew our charge and a small cloud of black smoke drifted down the road. A moment later the firing stopped. We looked out into the brush, watching for movement.

"Everybody," Lieutenant Goodkin said, "come here."

"What's up, Lieutenant?" Glock asked as we crowded around.

"Fourth Platoon got caught out on the road. They have some dead and wounded. They estimate there's a company-sized force of enemy around, with more on the way. So, be real careful from here on out, okay?"

We moved off into the bush. We passed a little clearing and I saw Grimaldi and his people inspecting the still-smoking hole their shape charge had made. It looked like it'd been dug with a post hole digger. Ahead, Captain DeVoors, the Top Sergeant, Ted, and some of the CP guys, huddled together, talking softly. On the ground around them lay a half dozen guys. One was obviously dead, with a towel draped over his face. A medic was working on another guy. Three others lay on makeshift litters and another sat against the dirt bank with a white bandage wrapped tightly around his head, covering his eyes. About a dozen other guys lined both sides of the road, facing out into the jungle in a loose perimeter.

Captain DeVoors looked up when he saw Lieutenant Goodkin. "I'm taking you with us," he said. "I'm leaving two squads with the Engineers to help them finish up. But you and I will make sure the wounded are medevaced."

"Yes, Sir," Lieutenant Goodkin said. He looked over at the guys laying on the makeshift litters.

The Captain poked Lieutenant Goodkin in the chest. "I want your platoon out front; your people are in better shape than anybody else's, okay?"

"Yes, Sir," the Lieutenant said. "Do you want to start now?"

The Captain shook his head. "They're bringing up some more wounded now. When they get here we go."

"Yes, Sir." Lieutenant Goodkin moved off a bit. He waved us over and looked at Glock. "You take the point."

Glock nodded.

The lieutenant looked at Ron. "I want you right behind him."

Ron smiled in reply.

I heard something and turned to see the other guys arriving. One of them had his arm in a sling. The Lieutenant tapped me on the back. I turned and quickly followed him and Ron and Glock.

We were evidently taking a different route back; I didn't recognize anything. After a half hour, we came to an area dotted with mogul-sized, palm-fern-covered hills. We went over and around them. The light was weak, the way it would be in a house at midday with all the shades down. I was one of the few people who still had a canteen of water left and I shared it with Ron, Bubba, Glock and Chico. We were walking between two small hills when small arms firing erupted somewhere behind us in the middle of the column. Again, the enemy had evidently let most of our column pass before they hit us.

We flattened ourselves against the ground and listened to the firing.

Every now and then I'd hear angry hornets whizzing through the brush and then I realized with shock that they were stray rounds. I wondered when they were going to blow the cratering charges. Why were they taking so long, I wondered? Every time someone got wounded or killed I felt as if my turn was coming closer.

Somebody tapped me on my leg. It was Ron. I followed him over to where the Lieutenant knelt, talking into the radio.

The Lieutenant put the handset down and turned to us. "The middle of the file is pinned down. I want you two to work your way up this ridge and drop some M-79 rounds in on the enemy position, okay?"

I nodded. My mouth was so dry I would've croaked if I tried to say anything.

Ron pursed his lips as he looked over the Lieutenant's shoulder at the map. The Lieutenant tapped his finger emphatically at a smudge of ridge lines. "The Captain figures they're here. He thinks he's pinpointed them."

Ron stared at the map and said nothing. Lieutenant Goodkin handed it to him. "Take this with you and help direct Carl's fire."

Ron nodded.

We started up the ridge and I felt strange. I thought of my theory and how everything that had happened so far could have been faked. I suddenly felt like I was a boy again, playing war games. I noticed the cartoonish, turtle-ish way Ron looked and moved. He pulled his head into his collar and hunched over under the big shell-like curve of the ruck. Under the green helmet he looked like a turtle. I saw him swallow a couple of times the way a turtle does, his Adam's apple moving up and down slowly, and I laughed. He looked at me like I was crazy.

We reached an opening in the brush and Ron stopped. Below us, the firing continued. Crouching down, I waited while Ron peered at the terrain below. He ducked back down and studied the map. Finally, he pointed to a spot where the bushes seemed a slightly lighter shade of green.

"Try there," he said. "Put a couple rounds in there."

It appeared to be about fifty meters distant and I flipped the sight up and adjusted it accordingly. The first round went high and I moved the slide on the sight down a little. The next one was right in there.

"Good," he said. He looked behind us nervously. "Put some more in there now."

I started popping the rounds down there as fast as I could reload, maybe one every five seconds or so. *Crash, crash, crash!* I could see the wispy puffs of black smoke rising up. I laughed and a round went wild.

Ron grabbed my shoulder and his angry face looked into mine. "Be cool," he hissed, "be cool."

I laughed again, I don't know why, and Ron's face twisted in disbelief. I put another half dozen rounds into the light green area.

When we came back down they were all sitting or crouching, looking out. Lieutenant Goodkin slapped Ron on the back and reached out and patted me on the shoulder. "They managed to disengage," he said, "you did it!"

Ron and I looked disbelievingly at each other.

"Take five," the Lieutenant said, "and eat something. The Captain wants us to hold here for a while."

Ron and I sat down. I took a swig of water and wondered when the next flare-up would come.

CHAPTER 15

The light was growing weak as the column snaked along. We moved slowly because of the wounded but, despite that, people were beginning to stumble and make noise. Hardly anybody had any food left. Bubba gave me some canned cake. I ate it as we walked, but it was so dry I barely managed to get it down. We were still a half day from the firebase when the column stopped again. Everybody was so tired and thirsty they sprawled on the ground. As we stared into the shadows, Lieutenant Goodkin walked over to Bubba. "We're taking the point now. I want you up front."

Bubba nodded grimly and got to his feet.

The Lieutenant turned to the rest of us. "We're going to a hill about a klick from here. When we get to the top we'll medevac the wounded out." The Lieutenant looked at me. "I want you behind Bubba."

I got to my feet wishing he'd forget about me for a while. It was always "you go up there," or "I want you here." I wished he would pick somebody else for a change.

I took my place behind Bubba. Chico, Ron, Glock and the Lieutenant followed along behind us as we made our way to the head of the column. I was very tired, but some of the guys we passed looked a lot worse than me, especially the ones carrying the litters, and I felt a little guilty.

We spent about twenty minutes crossing some flat land and then we picked up a trail at the bottom of a ridge and started up. About halfway up, the undergrowth grew very thick and the trail turned out to be a zigzagging game trail that we had to squeeze ourselves through. Visibility was very bad. The ridge grew steep and it was a tough climb. I was following closely behind Bubba when he suddenly fired a burst on automatic and backed up into me, knocking me down. We crawled behind some tall bushes.

I was dizzy from the crack on the head he'd given me. "What was it?" I said. As I spoke I could taste blood.

Bubba looked up anxiously through the bushes. "Enemy. I damn near stepped on one of them when I came through that bush."

I wiped away the blood pouring from my nose. "What should we do now?"

"I don't know, Carl." We looked down the hill behind us.

The Lieutenant, Ron and the others peered anxiously over some bushes back up at us. "How many?" the Lieutenant mouthed silently.

"I saw three," Bubba whispered softly, "and I think I got one."

Lieutenant Goodkin picked up the horn to report to the Captain. Bubba and I turned and continued looking up through the bushes. I wondered what they were doing up there, and how many there were. If it hadn't been for Bubba's wide back, I finally might have seen one.

We waited a while longer and I heard a little sound that took me back to when I was a kid. We had just taken refuge behind some bushes during the rock fight with the black kids. This was the same sound, a little clipping noise, as something came through the leaves overhead.

I turned to Bubba and frowned. A rock? Of all the crazy things . . . they were throwing a rock!

Bubba looked at me blankly, then realization twisted his features. "Grenade!" he yelled.

I turned to dive out of the way when a flash of light and sound picked me up, rolling and pummeling me like a huge wave. I landed against some bushes. I didn't know where Bubba was.

I was lying on my back and my ears were ringing. For a moment I couldn't move. Then I turned my head and saw my M-79 a few inches away. I grabbed it. The stock was split and the end of the barrel seemed misshapen. Lieutenant Goodkin and Ron were looking down at me. "Are you okay?" the Lieutenant asked.

"Yeah." I tried to get up.

"Wait, wait," the Lieutenant said, "let the medic look at you." He turned away. "How's Bubba?" he said to somebody.

"He's dead," came the reply.

I turned and looked in the other direction and saw them bent over Bubba. It didn't seem possible to be talking to the guy one minute and to hear that he was dead the next. I felt sleepy all of a sudden.

The same pudgy-faced medic I'd seen earlier looked down at me and smiled. "Where do you hurt, man?"

I thought for a minute, but I couldn't feel any pain. "I don't know. My foot is cold."

He nodded and helped me to a sitting position.

I saw that my left boot had come off, my sock, too. The left pant leg was torn and frazzled in the back. The medic turned my leg. It felt numb. It was hard to get a good look at the wound, but there appeared to be some deep scars in the calf.

"You caught some shrapnel down there," he said, "but the artery seems okay. C'mon and let's get a bandage on it."

He quickly tied a square cotton bandage to my leg and, together with Chico, helped me stand up. I felt okay, but my leg was numb, and my foot pointed toe first down at the ground, despite what I tried to make it do. I lowered it flat on the dirt and tried to put some weight on it and I almost screamed from the pain. It was sharp as a knife.

"Let's sit him back down for a minute," said the medic.

I looked around at the others. Lieutenant Goodkin was talking on the radio. Ron and Glock knelt and talked as they looked up to where the grenade had come from. What were they doing, I thought. We had to get out of here. I heard some firing and turned to see Glock spraying the bushes with his weapon like he was watering them with a hose. He turned and smiled and mortar rounds began falling all around, erupting into thunderous orange mushrooms.

The Lieutenant yelled at us to get to the bottom of the ridge. I started crawling as fast as I could. Ahead of me, two guys carried a wounded guy on a litter and then they were gone in a flash of orange fire and black smoke. Gunfire roared all around us. As I crawled, I prayed the bullets wouldn't find me. Somebody grabbed me and helped me to my feet. It was Lieutenant Goodkin and Chico. They helped me hobble down the slope. Captain DeVoors was down there, his face flushed and wild-looking. He grabbed some guy that ran by him, whipping him around.

"Out there," he screamed at the guy, "put some fire out there!" The guy got down on one knee and fired a magazine into the bushes. The

156

Captain turned away for a moment and the guy got up and ran off. I heard a little LOH helicopter overhead. Through a small opening in the trees, I watched it make a fast, banking turn. The Captain talked loudly into the radio as the chopper continued to circle. Someone said it was a Colonel from Battalion Headquarters directing the action.

A bunch of guys came running down the slope toward us. Captain DeVoors put down the handset. "Hold it!" he shouted. "Form a line here!" He lined them up facing into the jungle. "Now put some fire out there!"

Lieutenant Goodkin and Chico helped me to a clearing about fifty feet away where the wounded were gathered. The others wore bloodied, raggedy bandages, but they could all stand on their own.

Chico helped me sit. The Lieutenant walked off to where Ron, Glock, the Fourth Platoon Lieutenant and Sergeant Brucker, the Fourth Platoon's NCO, and some other guys were having a powwow. I wondered what they were planning.

The medic walked up to me. He smiled and knelt to look at my leg. "Your bandage is gone," he said apologetically, "and I don't have another one to give you."

I saw that he was right, but I didn't care. The thing that worried me was that none of the wounded guys knew me, and I was afraid they'd run off and leave me if something happened.

Up on the ridge, the firing was dying down. Lieutenant Goodkin came over. "I understand your weapon was damaged?"

I nodded.

He took his .45 from its holster and handed it to me.

"Thanks." I put it in my pocket.

Not far away, the Captain sat alone with his head in his hands. Everybody kept a distance from him. I'd never liked the guy, but I felt sorry for him now.

Lieutenant Goodkin turned to the medic. "Okay, let's get going."

Chico threw me a wink as he and two other guys started down the trail. The wounded followed closely behind. Lieutenant Goodkin and the medic helped me to my feet and we joined the column. Some guys from another platoon took up the rear.

"Where's Ron and Glock?" I asked the Lieutenant.

"I sent them and six other guys back to the road," he said. "The engineers got pinned down and haven't been able to blow the cratering charges."

After we'd hiked for a while I didn't hear any more firing. It was getting dark. The trail straightened and I spotted Chico up on point. The sight of him made me feel safer.

It became too dark to go any farther. Lieutenant Goodkin had some of the guys form a protective perimeter, while the others cleared the ground of rocks and brush so we could sleep. There was hardly any food or water left and we were all very hungry. Somebody passed me some food. It was too dark to see what it was, but I think it was a slice of pork roll and I gulped it down. One of the newer guys claimed that you could get water from bamboo and they started hacking the stuff down. The medic gave me a six-inch section of bamboo as wide around as a shot glass. There was enough water in it to take my mind off my thirst.

Everybody was edgy and nobody had any sleeping gear; we just lay on the ground. The guy next to me said that the enemy had brought tanks up on the road. One of the wounded had a crying jag sometime in the night and the Lieutenant spent an hour trying to quiet him. Another time I woke to hear disembodied voices whispering nervously about movement. I took out the .45 and listened closely. After about twenty minutes nothing happened and I fell back to sleep.

When I woke everybody was talking about the water we'd drank. Chico gave me another section of bamboo. Inside, about a dozen little, black bugs swam around. I wondered how many I'd drank the night before, but I didn't really care. Now, like everybody else, I just picked them out and drank it anyway. There was no food.

We moved out and headed for a hill the Lieutenant had chosen for the helicopter to land. The sound of two distant explosions reached us. Everybody looked around nervously.

Lieutenant Goodkin got a call on the radio. He held his hand over the mouthpiece and smiled. "They blew the road," he said.

A few guys cheered but most seemed not to care. I was proud that Ron and Glock were back there and had helped them do it. I hoped they'd catch up with us before we were medevaced. I really wanted to see them and congratulate them.

We got to the top of the little hill without incident. It was covered with a lot of bamboo and elephant grass.

Lieutenant Goodkin called to Chico, "Get a couple of guys and start clearing all this bamboo away." Then Lieutenant Goodkin got on the radio and started calling for the chopper.

Chico turned to the others. "Okay, you heard the Lieutenant. Let's get chopping."

It took them a half hour to knock all the bamboo and grass down. It lay in a tangled mess, about knee high. Just as they were finishing, we heard faint "thock-eh-ta, thock-eh-ta" sounds in the distance. The wounded guys looked around, licking their lips. Soon I could hear the chopper clearly and realized that the enemy could too.

Lieutenant Goodkin kept his ear pressed to the handset as he watched us. "Get ready to pop smoke," he said.

Some guy pulled a smoke canister from his web belt.

"Pop smoke!"

A shower of sparks issued from the bottom of the can along with the yellow smoke, which was already drifting across the hill in a low cloud. He dropped it and it ignited the chopped-down bamboo and litter. Flames spread and gray smoke mixed with the yellow smoke from the grenade. By this time the chopper was in sight, making a wide sweeping turn to come in against the wind. I yelled to the Lieutenant that the bamboo was on fire, but he didn't hear me. A moment later the chopper was above us, its downdraft fanning the flames. The wounded surged forward, hoping to pull themselves aboard, but the pilot had seen the fire and wouldn't land. One of the wounded guys grabbed onto the skid and pulled himself up, wrapping his legs around it. He hung on with closed eyes as the flames licked up at him.

Lieutenant Goodkin and the medic rushed over and pulled him off. The chopper banked slightly and flew off, and we quickly moved upwind of the sooty smoke. As the chopper circled in the distance, Lieutenant Goodkin consulted with the pilot on his radio. Everything was so messed up. It was all on-the-job training. Nobody knew what the heck they were doing. Now the enemy knew exactly where we were and what we were up to. And we were just a gang of wounded and a handful of 'cruits.

Lieutenant Goodkin put down the horn and turned to us. "They spotted a good place to set down not too far from here. We have fifteen minutes to get there." The Lieutenant consulted with Chico and some others as we formed up. With the Lieutenant and the medic on either side of me, I followed the others down the slope. It took us about twenty minutes, but finally we reached the spot, a small hill covered with elephant grass. I couldn't hear the chopper any more and wondered if they'd had to go back to base. For the next few minutes everyone watched and listened anxiously. Finally we heard the chopper and I felt a flood of relief. The Lieutenant ordered everybody into the bushes behind the clearing.

We could hear the chopper racing toward us. Then it suddenly appeared overhead and touched down with a little bouncing dance.

The wounded guys leapt out from behind the bushes and ran for it. They were clambering aboard before Lieutenant Goodkin, the medic and I were even halfway there.

They got me aboard and I heard firing. Our guys were in the bushes, firing out. I heard the ominous "pock pock pock" sounds as enemy rounds struck the metal of the chopper. The door gunner on the left opened up with his M-60 and we flattened ourselves on the floor. The pilot pulled back on his stick and the chopper shuddered. I was afraid he wouldn't get it off the ground with thirteen of us aboard, but, miraculously, we rose slowly, maybe an inch at a time, as I prayed my guts out.

I looked down at Lieutenant Goodkin and the medic and Chico and the others as they followed our ascent with worried eyes. A deep sadness welled up in me. When we were twenty-five feet in the air we began to move forward and I knew we would make it. Five minutes later we were up high and out of danger and I couldn't see them anymore. My sadness lifted and an intoxicating relief flooded through me.

The Aid Station was a madhouse. The tents were jammed with wounded, and some had to be put on cots outside in the shade. There were body bags everywhere and medics running around, yelling, as they loaded and unloaded the choppers. Some of the less seriously wounded sat in groups and talked as they smoked cigarettes and played cards. I lay on a metal table under a big tent that had its canvas sides raised to let in a breeze.

As the doctor looked at my leg I asked the medic why there were so many wounded.

"The enemy hit every American installation in the area," he said as he handed a bandage to the doctor.

"And all at the same time too," added the doctor. "They're calling it the Post-Tet offensive." The doctor rubbed something wet into my wound and bandaged it up.

I sat up and looked at him. "Are you sending me to Dak-To?" I said. They had a medical facility there. Maybe I could get out to visit Chantal.

The doctor didn't even look at me as he spoke to the medic. "Tag him for McGernity."

They put me on another chopper for the ride to McGernity. Both doors were rolled back and a wonderful cool breeze washed through the moment we lifted off. There was only me, and four body bags aboard. They lay on the floor like green mummies. I looked up at the Pilots who were chatting calmly as they watched the instruments and the terrain below. I looked back at the body bags and wondered who they were. My back hurt and I wanted to lean against the bulkhead but they were in the way. I wondered if they were still warm or if they had grown cold and stiff like bodies are supposed to get after awhile.

I touched the nearest body bag. Supposedly they were made by DOW chemical company, the same people who made Saran Wrap for sandwiches. I thought of that commercial about Saran Wrap, "sealing in the freshness," and another cold blade of guilt stabbed through me. I tried to stop thinking such things, but I couldn't. It was like the time Ron and them got caught in the barbed wire up on Firebase 15 and I couldn't stop laughing. Once my mind got fixed on something, it didn't want to move on.

I read the tag on the nearest body bag—Brook O'Brian, PFC. I stared at it, puzzled for a moment. Then, sadly, it dawned on me—it was

Beobee. He had told me the meaning of his initials so long ago that I had forgotten. He had "Esquire" or "the third" or something, tacked to the end, but to the Army he was just "Brook O'Brian, PFC."

I looked away. Beobee used to get on my nerves, but I'd really gotten to like him. I moved as far away from him as I could and looked out. We had left the jungle behind and now flew over a reddish plain, approaching some distant buildings. Off to the left I saw a small spotter plane taking off from a runway. We descended, passing between some tall warehouses. I looked out the other door to see what was on that side and caught sight of a guy wearing a pair of red swim trunks, frozen in the middle of a really beautiful jackknife dive. He plunged into a pool of blue water, around which guys sat in deck chairs, cans of beer in their hands. It was the pool they had been talking about putting in when I'd first come in-country.

A building flashed past, blocking my view, and then we landed in a courtyard on a concrete landing pad painted with a big red cross. There was no one to help me out of the chopper, and I edged off the floor and lowered myself to the grass. The pilots turned off the turbines and started winding down. Across the way, a set of double doors banged open and a nurse raced out pushing a wheelchair. She helped me into the chair and pushed me to the building and through the doors.

Inside, doctors and medics in blood-smeared green outfits rushed around. With a quick movement, the nurse swept a dampened string of blonde hair out of her eyes and said, "Let's get you on a gurney."

I was trying to hoist myself up when she lifted me onto the gurney herself. Working quickly, she pulled my shirt off and cut my pants away with a pair of scissors. When I saw how skinny I'd become, I was embarrassed. She jabbed a needle in me and that was the last thing I remembered for a while.

Somebody was shaking me. I opened my eyes. An Air Force Major looked down at me. The lights were on and it was dark outside. I had no idea what time it was.

"You're flying out tomorrow," he said.

A feeling of deep longing came over me. "Home?"

He looked surprised. "Oh, no. You're going to Japan."

"Oh." I'd hoped to recuperate here at McGernity. It was only about fifty miles to Dak-To and that would have meant that Chantal could visit me. I was about to say as much to him, but I felt odd, very tired and very calm. I realized that I had already been operated on and was still feeling the effects of the anesthesia.

There were ten beds in the room, five on each side. In the bed next to mine, the last one on my side of the room, there was a guy in a full body cast. He looked like King Tut's mummy, except that one of his legs was raised in traction. Two guys in pajamas shuffled down the aisle toward me. One of them was on the fat side, probably a Base Camp Commando. The other was thin and wiry. His nose was long and reddened and his ears curled around, giving him a kind of rodent-like appearance. They stood at the foot of the mummy's bed and looked down at him.

The fat guy nodded to me. "You know who's bunking next to you?"

I shook my head.

He smiled like I was supposed to know the guy or something. "Charley."

"Charley who?"

"Charley, man! Victor Charley, VC, an enemy."

I turned and looked to see if he was right, but I couldn't see the mummy's eyes. His bed was up too high. I had never seen a live enemy and I had to get a look. I raised myself and saw that it was true.

The two guys came around to the side of the VC's bed and looked down at him. His eyes jumped around like two little live things trying to detach themselves and escape.

The rodent-looking guy turned to me. "We're gonna kill him tonight." He bent down to the VC. "Tonight you die."

"Are you serious?" I said.

He gave me an angry look. "Damn right, I'm serious."

I shook my head.

"What?"

I continued to shake my head. "You ain't killing anybody who's laying wounded in bed while I'm here." I wondered if I should tell one of the medics. I looked around but I didn't see anyone. The fat guy smiled as if it had all been a big joke, but the little rodent guy was still looking at me like I was crazy. I kept shaking my head.

They both stared at me for a minute and then sirens sounded in the distance. The lights went out and a dim, red emergency light came on, casting angry shadows. Two medics ran in. "Under your beds!" they shouted. "Quick! Everybody under their beds." They helped me get under my bed and left the VC in his.

The attack lasted about ten minutes, the rockets booming like thunder. I prayed there wouldn't be a ground attack. I didn't have a rifle and I couldn't walk. I'd be a sitting duck. Finally it was over. The nurse helped me back into bed and gave me another shot. Just before I passed out, I told her they were going to try and kill the VC. She asked me who was going to try and I told her I couldn't say, but that they were going to try tonight. Then I passed out.

When they woke me in the morning for my flight, I saw with relief that he was still alive.

We were to fly out of Vietnam in a huge Air Force jet, a C-141. They carried us up the ramp in the back and hung the litters we lay in from these wire racks that resembled a bunch of coat-hangers hooked together, one litter suspended over another, three high. There was only about six inches of space between the tip of my nose and the bottom of the litter above me. The post-Tet offensive had been pretty bad. There must have been a hundred wounded on the flight.

The moment the jet lifted off, everybody started whistling and cheering like a bunch of idiots. All it would've taken would have been one SAM missile and we would've all been right back down on the ground again. I would save my cheering until we got to at least twenty thousand feet. I asked the nurse to tell me when we got that high, but I fell asleep. They must have been pumping a pretty powerful sedative through my IV because I was out like a light until they carried us down the ramp in Japan.

CHAPTER 16

It rained as they drove us to the 9th Field Hospital, on the outskirts of Tokyo. They used the same hanging litter arrangement on the buses, as on the plane. But in spite of being flat on my back, and not being able to see much, I could still feel a big difference between this place and Vietnam. Part of it was the wonderful damp chill in the air, but mostly it was the noise. The noises here were safe noises—horns honking, the tick of engines idling at a traffic light, a police whistle—noises that made you want to cry. It really was something. Nobody said a word, but I know the others were blown away by the feeling, too. I saw the reflection of the guy below me in the window glass. He was a gut wound with a lot of tubes and bags attached to him. He couldn't move, but his eyes were darting here and there at the colorful blurs of car brake lights and traffic lights in the wet streets.

They put me in Ward Three. There was a big window behind my bed. It had stopped raining. I turned and stared out. After a while I felt like I was floating over the complex of hospital buildings. Then I was hovering over the busy streets of Tokyo, then sailing out over the distant plains to where Mount Fuji rose up covered with white snow. Its pure, white form soothed the pain and noise in my head the way the sound of the wind or the surf would, and it put me into a sort of trance.

"It's beautiful, isn't it?" It was the guy in the next bed. He had been sleeping when I arrived. I nodded and then looked back out at the mountain.

"You know," he said, "the Japanese worship that mountain."

"I can see why." I continued to stare at it. It was so calming. I'd never seen anything as peaceful and pure as that in Vietnam. I turned away from the window.

"What's your name?" he asked.

"Carl Melcher. Call me Carl."

He sat up against his headboard. "I'm Jack Krouse. They call me a lot of things around here, but you can call me Krouse."

He looked my age. He was on the pudgy side, and his hair was greased and curled up into a little pompadour. He had bright, playful eyes, and he looked like a wise-cracker, the kind of guy who was always playing tricks on people.

Another guy came in and sat at the foot of Krouse's bed. Krouse introduced him as Greg Mills. Greg was tall, about six foot, with blond hair and blue eyes, the good-looking surfer type who gets his pick of the girls when he goes to a dance or to the beach.

"Wow," Greg said. "Must be a mile of bandage on your leg."

"Yeah," Krouse said, almost jealously, "it must really be messed up. What happened?"

"Grenade. They had to remove a lot of muscle tissue." I was about to tell them how the grenade had killed Bubba but I didn't go into it. It was too depressing. I wondered how Ron and the others were taking it.

"Will you regain the use of it?" Greg asked.

"Oh, yeah. There's no bone damage. That's what they said in McGernity. They said I should be walking on it in a month."

Krouse rubbed his lower lip thoughtfully. "Hmm, I think you have the proverbial million dollar wound there, pal."

"Oh, yeah?"

Krouse inspected my leg as if silently calculating the time of my recovery. In its swath of bandages the leg had the shape of a python that had just swallowed a basketball.

"How long have you guys been here," I asked.

"Not long enough," Greg said, laughing.

"Same here," Krouse said. "If we could manage to stay here for six more months we could go home. But that's pretty unlikely."

"What happened to you?"

Krouse reached around to pat his buttocks. "A piece of shrapnel in the left cheek. I was in a convoy to Phan Thiet when the enemy ambushed us. We didn't have a chance. They hit us with everything they had for about a minute. Mortars, machine guns, B-40's. We had fifty percent casualties. I ended up in a rice paddy with the dead body of the

166

guy that'd been sitting beside me." He shook his head and looked out the window.

I looked at Greg. He lifted his pant leg to reveal a scattering of shallow-looking wounds, like he'd been hit with buckshot. "Shrapnel from a B-40 rocket," he said.

The swinging door at the end of the ward banged open and a baby-faced orderly entered. He walked hurriedly down the aisle, looking back over his shoulder every now and then. When he was almost to the other end, the doors he'd come through banged open again and another orderly with a kid's face walked in. The first one giggled loudly and rushed out the doors. The second grew red-faced when he saw us watching him, then laughed and gave pursuit.

Jees! They looked so young. I was reminded of the beginning of my senior year at East when my buddies and I would see the new, rosy-cheeked freshmen wandering wide-eyed through the halls.

As the pursuer went out the far door, Krouse shook his head disdainfully. "One of them's named Chip. We call the pair of them 'Chip and Dale,' like the cartoon characters."

Greg nodded.

The doors banged open again and the two of them entered the ward pushing carts full of lunch trays.

"The smaller, chubby one is Chip Taylor," said Krouse.

Chip was about my size, with blond hair and blue eyes and big rosy cheeks that were kind of chipmunk-ish. Greg told me that Dale's real name was Alfred Deavers. He was about two inches taller than Chip, thinner, with light, brown hair and brown eyes. He had prominent incissor teeth.

The two of them moved down the aisle, having a "did so, did not," kiddy-type of argument as they distributed the trays. I smiled as I recalled the *Chip 'N' Dale* cartoons I'd watched as a kid, with the two chattering, ever-so-reasonable chipmunks. There certainly was a resemblance.

Krouse turned to me. "They never advanced beyond puberty."

We fell silent for a moment. "How're your wounds doing?" I asked after a while.

167

Krouse shook his head and stared at the floor. "Unfortunately, great." He looked to Greg who nodded in agreement. "Pretty soon they'll try and transfer us up to Ward Nine."

"So?"

"Ward Nine is more of an army barracks than a hospital," said Greg calmly. "They have physical training, rifle drill, dress inspections, formations, the usual stateside stuff. They even get weekend passes."

"That last part sounds pretty good," I said.

"Of course it does," Krouse said. "It's supposed to. That's the bait."

"What do you mean?"

"When you've been laying around here long enough, you'll know."

Greg nodded. "It gets pretty boring around here."

"Boring?" said Krouse, "it's worse than that. All you got to do is play Gin Rummy with the other dummies. After the first week you get to thinking about the Ginza and those cute little, Japanese girls, and that puts your head in a whirl, so you be a good little wooden-headed soldier and take your medicine, go to physical therapy and stay on the dime, get stronger and better and transfer to Nine, then the Army says, 'game's over pal, your butt is mine . . . ' "

He was getting his anger out in a sort of singsong tirade and Greg let him go on.

"The green machine got you, man; they hold all the aces. Those dummies in Nine are goin' to dangerous places; they're in such a hurry to go out and play; the enemy'll get another chance to blow them away."

He was red-faced and breathing hard. "Stupid idiots!"

"You think about that stuff too much," said Greg, smiling at me. "Take a deep breath and hold it."

Krouse glared at him.

I felt like I should try and help calm him, too. "Well, you never know," I said softly, "the war could wind down in a few months. The Paris Peace talks are still going on as far as I know." I thought about all the guys I knew who had died or gotten blown up or shot while the so-called leaders were sitting in Paris talking peace and I began to get upset myself.

Krouse's eyes were wild-looking. "Maaannnnn," he said slowly, "winding down or winding up, it don't make any difference to me. I'm not going back there to bleed to death in some rice paddy."

I didn't say anything further to him. How could he say he wasn't going back? He'd only done one week in Nam. He was healing and he had more than eleven months left to his tour. What choice did he have?

I was probably going back too. I just hoped that by the time I got back things would have calmed down. Maybe when I got back it would be like the old days on Firebase 29 with Ron and Glock. I really missed those guys. We'd been through so much together. Maybe if I went back I could get down to see Chantal. Maybe I could somehow spend my R&R in Dak-To with her.

A bunch of doctors and medics entered the ward. They started four beds down from us, consulting charts and talking to the patients. One of the Doctors paused at my bed. He was about fifty, with a kindly face and a bald spot on his head the size of your hand. He looked at my chart, then glanced over at Krouse and Greg. He smiled. "Is Captain Avery taking good care of you, Krouse?"

Krouse smiled playfully. "Yes, Sir. He certainly is, Sir."

By the doctor's tone of voice, and by the way Krouse called him "Sir," I knew this was some kind of game they played. The doctor put my chart back and introduced himself as Captain Walker. He unwrapped the bandages on my leg. It was the first time I'd seen it since the operation. There were two good sized holes in it and the exposed red flesh looked like the steaks you'd see wrapped in plastic at the supermarket.

Dr. Walker took a long look at it. "It'll be at least two more weeks before we can sew it closed. The tissue will have to build back up first."

"How long before I'll be able to use it?"

"A month, maybe less."

He moved to the other side of the ward and one of the medics in his party stayed to bandage it. Krouse and Greg watched the medic work. When he left they came closer.

"How long were you in Nam, Carl?" Krouse asked.

"About six months."

He looked at Greg and nodded his head thoughtfully. "He should make it back to the States."

"You think so?" Greg asked.

Krouse nodded again.

"How do you figure that?" I said.

Krouse looked at me. "If by the time you're healed you have less than five months left to your original tour, they send you back to the States."

"That's right," Greg said. "I've been here a month and I've seen a lot of wounds. With a leg like yours I'd say you have a pretty good chance of going home."

"Yeah," I said, "but if it heals in less than a month like he just said, that gives me more than five months left." These guys always made these things sound so easy, too easy for a peon PFC.

Krouse gave me a look like I was crazy. "Look, you're right, it is kind of iffy in your case. The really bad cases get sent straight back to the States if they can travel. But cases like yours . . ." He shook his head again and leaned closer. "I'm telling you, man, they're not sure. It all depends on how quickly you mend or . . ." He looked at Greg then leaned closer to me. ". . . or how slowly you mend. You dig?"

I didn't say anything. I knew guys in basic training who pulled all kinds of stunts to get discharged, like taking drugs or acting crazy. I figured that was their business, but I could never do anything like that. I'd gone through Basic and Infantry School and five months of Nam because I wouldn't cheat like that. Either my leg healed and they sent me back, or it didn't. If I went back I would be with Ron and Glock again, and I might get to see Chantal. It was up to my damn leg and my karma and that was that.

"We'll see," I said. "How long were you in Vietnam, Greg?"

He laughed. "About six weeks."

"Wow," I said.

Krouse sat up on the edge of his bed. "Yeah, we're a couple of crusty old vets."

I laughed. "Dig it. Where were you stationed?" I asked Krouse.

"The Delta."

"I heard it was pretty bad down there," I said.

"Well, for one week it was, that I can tell you. I believe ninety percent of the civilians were VC and about eight percent VC sympathizers."

"Really? Up in the Central Highlands, the civilians were okay." I thought of Chantal and all the little ragamuffin kids.

"Jees," Krouse said, "there's no such thing as a civilian in the Delta. I kid you not. I was in-country two days when I went to the market with these two other Johnny-new-guys. We were wandering around like tourists. Two of the prettiest girls I've ever seen walked up to us selling cold bottles of Coke, right, and these guys buy themselves one. I didn't bother, though. Wasn't thirsty. That evening I saw both those guys on the chopper pad on stretchers. The Coke had been loaded with ground glass, man. Sliced their intestines to spaghetti."

He shook his head sadly and looked out the window at Fuji. We were all silent for a moment and then Greg smiled. "C'mon," he said to Krouse, "let's get Carl a wheelchair and take him on the grand tour, okay?"

"Nah, that's okay," Krouse said, without turning to look at us. "You guys go without me."

"C'mon," I said, trying to coax him. I noticed Greg shaking his head and I said nothing further.

After Greg found a wheelchair for me and we had rolled out of earshot, he said, "Once he gets like that you just have to leave him alone for awhile."

I felt bad about leaving Krouse there. When he wasn't talking about the army or Vietnam he was a lot of fun. He reminded me a little of Lee, at least his troubled side did. But Krouse had a better sense of humor.

Later that evening Krouse had regained his spirits. We played cards and then I wrote my parents. I told them right off that I was okay, no legs or arms missing, so that they wouldn't freak out when they saw the Red Cross stationery. I told them I had shrapnel wounds, but that I'd already been operated on and was healing. Then I wrote a letter to Lieutenant Goodkin. I asked him if he'd had any luck tracking down Chantal. I told him I'd probably be coming back to the field in a month and to give my address to Ron, Glock and Chico, and to tell them to write.

When I finished, Krouse watched me tuck the letters into their envelopes. "Want to send them a picture?" he asked.

"Sure."

He got out his Polaroid and took two shots. I put one in each letter and sealed them.

"Give me your letters," he said. "I'll mail them for you."

"Thanks." I watched him walk off with my letters, his slippers slapping the tile floor.

Later the head nurse came through the ward. She paused at Krouse's bed and gave him two pills. Then she was at my bedside. She gave me a paper cup with my medication in it. She poured some water for Krouse and me, and moved on.

"Look," Krouse said, holding out his hand. He still had the pills she gave him in his palm.

"Aren't you going to take them?"

"I'm saving them for when I really need them." He pulled the night stand drawer open and tossed them in. There were already a couple dozen of them rolling around in there.

I lay back and tried reading but I grew tired and closed my eyes. I luxuriated in the clean sheets and the soft mattress, the warmth and dryness, the quiet. It was strange and wonderful.

Chip and Dale, the orderlies, were at the far end of the ward, collecting the dinner trays. Krouse and Greg played poker on Krouse's bed, crumpled-up dollar bills and silver coins on the blanket between them. I was writing another letter to the Lieutenant. It'd been about a week and I still hadn't heard from him, but I think it took about that long for a letter to reach a line company in Vietnam. I included a note for him to give to Chantal, just in case he'd managed to get her address.

One thing that bothered me was the fact that I hadn't had time to go back to the firebase and get my personals—my binoculars, my radio, my CIB and my pictures. I'd been telling Krouse and Greg about the squad and wished I could have shown them some pictures. My favorite was of Ron and Glock boxing at the bridge, Glock with this forced, grim expression on his face, and Ron, smiling and, for once, without his sunglasses on, while all around them the raggedy-clothed little kids jumped and mimicked.

I looked up and saw Chip and Dale coming closer. "Be careful," I said to Krouse and Greg, "You better get that money off the bed." We were allowed to play poker, but not for money.

Krouse and Greg went on with their game without looking up. I started a letter to the Battalion Commander. I figured he'd know where everybody was and could get them to write.

"Hey, you're not allowed to gamble on the ward!" It was Chip. He and Dale glared angrily at Krouse and Greg as Greg calmly pocketed the money.

"We're not gambling, idiot," Krouse said. "That was money I owed him."

Chip's red cheeks turned redder. "Who you calling an idiot, war hero."

Chip had evidently expected his taunt to hurt so when Krouse, Greg and I all laughed, he seemed a bit flustered. Dale went back to work, gathering up trays, but Chip lingered in front of the bed.

"I hear you're getting the Medal of Honor," he said to Krouse.

"No," Krouse said, "just the Marksman's Badge."

"For what?"

Krouse had a spoon full of mashed potatoes in his hand. "For this." He flipped a glop of it squarely in Chip's eye.

We laughed.

"Go ahead and laugh," said Chip as he wiped the potatoes away, "but I'm reporting you for gambling." Chip's eyes met mine and narrowed. I had made his enemies' list, but I didn't care. I had tried to stay out of their little feud, but hadn't succeeded. It was inevitable. A lot of it had to do with the fact that we had been to Vietnam and they hadn't.

Krouse and Mills were trying to forestall going back and Chip and Dale knew it. They could never understand why. It was a death sentence for a lot of guys. But to Chip and Dale and people like them, Krouse was like some lazy guy trying to get out of KP or something. As I watched Chip and Dale walk off, I realized that Vietnam had made us totally different from them, like night from day, and we would never be the same again.

Later, the medic was busy anesthetizing my leg with a needle while I looked away. Across from me, Greg sat on Krouse's bed, listening to the little radio I'd bought at the PX. Krouse was off somewhere. There was a card game going on two beds down. At the end of the ward a couple of guys stood around in their bathrobes, rapping.

My wound was now numb and I turned to watch the medic push a curved needle through the skin with a pair of long-nose pliers. It left a little dot of blood where it entered and exited. As he pulled the thread through I felt no pain. It was like he was sewing a sock I was wearing, and not my leg. After he finished, the Japanese lady who worked on the ward came by with the mail cart. There was a letter from my sister, but nothing from the Lieutenant or the squad.

Krouse returned and leaned against his bed.

Greg pulled the radio earplug out. "What's up?"

"This," Krouse said. He looked around furtively, and then removed a moist, stained cotton swab from the pocket of his bathrobe. "This is up. It may just up your temperature a little. I managed to get it off a drinking fountain over by Ward One."

"Oh," Greg said.

"What's the big deal about Ward One?" I asked.

"Malaria."

Chip and Dale entered the ward by the far doors.

"Be careful," I said.

Krouse turned to watch them. When Chip bent down to grab one of the trays, Krouse lifted his bathrobe aside and inserted the swab through the sutures of his wound. He smiled. "The Lord helps those who help themselves."

Chip looked over. His nose twitched a little, as if he suspected something. He watched us suspiciously for a few moments and then continued working. Krouse offered the swab to Greg, who shook his head.

"What's the matter?"

Greg shrugged. "It wouldn't do me any good anyway."

"What do you mean?"

"They're transferring me up to Ward Nine."

"Jees!" Krouse said loudly. A few heads turned our way. Ignoring them, Krouse slammed his hand down on the night table.

"Isn't there anything you can do?" I said.

"No. I already talked to Doctor Sellers about it and it's final."

"That son-of-a . . ." Krouse said. "I swear! Put a doctor in a uniform and he becomes as big a Nazi as any officer."

"It's not his fault," Greg said. "If he could've kept me down here he would have." Greg looked at me and laughed. "I'm just too damn healthy, that's all."

Krouse looked horrified. "You can still do something, man. You gotta keep trying." His voice broke as he gestured at the other guys in the ward, "They'll send these dummies back there, but not everybody. If you're smart you can beat them."

Neither Greg nor I said anything.

Krouse shook his head sadly. "I'm going for a walk."

Greg looked at me and shrugged his shoulders.

"When are you going?" I said.

"Tomorrow."

That was the army, always breaking up friendships. I decided that from now on I would never go out of my way to make friends. It was just too painful.

Greg got up to go. "I'll come around as often as I can."

I nodded.

"Keep an eye on him, Carl?" he said. "I worry about him."

"I will."

CHAPTER 17

Two days after Greg moved up to Ward Nine he came back down for a visit. It was right after dinner.

Krouse looked around slyly and pulled a pint bottle of whiskey from his robe pocket and showed it to Greg.

"All right!" Greg said.

Krouse looked at me. "Carl, do you have a pair of slacks and a sports shirt?"

"No." I'd been living in my robe and pajamas and the thought of buying a shirt or pants had never even crossed my mind.

"I have a shirt that the laundry shrunk that I can loan him," Greg said, "but he'll have to go to the PX and buy himself a pair of slacks."

"What's up?" I asked.

Krouse turned to me with a wild look in his eyes. "We're gonna go out and get drunk."

"Oh yeah?" It was good to see Krouse being his old mischievous self. Then I realized I couldn't go. "I can't get off post."

"You don't have to," Greg said. "We're going to the NCO club. It's on the hospital grounds."

I got on my crutches and went down to the PX to pick out a pair of pants. They had only a half-dozen pairs. There were only two that fit me, a gray pair and an orange pair. I wanted something as far away on the color spectrum from army green as possible so I picked the orange.

I put them on as soon as I got back. Krouse and Greg laughed when they saw them.

"God, they're loud," Greg said.

"Loud don't cover it," said Krouse. He shook his head in wonder. "Jees, Carl, that's the first pair of international orange slacks I've ever seen."

I laughed. They had looked good in the dingy light of the PX, but now I realized they were a bit too much.

The NCO club reminded me of the Student Lounge back at State, high vaulted ceilings, with wood paneling throughout. The walls were hung with lots of the unit's pictures—pictures of people at flag-raising ceremonies, pictures of people receiving awards and such. There was a big mahogany bar at one end of the room, and at the other, a stage. Nickel and dime slot machines lined the walls, and tables and chairs filled out the place.

A Japanese waitress seated us by one of the few windows in the place. She went away and we studied the menus. Five minutes later she showed two guys about our age to the table next to us. When Krouse turned to her she had already started away. "Dag," he said.

"Whistle," Greg said.

"No, that's low class," Krouse said. He waved his hand instead, calling out, "Hey baby . . . over here!"

She turned to us and smiled.

"We'd like to order now, please," Krouse said when she returned.

"Good. I take order, please."

Her English wasn't too good. I ordered brook trout with glazed white potatoes and asparagus. Krouse and Greg ordered ground sirloin steak. She started to walk off again and Krouse touched her on the elbow. "Could you bring us a bottle of white wine with that, please?"

After she left, Krouse stood and poured three shots of whiskey into the water glasses. We drank a toast to the three of us. I didn't like whiskey and had a spasm as it went down. I drank a glass of cold water to get the taste out of my mouth. The waitress soon brought our dinners and the bottle of white wine.

The food was delicious and I relished every bite. Later, after quickly looking around, Krouse took the whiskey bottle out again and took a drink. He extended it to me.

I declined. The wine was enough. I didn't want to get sick.

Krouse poured more whiskey into his and Greg's glasses. I toasted them with the wine I still had. Krouse looked around the club playfully and then poured himself another. He stood and raised his glass. "Here's to the war . . . over one million killed!"

He laughed drunkenly and sat back down. The guys next to us, who had been talking quietly, looked over and smiled.

"Whatsamatter?" Krouse said to them, "it's goin' better than McDonald's, ain't it?"

Greg smiled at them apologetically. "It's okay. He's a Ward Seven patient, you know . . . head case, schizophrenic. Half of him is Green Beret killing machine, the other half San Francisco hippie."

"Head case?" Krouse shouted in mock anger.

The waitress heard him from way over at the bar. She came over to our table.

Krouse poured the last of the wine into my glass. "Would you please bring us another bottle?" he asked.

The waitress smiled politely. "In five minutes I ask, okay." She went two tables over to take a new party's dinner order.

Krouse looked at Greg and shook his head. "I'm gonna miss you, you son of a gun."

"Thanks," Greg said.

"Me too," I said.

"It just ain't fair," Krouse said.

"Leave it," Greg said, "life ain't fair. You should know that by now."

"Damn!" Krouse said. "I can't leave it and neither should you. That's what the problem is. Everybody just goes along with the program."

"Not everybody," I said, "there are some people back home who are trying to change things."

Krouse looked at me, his face red with anger. "You know, Carl, you're too damn trusting for your own good. You better wise up and start looking after yourself before it's too late."

I laughed, taken aback by his anger. I wasn't any more trusting than the next guy. At least I didn't think I was.

Greg frowned at Krouse. "Can't you just forget about that stuff for one night?"

"No," Krouse said loudly. "I can't." He pulled a letter from his shirt pocket and flipped it open. "Listen to this. It's from a friend of mine,

Bud Quint, old Bud the stud. He's going to Burnham College. Listen to how concerned he is. Where was it . . . oh, here. 'Cheryl's old man won't let her go out with me any more. I brought her home from a frat party high as a kite. Cathy's in Boston. I'm trying to scrounge up somebody for the Spring dance. I'm not even sure I can get the old man's Mustang.' " Krouse paused. "The whole letter is fulla crap like that . . . his new Triumph motorcycle, who he saw in concert, where he intends to work when he graduates, just b-s like that. And at the end he asks me if I killed anybody, as if we were all over here lining people up against the walls and shooting them for target practice. I swear to God, when I get back I'm gonna find him and bust him in the chops."

He crumpled the letter in a ball. "Oh, man, look what just walked in."

An older Master Sergeant, skinny, with a pencil-thin, Clark Gable-style mustache, walked over to the bar and consulted with the bartender. Our waitress completed her rounds and made her way back to the bar. She spoke quietly with the Master Sergeant and they both looked over at us.

She came back empty-handed. "Sorry. He say no more." She bowed her head a little. "I very sorry."

Krouse took her hand and looked up at her. "Don't take it so hard, sweetheart," he said.

I started laughing; I couldn't help it.

"You tried," Krouse went on, "and that's what counts."

She looked confused but kept a polite smile on her face.

Krouse turned to us. "She tried, didn't she, fellas?" he said, sounding like the MC at some amateur night talent show. "She really gave it the old college try, right?"

We shook our heads in agreement and she covered her mouth in embarrassed laughter.

Greg looked at his watch. "It's just as well. I have to get back soon."

"What's the matter?" Krouse said.

"We have a formation at seven. If I want a weekend pass I have to be there."

Krouse looked at me and wagged his head high with mock haughtiness. "Well, la de dah."

Greg and I laughed.

Krouse pulled his whiskey bottle out and took a swig. "Well, then, one more drink," he shouted, "one more drink."

He stood and yelled over to the Master Sergeant, "Hey, Sarge, c'mon over and have a drink with us."

An annoyed look crossed the sergeant's face as he tried to ignore him and continue his conversation with the bartender.

"Jack," Greg said, "he's the manager. You want to get us all in trouble?"

Krouse waved his glass at the sergeant. "Hey, lifer. C'mon and have a drink with the troops." The sergeant continued to ignore him, but his face was getting red.

"Let's get him out of here, Carl," Greg said.

We got up to go, but before we could get to him, Krouse had climbed onto the table. The GIs beside us started clapping. "Speech, speech," one of them yelled.

"I wanna propose a toast," Krouse shouted, "to the green machine, and to all the men that keep it well lubricated . . . men like the Master Sergeant."

"Oh, Jees," Greg said.

"Here, here," one of the guys at the next table said. They were egging him on, enjoying the spectacle, as Greg and I tried to get him down off the table.

"Screw the President," Krouse shouted, "screw the Congress, and screw the Army!"

The GIs next to us were almost falling out of their chairs laughing. The Master Sergeant quickly advanced on our table. He ignored Krouse completely and looked at Greg and me. "Get him the hell down from there!"

"Yes, Sergeant," we said in unison. Greg grabbed Krouse around the waist and pulled.

The sergeant glared at Krouse. "All right punk, what's your name?"

Krouse came to a campy kind of attention, looking straight ahead as if he was in a formation on the parade field. "Krouse, Jackson," he shouted, "Private First Class, US60836652, Saarr-gent!"

The sergeant wrote it all down on the back of a business card. He turned to Greg. "What ward is he in?"

My heart sank.

"Ward Three."

He wrote that on the card and put it in his pocket. "Get him the hell out of my club right now or you'll both go on report!"

I followed on my crutches as Greg pushed Krouse along in front of him. Once outside, Krouse seemed to run out of steam. We got him back to the ward without too much trouble, about five minutes before lights out.

We pushed him into the bed and got the covers over him. Krouse opened his eyes. "Greg?"

"What?"

"They're gonna send me back to Nam, man. Sure as hell."

"Go to sleep, Jack."

Krouse looked at me. "Right, Carl?"

"I don't know."

"Hey, Greg?" Krouse said plaintively.

"Yeah?"

"When you goin' downtown?"

"Friday night."

"You gonna get a girl?"

"I'm going to try."

"Well, I ain't gonna make it, so you know what?"

"What?" Krouse said tiredly.

"Give her a kiss for me, will you buddy?"

Greg looked over at me and laughed. He shook his head. "Yeah, okay." He waved me over and I went out the door with him.

Greg paused. "Keep an eye on him, will you, Carl?"

"I will. Don't worry."

Greg smiled sadly and extended his hand. I shook it.

They put the lights out a few minutes after Greg left. I got my radio out of my dresser and put in the ear plug. I looked over at Krouse. He was sound asleep. I got into bed and turned on the radio. Some Japanese newscaster was talking animatedly about something in his own language. I listened to him, fascinated for some reason, and soon fell asleep.

That song, "Lovin' Your Lovin,'" by Steem Masheen, was playing, and the strangest thing happened. It started getting louder and louder and all of a sudden people were sitting up in their beds, looking around.

"Where's that music coming from?" asked the guy two beds down, a concerned frown on his face.

"Got me," his neighbor said.

The music grew louder until everybody in the ward was looking around like they were going crazy. The head nurse and some new guy started dancing out in the main aisle. I saw the Japanese waitress down at the end dancing with Krouse. I felt like I had to get up and move. I left my crutches behind and moved to the beat. The music picked up and I wanted to laugh and cry at the same time. I moved faster and felt something tugging at my leg. The stitches had come loose and a big chunk of flesh flapped up and down. I ignored it, continuing to dance faster and faster and then I felt a burning sensation as it ripped away. It lay on the tile floor and I danced away from it, ignoring the thin red line of blood that poured from my leg.

After our crazy night at the NCO club, it was three weeks before I saw Greg again. He came by to see Krouse once, but I was down at Physical Therapy and missed him. My leg was healing nicely. I'd written four letters to the Lieutenant and still hadn't received any response. I missed Chantal, but it was getting harder and harder to visualize her. One evening as the sunlight faded from the window Greg appeared at the foot of my bed. He was wearing fatigues and looked regular army, not like a hospital patient at all.

"Where's Krouse?" he said.

"He's off on one of his germ-capturing patrols."

"C'mon. Get your crutches and let's go to the PX for a Coke."

We sat in one of the booths. "How's Jack been?" Greg asked.

"Okay. He's been awful quiet, though."

"Really?"

"Yeah. He seems to need to talk a lot about things. But I'm not much of a conversationalist. I don't know what's the matter with me. I just want to read and sleep."

Greg laughed. "Don't worry about it. Some people are quiet and some people talk too much. It all evens out. He worries me, though. He dwells on things too much, and he's so bitter."

"I know." A lot of what Krouse had said over the past weeks had gotten under my skin, and was starting to bother me. He talked a lot about death and about how unfair life could be.

Greg took a swig of Coke. "A lot of what he says makes sense, but what good is saying it? It doesn't make you feel any better."

"I know. So, how're things up on Ward Nine?"

Greg looked off in the distance. "Not too bad. We have formations, inspections, all of that. But it's not as bad as you'd think." He looked at me. "I was going out of my mind doing nothing down here, and now at least I'm busy." He smiled. "I've been downtown the past two weekends. I've gone to the movies, to the dance clubs, rented a car. I even met a girl."

"Really?" All of that seemed unreal to me, like life on another planet. It had been a long time. "What's her name?"

"Noriko."

Noriko. I liked it. The Japanese women all had such beautiful names. I thought about Chantal back in Tin Can City and felt a twinge of sadness. "What's she like?"

"She's beautiful. Really. Not just on the outside, but on the inside, too. She was telling me about affirmations."

"What's that?"

"They're like positive thoughts. It's from a book she's reading. You put them into words and say them aloud. Then they come true."

"Like what?"

"Like, 'I will not go back to Vietnam.' "

"Really?" I tried not to smile, but I couldn't help it. He seemed a little embarrassed. I wasn't trying to be a wise guy, but it was a little bit too much.

"I know it sounds dumb," he said, "but there's something to it, Carl."

I didn't say anything and he went on quickly, as if he had to get it all off his chest.

"You are what you think. That's what they say, you know. Noriko said that if you think positively like that you can change your karma."

I knew a little about karma and you couldn't just change it like you did your underwear. It all sounded too simple, but I really respected Greg so I didn't say anything.

Some redheaded guy wearing a Spec Four patch on his arm approached us. "Are you going down soon?" he asked Greg.

Greg looked at his watch. "Oh, Jees." He turned to me. "I have night shift laundry detail down in the basement. C'mon, I'll walk you back to the ward."

Something brought me out of a deep sleep. The ward was totally dark. A voice cried faintly and pitifully, and my skin crawled as I realized I'd heard it before. It was the same voice that had accosted me as I walked to the showers that night so long ago in Camp McGernity, the same, totally hopeless sobbing. It came from the direction of Krouse's bed. It stopped suddenly. I listened a little while longer and then I fell back to sleep.

Something crashed to the floor and my bed was jerked noisily sideways. The lights were on. Doctor Walker and two medics were leaning over Krouse's bed. Greg stood at the foot of the bed dressed in civies.

"Get him on the floor. On the floor!" Doctor Walker ordered angrily.

Krouse's face was somewhere between beet red and purple. Saliva glistened on his cheek and his open eyes bulged. There was a grotesque, rubbery smile on his face, like one of those Jerry Mahoney ventriloquist dummies.

"Look in the night table," Doctor Walker said.

One of the medics pulled out the drawer and took out a couple of pills. There were only three left. "Seconals and Darvons," he said.

"Damn it," Doctor Walker hissed. He ripped open Krouse's pajama shirt and pounded on his chest. With each thump, saliva bubbled out of Krouse's mouth. The head nurse ran in with a needle and handed it to

Doctor Walker. He jabbed it into Krouse's chest. The swinging doors banged open and Chip and Dale raced in with a heart machine on wheels. After they'd plugged it in, the nurse held the two electrodes to Jack's chest. "Hold!" said Doctor Walker, as he pushed a button. Krouse flopped spastically, like a marionette. Doctor Walker did that about three or four times, with the same effect, and the entire ward was up and crowding around. Doctor Walker looked up suddenly and saw the crowd. "Get them the hell out of the way!"

He continued to pound on Krouse's chest with his balled fists for another five minutes and then slowly got to his feet. Greg hung his head. Everybody was talking excitedly and looking around. I went into the latrine. I couldn't be around anyone and there was no other place to go.

CHAPTER 18

I sat on the bed, reading. I scratched my head and a blizzard of dandruff flakes fell down. It was due to a fungal infection I'd picked up from being out in the field so long without being able to shower. We'd fill up our steel pots with a couple quarts of cold water and wash up that way, but it didn't really do the job.

Someone walked up and sat on the edge of my bed. It was Greg. He had a large manila envelope with him. "How you doing, Carl?"

"Not bad, and you?"

He nodded slowly and forced a smile. "Things are looking up," he said softly. His look grew serious. "How's your leg?"

"Almost healed. Doctor Walker said he's giving me another week down here with the crutches and then I'm going up to Nine with a cane."

Greg frowned and grew silent. I liked Greg. He was one of the most serious, mature guys I'd known since I'd been in the army.

Greg opened the manila envelope and pulled out a stack of letters wrapped with a rubber band. They looked familiar. "You know," he said, "after they took Jack away, the ward nurse went through his night table and found these." He handed them to me. They were all my letters to the company, to the Lieutenant, to Battalion Headquarters. They were all sealed and untouched.

"He never mailed them?"

Greg nodded.

I looked through the letters. I didn't see the ones I'd written to my folks. "This isn't all of them."

"He only kept the ones going to Nam."

I looked at him in a daze. "Why?"

Greg shrugged. "Who knows? I have an idea, though. He was trying to help you make a clean break with all of that, so that you wouldn't want to go back."

It didn't make sense to me. What did "want" have to do with it? Did Greg's not wanting to go up to Ward Nine, and not wanting to go back to Vietnam make any difference? Did Krouse's?

Greg and I stared out the window at Fuji's cold white form. I felt a tiny twinge of relief. I'd been worried about why the squad and the Lieutenant hadn't answered my letters. At least they were okay. I took the letter to Battalion and the one to the Lieutenant and put them up on the dresser. There was no telling where the company was now, but they would find out. I dropped the others in the waste can.

Greg pointed to the letters I had put on the dresser. "You sure you want to send them out?"

I nodded.

"You know, you're still a borderline case. If you really tried you might be able to tip the scales and not go back."

"Maybe." I didn't want to talk about it anymore. It was too depressing. "So," I said, trying to get the topic of conversation off of me and on to him, "have you heard anything about going back to Vietnam?"

"I'm not going back."

"What do you mean?"

"I'm going to Okinawa."

"You're kidding!"

He had a big smile on his face as he shook his head from side to side. I was amazed. He'd only been in Vietnam a month and then a month here. And now Okinawa?

"Pretty lucky, pal," I said.

"Yeah." He laughed. "Noriko says it's the result of having a positive spirit, a positive mind."

I shook my head in wonder. That was the Army for you. There were always a couple of guys who'd get over with incredible luck.

"Well," he said, "you're on your own now. I have to go." He slapped me on the back and extended his hand. "Good luck, man. Take care of yourself."

"Yeah, Greg. It's been great knowing you."

Later, the Japanese lady came by and I asked her if she'd mail my letters for me. I'd felt really low since Greg left, but now, as I watched her walk off with the letters, I felt hope again. Soon I'd hear about Ron and Glock and Chico, and the Lieutenant, and, maybe even Chantal. I couldn't wait.

After Greg left, time seemed to stop. I had no friends and nothing to do but lie around and read, and I was too depressed for that. My world became a quiet, uneventful hell.

Then one day Chip pushed a gurney awkwardly through the far doors. The guy lying on the thing quickly yanked his hand away as one of the doors closed on it. Chip pushed the gurney closer. The wounded guy's head rested on a pillow and he had his two yellow iodine-stained, skinny arms folded behind his head. He looked familiar. When he was about ten feet away I realized he was from my company.

He recognized me and turned to Chip. "Whoa, hold up there. I want to talk to this here fella." Frowning impatiently, Chip stopped the gurney by my bed. The guy smiled at me. He was very skinny and pale and his hair was long and dirty-looking. He reminded me of a painting my parents had of Jesus Christ dragging his cross up a hill.

"You're from company B, aren't you?" he said.

"Yeah. So are you."

"Well, I'll be damned!" He smiled. "We did a patrol together."

"Dig it. What's your name again?"

"Arley Hayes. Yours?"

"Carl Melcher."

Chip started pushing him away and Arley turned to him angrily. "Hold up there, will ya, sport?"

Chip stopped and glared at me.

"We'll have to talk some," said Arley. "You come on over and see me tonight after chow. You hear?"

"I'll be there," I said excitedly. I'd been dying to talk to somebody from the company and here he was! I watched Chip push him away and noted what bed he put him in.

* * *

After they took my meal tray away I went to see Arley. He was tall, too long for the Japanese-sized bed. He extended a skinny hand to me to shake. "Pull up a chair, buddy," he said.

As I sat down, he popped a chaw of chewing tobacco in his mouth. "Wanna plug?"

"No, thanks. When did you get wounded?"

"Last week, up at Ban Me Thuet. A couple Sappers got through the perimeter, but we tore 'em up." He smiled as he chewed happily. A trickle of brown saliva ran from the corner of his mouth. "You got hit on the road, didn't you?"

"Yeah, me and about twenty other guys."

He nodded. "It was bad up on the Firebase, too. They kept hitting us the whole time you were down there."

"Really? I never knew that. I was medevaced out. How's the rest of the company doing?"

"The rest? There ain't hardly any old timers left." He turned and spat into a can on his bedside table. "Yeah, that was bad. And we ain't never had it that bad since." He shook his head in wonder. "The whole time you all were down there, they were trying to get through our wire. I shot three myself. I thought we'd never get off that darn hill."

"What about the guys from the road, how'd they make out?"

"A lot of them did, a lot of them didn't. The Lieutenant was okay, the young one. I forget his name."

"Goodkin."

"That's right, Goodkin. And about twenty others, I don't know their names. They brought back eight bodies."

"Beobee was one of them."

"Yeah. I knew him, a good ole Southern boy."

I nodded. "What about Ron Jakes and Glock?"

"Glock?"

"McLoughlin. We called him, Glock. And Ron Jakes."

"Oh, yeah. We called them Salt and Pepper. Ron was the black fella, right?"

"Yeah."

He shook his head sadly. "They both died down there on that darn road."

I felt dizzy.

"That Puerto Rican fella from New York helped bring their bodies in. What was his name?"

"Chico."

"Yeah. He carried one of them back hisself. He got blown up later, though. Enemy grenade landed in his hole. Lordy, lordy, I thought I'd never get off that darn hill. Are you okay, buddy?"

"Yeah." I got to my feet. I thought I was going to be sick and started for the latrine.

"C'mon over later and we'll play some cards, okay, buddy?"

I waved without turning.

There was a full moon and we could see the submarine out there past the breakers, its stick-like black form floating on the silver sea. We knew they'd be coming and we were all straining our eyes in the dark, watching for them. Would they come in rubber rafts? I wondered. Or would they swim?

The sand was still warm from the sun that had burned down on it all day, and a warm breeze was blowing in off the sea. As I listened to the gentle roar of the breakers, I wondered if I had enough bullets. I asked the guy next to me if he had any extra bullets and he wouldn't answer me. I thought it was Glock but I couldn't be sure. Maybe it was Beobee.

We waited for what seemed like an hour and I looked up and noticed that the disc of moon was higher now. Still, I couldn't see them. Then I heard a shout.

"There's one!" someone said from up in front.

"Where?" another voice said.

"Over there. No, two . . . three of them. Over there, see!"

"There's at least a company of them," Ron said.

Around me the others made a heck of a racket, slamming

magazines into their weapons, releasing the bolts and chambering rounds.

I stared at the surf in the distance and finally I saw their black shapes, scurrying quickly, bug-like, here and there, and then dropping and disappearing for a moment and then scurrying in the other direction. Someone in front of me fired a round at them and then everybody else started shooting. I was trying to get a clear shot between the two guys in front of me. When I finally saw one I pulled the trigger. Nothing happened. I tried again and again but my rifle wouldn't work.

I noticed the others falling back. Not wanting to be left behind, I grabbed my rifle and followed. We ran into an old barracks and up the stairs. Looking down between the wooden balusters of the balustrade, we watched for them, waiting for the door to come crashing down. Suddenly the lights went out and someone cursed. Downstairs the door crashed open and all the windows seemed to shatter at the same time. There was only the red glow of the little emergency light by the door and I could see their dark shapes down there, moving around, scrambling toward the stairs.

"They're coming up!" Glock shouted.

"Where?" Ron asked.

"Like hell they are!" Beobee said. He popped the pin on some kind of grenade and I briefly saw him, Ron, Glock and Chico in the orange flash before he threw it downstairs. There was a rushing hiss as a rosy, glowing foam erupted, quickly engulfing the downstairs area. I could hear them thrashing about under it, an occasional black, tentacle-like limb breaking the surface.

"I think it's working," Glock said, as we watched the tumult below.

I wanted to believe him but I could see that the stuff was beginning to dry up and recede. "Do you have any more?" I asked Beobee.

"No."

"Look, they're starting up the stairs," somebody said.

"Oh, Lordy," Beobee said. "Sweet Jesus help us."

I awoke from my dream abruptly. The ward lights were on and my dinner tray, still covered, sat on the bedside table. I looked at my watch. It was ten minutes after seven. My new neighbor, a black guy named Johnson, lay in Krouse's old bed. Krouse had only been dead one day when they brought Johnson in. I guess they really needed the beds.

I decided to go out to the main corridor to the candy machine. I hadn't been able to eat much the past couple of days. Candy bars were about all I could get down. After Krouse died, and after finding out about Ron and the others, I just didn't care about anything.

I sat up and reached for my crutches. I always leaned them against the wall beside my bed, but they were missing. I stood on one leg and got down and looked under the bed. Nothing. They were gone! Just yesterday Doctor Walker had said that he'd keep me on them for another four or five days.

"What's the matter?" It was Johnson looking over at me.

"My crutches, they're gone."

"The orderly took them."

"Which one?"

"The little, chubby, blond-headed guy."

"Oh." I knew it! Chip was messing with me because I'd been Krouse's friend. He was hassling me because he thought I was malingering. He'd done the same thing to Krouse and Mills. Both he and Dale had. They just couldn't understand. The more I thought about it, the more angry I became. I'd never cheated the Army. I'd always played by the rules. I'd done everything they'd told me to. And the only thing that had made it bearable was the thought that I would be going back with my squad, and maybe seeing Chantal.

Still, I hadn't cheated. I'd continued to go to Physical Therapy. I hadn't tampered with my wound. And now they were treating me like I was some lazy slob trying to get out of doing KP or something!

Chip entered the far door, pushing the big dinner tray cart. He looked in my direction. Even from that distance, I saw his face change. He knew that I knew. I took my tray off the table and lay it across my lap as I waited for him to work his way down the ward.

He took Johnson's tray without looking in my direction. He slid it into the rack and walked up to me, never making eye contact. When he reached for my tray, I held it fast. He blinked in confusion.

"I want my crutches back," I said.

"What?"

"Don't 'what' me, man." I looked deep into his eyes. "This guy over here said you took my crutches. I want them back now. Do you understand?"

I could see his nostrils dilating. He swallowed. "When I finish collecting the trays."

"Good. I'll be waiting." I released the tray.

About ten minutes later someone approached. It was the Japanese lady. She leaned my crutches against the wall and went away. I lay back down and stared at the milky white globe of one of the overhead lights. Images formed. Ron and Glock boxed playfully in the dusty street at the bridge; Chico sat on the trail, totally exhausted, an olive green washcloth on his head to soak up his sweat; Papa ate his chow from a paper plate in the sun on the bunker roof; Chantal walked hand in hand with me down the dusty road to Tin Can City. I closed my eyes. They were all gone from me now and I was alone. More alone than I'd ever been in my life.

Someone started shaking my bed back and forth, back and forth. I refused to open my eyes, wanting instead to look on the faces of my friends from the past. Their images faded as the glare of the ward lights penetrated my eyelids. They continued to shake the bed, saying nothing.

I quickly sat up. There was no one there, yet my bed continued to shake by itself. Then I noticed the moving reflections of the lights in the blackened windows; the windows bowed in and out slightly, chattering like a huge set of teeth.

"Earthquake!" somebody shouted.

In the middle of the ward, Chip had his arms wrapped tightly around one of the columns, his mouth open in fear. All the guys in the ward were sitting up in their beds, horrified as the building bounced and shook. The tremors stopped suddenly and I heard someone saying something over and over again. "I'm goin' home," they said. Over and over came the refrain, "I'm goin' home, I'm goin' home," and then I realized it was me.

A quiet calm came over me. I'd reached the bottom of a deep, deep cave and could go no lower. There was only one way to go and that was up. Everything was very clear now. I would go home. It was all up to me, just like Ron had said so many times, just like Krouse and Greg had said.

I got my crutches and started for the door. I saw a lot of the others looking at me.

"I'm goin' home," I shouted at them, "I've done my time!" There were tears coming down my face, but I didn't care. They continued to stare at me and I laughed. I turned and went out the double doors to find Doctor Walker and tell him.

The door to the doctors' office wing was open and the lights were on, but there was no one around. I waited for about five minutes. The muted sound of a siren penetrated the hospital's walls. I was about to leave when I heard a noise in the back. I went in farther and saw Dr. Walker soaking up a spill of water on his desk with a hanky. A vase of flowers had tipped over. He looked up suddenly and saw me.

"Quite a shaker, wasn't it?"

"Yes, Sir," I said.

He threw the flowers in the waist can, wrung out his hanky, and gave his desk another wipe. "Get them all the time here. Sit down, son."

He sat down when I did and made a little triangle with his fingers and thumbs. "What can I do for you?"

I was a little nervous. "I wanted to talk to you."

He touched his fingers together a few times as his eyes looked into mine. "You want to go home. Is that it?"

"Yes," I said.

He leaned forward and scribbled something on a note pad in front of him. There was already a bunch of handwriting on it. "There's a flight

Monday. You'll have to get your things packed and ready for pickup tomorrow. Can you do that?"

I had a lump in my throat and couldn't talk. I nodded.

He smiled sadly. "Go on back to the ward and get some sleep."

"Thank you, Sir," I said hoarsely as I grabbed my crutches and got to my feet. I went out.

A month later, in Philadelphia

I was in the recliner watching the news when my mom brought me a tall glass of iced tea. My parents had bought a color TV. It was our first, and it was really neat. A bunch of people were demonstrating against the war. Some long-haired guy ran up to the police barricade and threw a bottle at the cops. That did it. The cops knocked the barrier down and charged, batons swinging. I watched in fascination.

My mom shook her head. "Carl, do you have to have that on? You ought to take a break from all of that and just rest." She looked at my leg worriedly.

"Okay," I said. "You mind turning it off?"

She smiled and turned the set off and went back to the kitchen.

They had given me a two-week medical leave. I could walk okay, but not too far. And I still had to do these physical therapy exercises. When I came back from my leave they would cut orders for my next duty assignment, somewhere stateside. I only had four months left in the army.

The door bell rang. "I'll get it," my mom called.

I heard her greet Jimmy Byrnes. "He's in here," she said.

He had a big smile on his face when he came in. He was dressed nicely. He'd always been a sharp dresser. He wore a maroon three-quarter-length leather jacket and Beatle boots. He extended his hand. "Hey! You're lookin' good, man."

"Thanks."

"Can I get you some iced tea?" my mom asked him.

"No thanks, Mrs. Melcher."

My mom went back into the kitchen.

"How was it over there?"

"Not too bad."

He nodded. "You hear about Joey Sheehan?"

"Yeah." My mother had already told me. He lived a couple blocks away and had died in Vietnam the week before. I had never liked the guy. He was a year ahead of me in grade school and the worst kind of bully. Just about every kid in the neighborhood had been worked over by Joey Sheehan at some point.

"How long you home for?" Jimmy asked.

"Couple weeks."

He nodded at my leg. "How is it?"

"Pretty much healed now."

He smiled. "So, you ready for 'Chez Vous' Friday night?"

I smiled. "Maybe next week." Even if my leg were completely healed, though, I still wouldn't go out. I didn't want to.

"Mike Bennet and Frank Carey are flying out to LA to be on Bandstand."

"You're kidding," I said.

"Uh-uh," he said. "They've been saving up for six months."

"Any guarantee they'll get on?"

Jimmy shrugged. "I don't know." He pointed to the TV. "Mind if I turn it on? Bandstand is coming on."

"Go ahead."

It was already in progress. I was amazed by the colors of the clothes. The girls wore miniskirts and halters and the guys, bell bottom pants and vests. A lot of people had these psychedelic designs on their shirts and pants, like swirling vortexes of color. Tye-dyed, they called it. Dick Clark looked the way he always did.

Jimmy watched for about five minutes. Then he checked his watch and stood.

"Gotta go, huh?" I said.

"Yeah." He put a stick of gum in his mouth. He offered me one. I shook my head.

"Well, I'll stop by again before you go back."

"Good deal."

I heard my mom coming out so I wouldn't have to get up and see him to the door.

"I'll let myself out, Mrs. Melcher," he called to her.

My mom looked at the TV. "Those skirts. . . ." She shook her head.

"They're in California, Mom."

"Oh, that's right." She shook her head again and went back to the kitchen.

They were playing some new song I'd never heard before. It had a pretty good beat, and I knew I could dance to it. But not there, not with those people. There was something about them . . . They were older than me, a lot of them. The guys were taller than I was, and dressed nicer. But they had an intriguing look on their faces as they peered into the camera. What was it, I wondered. Where had I seen it before? Then I realized. It was the look of a child searching for his parents' face as he goes around on the merry-go-round, a look that says, "Look at me! Look at me!" They were kids, I realized, twenty-year-olds, but still kids.

After a few minutes I couldn't watch any more of it. I laid my head back and closed my eyes. Later I heard my mom click the TV off and I slept.

The End